FÜR ELISE

FÜR ELISE

A Novel

MARK SPLITSTONE

Amalgam Books

Published by Amalgam Books, Elmhurst, Illinois

Edited by Girl Friday Productions
www.girlfridayproductions.com

Cover design: Richard Ljoenes Design LLC
Editorial production: Alyssa Brillinger

Excerpt by Wolfgang Borchert, translated by David Porter, from THE MAN OUTSIDE, copyright 1971 by New Directions Publishing Corp. Reprinted by permission of New Directions Publishing Corp.

Image credits: Cover photographs: man by Joanna Czogala / Arcangel Images; woman by © Miguel Sobreira / Trevillion Images; bench by Nutnaree Saingwongwattana / Shutterstock; the ruin of Frauenkirche, Dresden by Alfred Strobel / Süddeutsche Zeitung Photo / Alamy Stock Photo; Dresden map by David Rumsey Map Collection, David Rumsey Map Center, Stanford Libraries; Für Elise sheet music by Ludwig van Beethoven {{PD-US-expired}}

ISBN (paperback): 979-8-218-56577-0
ISBN (ebook): 979-8-218-56578-7
Library of Congress Control Number: 2024926258

First edition

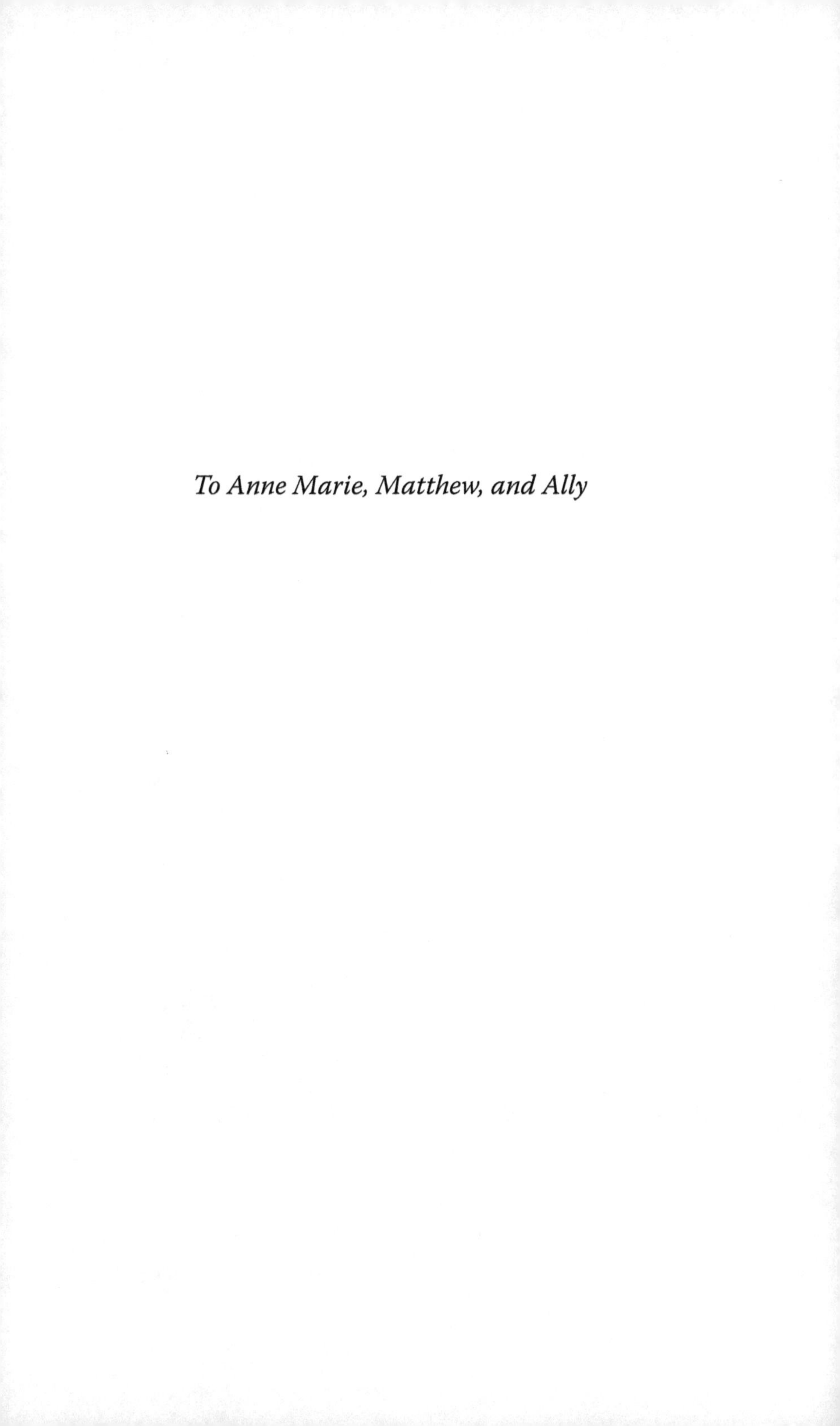

To Anne Marie, Matthew, and Ally

PROLOGUE

January 1956

Hans Becker had fixated on this day for fourteen years. He had planned for it, dreamed of it, obsessed over it, and fantasized about it. Thoughts of his return home were all that had kept him alive, but now that the day had finally arrived, he just wanted it to be over. No reality could live up to the fantasy he had forged in his imagination.

In the Soviet prisoner-of-war transition center the night before, he had been too excited to sleep, and now the chugging of the train's steam engine and the rocking of the carriage made him drowsy. His head lolled forward as the train decelerated, and when it surrendered its last bit of momentum and stopped, his chin hit his chest, jolting him awake.

During his first days of combat in 1942, when he was only eighteen years old, he had developed a habit of snapping from deep sleep to full consciousness in a matter of seconds, and he'd done so again. But even though he was wide awake, he couldn't immediately determine where he was or, for that matter, *when* he was. Time, like so many other aspects of his life, had lost most of its meaning long ago.

He wiped the film of ice off the window and saw that the

nearby railway station was painted orange. He frowned and muttered, "What the hell?" Odder still, the station, with its Tudor arches and turrets, resembled a castle, and while he hadn't thought about architecture in years, he recalled that this style was known as neo-Gothic. An orange neo-Gothic railway station. He began to think he was dreaming and turned to scan the faces of the other men in the half-filled passenger car. Nobody made eye contact, and while he recognized some of them from the transition center, he hadn't spoken to them there and didn't intend to here.

He had a feeling he had seen this station before, and as the train began to inch forward, he closed his eyes and tried to remember when. After a minute, it came to him—it had been in Breslau, a German city he passed through on his way to the Russian front in 1942. His current train now entered the dilapidated station, and as it approached the dimly lit, deserted platform, he thought back to that earlier day, when it had been bustling with dozens of Wehrmacht recruits saying goodbye to their tearful mothers and stoic fathers. They had been too young and stupid to realize what they were getting into, and so had he.

He leaned back, relieved to have solved the orange railway station mystery, but as the engine stopped and hissed its final burst of steam, he saw that the platform sign didn't read "Breslau." Instead, it read "Wrocław" in Polish script. Could there possibly be an orange neo-Gothic railway station besides the one in Breslau, or was he losing his mind?

A chill shuddered through his body, and he tried to warm himself by blowing into his cupped hands. After a moment, he picked up the canvas bag he had received at the transition center, pulled open the drawstring, and looked inside. It contained a set of Russian work clothes identical to the ones he was wearing, a toothbrush, toothpaste, a razor, and ten marks. The bag and its contents were his compensation for one year of war and thirteen years of captivity. *On balance,* he thought wryly, *probably not worth it.*

He dug to the bottom and retrieved a small bundle of envelopes bound with a string. He pulled out the top envelope, removed the letter, and reread it:

> Hans: I received your letter, and I'm happy to hear you're finally coming home. I can't believe how long it's been. Regarding your request to stay with us, that's fine, but you should know that it can't be a long-term arrangement. As I mentioned in my previous letter, my mother isn't well and our apartment is small, but we can certainly make room for you temporarily. I've noted your arrival time and will meet you at the station. Elise.

Hans skimmed his fingertips over the letter and tried to picture her writing it. All the images he could generate, though, were hopelessly out of date: teenage Elise sitting at the desk in her old bedroom, twirling a pigtail with one hand as she wrote with the other . . . relaxing on the couch in the parlor of her parents' house, with a Bach concerto playing in the background . . . swaying gently on the front porch swing, wearing a pink dress on a hot summer night. He stared blankly at the letter but then sighed and refolded it, realizing the futility of his attempt at visualization. He no longer knew what she looked like, and the old desk, bedroom, couch, parlor, house, and swing had probably ceased to exist in 1945.

He put the note back in the envelope and the envelope back in the stack with the other twenty-seven letters he had received from her. He knew exactly how many there were because he had read each one countless times. The oldest was from 1948, the year the Russians first allowed their prisoners of war to receive mail. Looking at the meager stack, Hans wondered how many letters he had sent to her in the past eight years. Three hundred? Four hundred?

The train began chugging westward, and he considered spending the rest of the journey reading Elise's letters one last time. But he had already memorized most of them, and it was pointless to try to find something in them that wasn't there. He wished he could read the letters she had sent him prior to his capture, but the Russians had immediately confiscated those. He remembered that the phrases "love you" and "miss you" were sprinkled liberally throughout, and in one letter, she even wrote that she forgave him for what he'd done on their last night together. She always closed those letters with "Yours forever." But while the past fourteen years had seemed like forever, he had no evidence that she still considered herself his.

He gazed out the window as the train trundled through a snowy countryside of fields, forests, rolling hills, and isolated farmhouses. Despite the sign he'd read in Breslau or Wrocław, or whatever city it had been, the landscape convinced him he was in Lower Silesia or Saxony and therefore not far from home.

The train rolled forward for another hour, making frequent unexpected and unexplained stops in the middle of nowhere. During one pause, Hans saw a village in the distance and was heartened that it appeared to be German. The half-timbered houses and red gabled roofs were much more appealing than the boxy, postwar Soviet architecture he had become accustomed to. But something seemed amiss. Then he realized what it was—no smoke was rising from the chimneys.

The train moved again, and as they passed the village, Hans saw it was deserted. Many of the buildings were scorched or partially collapsed, and the windows of the remaining ones were boarded up. Snow blew across the desolate streets, and the scene reminded him of an American Old West ghost town. The church was missing its steeple, and he remembered early in the war, as the Wehrmacht marched east into the Soviet Union, seeing German tanks blast the tallest buildings in every village and town in case they concealed snipers' nests. He wondered if the Russians had returned the favor later in the war when they'd marched west.

They eventually stopped at a town he was familiar with, Görlitz, and for the first time, he was sure he was in Germany. The signs here were in German, and the elderly couple who boarded the train spoke German. The next stop would likely be his, and he had to remind himself to continue to breathe.

When the train finally reached his hometown, he was initially relieved to see that the accounts of its devastation had apparently been exaggerated. As they continued toward the city center, though, each block looked worse than the one before. Many of the buildings he expected to see were gone, replaced by vacant lots overgrown with weeds. The blackened walls of the surviving structures made them look like the interiors of giant fireplaces.

They rounded the bend for the final stretch to the station but then stopped. He could see that the station's basic structure was intact, but the magnificent glass dome that once fronted it was gone, and its most distinctive feature, a trio of graceful arched roofs, was ruined: The glass of the arches had been replaced with plywood.

He looked around the passenger car and muttered a stream of curse words, as if that would get the train restarted. Finally, with an exhale of steam, the engine inched forward and chuffed into the station. Before the war, the station had been illuminated by sunlight filtering through the glass roof, but now the light came from haphazardly spaced industrial fixtures. As his eyes adjusted to the gloom, the grim state of the station's interior became apparent. Both clock towers were gone, and plaster and wood masked the station's exquisite brick and wrought iron framework. The place was nearly unrecognizable, and he began to question whether he was even at the right station until he saw the platform sign that read "Dresden."

Nearly all the people waiting on the platform were women, and Hans wondered if they were mothers there to greet their POW sons. But then he saw that in front of their chests, many of them held signs that displayed names, photographs, and military details. Were they hoping to get information about missing soldiers? The women's faces were as faded and worn as the signs, and he realized that they might have been coming to the station for more than ten years, showing up whenever each new batch of POWs was released. "Private Schneider, last seen at Kursk July 1943." "Sergeant Kohl, captured outside Moscow December 1941." And on all the signs: *"Wer kennt ihn?"*—"Who knows him?" By this point, they surely knew the answer, but they apparently couldn't stop asking the question. *Wer kennt ihn?* Hans shook his head. *Nobody. Nobody knows him.*

Other passengers began to disembark, but Hans continued to gaze out the window. Eventually, his eyes fixed on a woman standing alone and motionless as the crowd swirled around her. She wore a tan dress and black winter coat, and her blond hair was cut in a bob. He knew it was Elise, but he struggled to reconcile her appearance with his mental image of her as a pigtailed teenager.

He closed his eyes for a few seconds, took one more look out the window, and then picked up his bag and exited. They saw each other immediately, and Hans desperately wanted to run and take her in his arms. Instead, he kept walking, stopping a meter away from her. There were no tears, but no smiles either. Finally, he stepped forward and hugged her. He felt her flinch and realized that this situation was as awkward for her as it was for him.

She pulled herself from him, and after maintaining eye contact for several seconds, looked away. When she looked back again, Hans was reminded of old people whose eyes had deadened and lost their sparkle, perhaps because they'd seen enough.

Elise was still young. But perhaps she'd seen enough too.

PART ONE
1940–1942

CHAPTER 1

There—it just happened again. For the second time during that morning's youth orchestra rehearsal, Hans had made eye contact with the pretty oboe player. This interaction had occurred regularly during rehearsals, starting at the first one two weeks before, and while the oboe player didn't always meet his gaze, sometimes she did. Of course, she might have just looked at him because she could feel his eyes on her, but Hans wasn't sure that was even a real phenomenon. What properties of physics or biology could possibly make a person feel someone looking at them?

The first time the conductor took attendance, Hans had learned that her name was Elise Engel, and since one of Hans's favorite songs was Beethoven's "Für Elise," this felt like fate to him. They both sat in the third row, Hans with the violins and Elise with the oboes, and the orchestra's semicircular layout allowed him to glance at her without turning his head. While he was careful not to stare, he had been able to establish a mental image of her. She was above average in height but not quite what would be considered tall. She wore her blond hair in braided pigtails that landed a touch past her clavicles, or where he imagined her clavicles were—that is, when he thought about such things.

Her clavicles and everything else about her were enhanced by her perfect posture, which he assumed was the result of good genes, a classy upbringing, or both. Looking at her caused him to reflexively sit up straighter, although this usually lasted only a few seconds before he reverted to his customary slouch. "Proper"—that was the right word. She was a proper young lady, or maybe a proper girl. He wasn't sure where the line was between those two descriptions. Either way, he guessed she was his age—seventeen—or perhaps a year or two younger.

Hans was most fascinated, though, with her eyes. He imagined their color was like the green of the ocean, although he had never seen the ocean. Or perhaps they were the green of an emerald, although he had never seen one of those either. Jade, maybe? He wasn't even sure what jade was, but he had heard it was green. He decided to stick with the ocean analogy because in addition to being green, her eyes also conveyed a great depth. He could work out the details of the metaphor later.

Rehearsal concluded without further eye contact, but Hans was content with the day's progress. When he was younger, he used to go fishing with his father, and his shared glances with Elise reminded him of the nibbles of those fish. A split second of excitement that told him he was onto something and made him feel anticipation about what was to come. But his father had taught him to wait until he was sure the hook was set before attempting to reel in a catch, so for now, nibbles would have to suffice. The reward would come later.

As he began to put his violin in its case, from the corner of his eye he saw Elise stand up and walk in his direction. He suddenly realized that this was the first chilly day of autumn, and Elise had probably worn a jacket. The coatroom was behind Hans, so she'd need to walk past him to get to it.

He wasn't yet prepared to talk to her, so he lowered his head and busied himself with the violin and case in his lap. She continued down the aisle between the second and third rows, out of the oboe section, past the flutes, into the violin section—and then stopped just short of his chair. His gaze rose from her black leather shoes and white ankle socks to her pink gingham dress and finally to her face. The two of them maintained eye contact for a few seconds, and then she looked down at his feet. He blushed as he realized that his long legs and clown-like shoes were blocking the aisle. He retracted them quickly, and when he looked back up, she smiled and walked past. As he began breathing again, he wondered— what did that smile mean? Was it friendly, or flirty, or was she chuckling at his gangliness? Perhaps it was a combination of all those things.

He remained seated with his heart racing and watched her leave the auditorium, clutching her schoolbooks to her chest and trailing slightly behind a group of girls as they gabbed and giggled. As the door closed behind her, a montage of prior failures played in his head—turning down a kiss from Gertrud when he was fourteen because of an infatuation with Elisabeth that he never would act on; waiting in line at the candy store next to Inge, the girl he was smitten with when he was fifteen, but failing to think of anything to say; standing and watching a parade for an hour next to his crush Anna when he was sixteen but being unable to open his mouth.

He vowed to put those frustrations behind him and do something this time. He'd be eighteen in less than a year, and it was time to act. But things couldn't be rushed—first, he needed a plan.

CHAPTER 2

Hans grinned as he walked home from school. The crisp autumn air felt good in his lungs, and he enjoyed seeing the rich greens of the oaks and lindens change into vibrant reds and golds. If the trees could transform, he thought, maybe he could too. The afternoon sunlight flickered through the leaves, highlighting his neighborhood's elegant houses and townhomes. He wondered if Elise lived in one of them.

When he arrived at his house, he tried not to let its appearance dampen his mood. In any given neighborhood, some houses stood out, for better or worse, and his was definitely the latter. It was small and shabby, and the entire structure leaned a bit, like a ship listing ten degrees to starboard. He was frustrated that his father hadn't done more to improve its appearance, given that he was a mason who built houses for a living.

He climbed the porch steps, flecks of paint shooting off the wobbly wooden handrail as his hand slid up it. The porch was crammed with items his father had taken from various worksites—conduit, bricks, lumber, and pipes, all covered by tarps. Some of this material was for home-remodeling ideas that bounced around in his father's head but hadn't gained enough kinetic energy to escape and enter the physical world. Most of it, though, was earmarked for his father's ridiculous project in the backyard.

As Hans opened the front door, Greta, the family German shepherd, gave a perfunctory bark before trotting over to welcome him. She rolled onto her back, but as he bent down to rub her belly, a thwap! from the backyard prompted her to scramble to her paws. Hans stood up and walked through the front room and into the kitchen to investigate. He looked out the open window and saw that his mother was cleaning a rug. It hung from a clothesline, and she was using a wicker carpet beater to bash it senseless. Thwap!

The backyard was small and, besides the clothesline, contained only his father's toolshed, an apple tree, a well-maintained but undersized vegetable garden nearing the end of its season, and right in the middle, a five-meter-square area of dirt with a one-meter-square piece of steel atop it. This was the only evidence of his father's project.

The musical accompaniment to the thwapping and the dull hum of the city was provided by the jingling of wind chimes hanging from a rod affixed to the house. Hans's father had assembled the chimes by using fishing line to attach steel conduit to the rod, and his mother had once told him that when the wind was just right, the chimes would compose a song. The problem, as Hans saw it, was that the wind was rarely just right. The chimes were usually either silent or else creating a cacophony. Even with the right wind, he thought, their sound was rather mournful, and in classical-music terms, the songs they played would be categorized as dirges or requiems. He sometimes thought the backyard seemed haunted, and the premise behind his father's project reinforced this sentiment.

Now, though, as he looked out the window, he was mesmerized by the song spontaneously composed by the chimes. Rather than sounding melancholy, it reminded him of a delightful Mozart piano concerto. The beautiful music, the cool autumn air, the sunshine, the chemicals coursing through his brain as he thought of Elise's smile . . . Thwap!

Jolted out of his trance, he again focused on his mother. Her graying blond hair was pulled back in a tight bun, and she wore the same plain dress, stained apron, and grim, determined expression that she did every day. Hans didn't think she had aged in his seventeen years of existence, but perhaps that was because she had always looked old. He watched her thick, calloused hands choke the carpet beater as it arced through the air. Thwap!

Greta whimpered, and Hans bent down to pet her. The dog rarely left his mother's side, but the current thwapping, like all loud noises, made her anxious. After calming her down, he left the kitchen and bounded up the stairs, two at a time, eager to begin developing a plan to build on the momentum created by his recent interactions with Elise.

CHAPTER 3

When Hans came downstairs a few hours later, he saw that his father still wasn't home, which meant he'd have to wait for dinner. He turned on the radio, and as he sat down to listen, the orchestral melody was interrupted by martial music, signifying the start of a victory news bulletin. These interruptions happened routinely, and this time, the announcer reported that the Luftwaffe had once again bombed London. According to the report, the massive damage done made it unlikely that England would be able to hold out against Germany much longer.

Hans picked up the newspaper from the coffee table. Its headline parroted the news about the inevitability of an English surrender. The government-controlled media had been consistently trumpeting this storyline since the evacuation of the English and French troops who'd been surrounded by German forces at Dunkirk three months earlier, but it wasn't clear to Hans that the English were any closer to surrendering now than they had been then.

The smell of dinner cooking wafted in from the kitchen, and he watched as his mother, wearing a look of resignation, took the red cabbage and fried potatoes off the cast iron stove. Their lack of a refrigerator forced her to go to the market every day, and since the market didn't have everything every day, she never knew ahead of time what she'd buy. The one exception was cabbage, and Hans was amazed by the myriad ways she managed to prepare it: cabbage and potatoes, cabbage and noodles, cabbage and cabbage. Since the start of the war, the one combination they rarely had was cabbage and meat. As he watched now, his mother covered the food to keep it warm, then entered the living room, sat down, and silently began darning socks.

Ninety minutes later, the front door opened and Hans's father stumbled in. As he closed the door behind him, Greta trotted up and warily sniffed his pants. The aromatic blend of construction debris, sweat, spilled alcohol, and tobacco smoke seemed to fascinate her. He gave her a brief pat on the head and then unsteadily placed his woolen flat cap on the coatrack. His dark, usually slicked-back hair was tousled, and his normally sharp blue eyes were glassy. He straightened his suspenders and made a movement to roll up his sleeves but then looked down and saw they were already rolled up.

Hans and his mother remained seated as his father's eyes danced between them. "Olga. Hansh." He appeared frustrated that he wasn't able to pronounce three syllables successfully.

Hans's mother sighed and said, "August."

He straightened himself, threw back his shoulders, and said, "I'll go change." He ascended the stairs, moving carefully and purposefully. The intent of these deliberate movements was presumably to make him appear not to be drunk, but in fact they had the opposite effect. Greta, who'd lost interest, now followed Hans's mother into the kitchen as she went to rewarm their meal.

Hans looked up and tracked the sound of his father's movements, as if watching the ceiling would help him hear better. He glanced into the kitchen and saw that his mother was doing the same thing. The floorboards were creaky, and after a lifetime of living in the house, Hans knew which ones produced which noises. He listened as the clomps of his father's work boots proceeded in the direction of the bathroom the three of them shared, and shortly after, he heard the toilet flush. The water in the sink ran for a minute—his father was probably splashing it on his face. The clomps continued down the hall to his parents' bedroom, and Hans knew this was the decision point. The next noise would be either clomps heading to the closet as his father took off his boots and changed clothes, or else springs squeaking as he collapsed onto the bed, probably fully clothed and on top of the blankets. It was quiet for a minute, and Hans pictured his father swaying in the doorway, trying to decide what to do. Finally, the clomps advanced to the closet, and Hans heard the work boots thud on the floor.

When his father came back downstairs, Hans sat down with him at the small wooden kitchen table and attempted to gauge his level of drunkenness. This was a skill Hans had mastered over the years, and tonight he estimated it at moderate. He knew, though, that what was moderate for his father would certainly be considered excessive for most people. After Hans's mother served the meal and sat down, his father asked her for a beer, and she dutifully stood up and got him a bottle of Radeberger pilsner. Hans watched his father as he grabbed the bottle and took a swig. His hands were thick and calloused, with cuts and scrapes on his knuckles and dirt under his fingernails.

Hans could tell his mother was anxious, even more than usual, and after several minutes she asked, without looking up, "Who was at the pub tonight?"

"Why do you ask?"

She paused and then said, "Did you hear that Herr Weber was denounced? The Gestapo have him in custody, and his wife doesn't know what's happening."

"I guess that happens sometimes."

"He was denounced for a joke he made at a pub."

The words hung in the air as Hans looked to his father, who wiped his face with a napkin and said, "Well, his jokes aren't funny. Maybe he deserved to be denounced." He grinned, but neither of them returned the smile. "It was probably just someone settling an old score." She glared at him as he picked up his fork and stabbed another potato. "What? Everybody loves me at the pub. Who would tell all the funny jokes if I got arrested?"

She shook her head and looked down at her plate. "You need to be careful."

With his face reddening, he said, "What do you think I'm saying there? That Germany is run by a bunch of lunatics and morons who will ruin the country? How stupid do you think I am?"

She recoiled and didn't respond.

Hans hated conflict almost as much as his mother did, so he decided to change the subject. Pretending the conversation up to that point hadn't happened, he asked his father, "How long do you think it will be before England gives up?"

The man turned his glare from his wife to his son and huffed, "What makes you think they'll give up?"

"My teachers say it's just a matter of time. There's no way England can stand up to us. We've taken almost all the rest of Europe, and England is all that's left."

"I agree that if the English army was still in France, we could beat them. But did you know England is an island? They still teach you some things in school, right?"

"Yes, I know England is an island."

"The problem is that it's already September and too late to invade England because it'll be winter soon."

"We don't have to invade. We can just bomb them until they give up."

"Oh, I see. And what's to keep them from bombing us?"

"The Luftwaffe. Nobody can beat the Luftwaffe."

He shook his head. "You know that the British bombed Berlin last month, right? Did your teachers mention that?"

"Yes, but we're damaging London more than England is damaging Berlin. At some point, Churchill will realize he can't win and take whatever deal he can get."

"Churchill isn't our problem—Hitler is. He's not going to stop until someone stops him." His face reddened, and he raised his voice again. "England can't beat Germany, but eventually Hitler will pick a fight with the wrong country, and that'll be the end of him and probably the end of us. The man is addicted to conquest. Austria, Czechoslovakia, Poland, Denmark, Norway, France, Belgium, Luxembourg, the Netherlands. Everyone said 'He'll probably stop there' after each of those, but they don't understand that it'll never be enough for him." He glared at Hans. "You're not turning into a Nazi, are you?"

"Of course not. I just think it's impressive what the army has done. Your generation couldn't conquer France in four years, and this generation did it in six weeks." Hans knew he had crossed a line and braced himself for a slap on the side of his head.

His father's eyes flashed. "It'll be impressive right up to the moment when it all falls apart. And just so you know, the minute I think you're buying into that vile nonsense they're cramming down your throat at your Hitler Youth meetings, you'll be out on the street." He pounded his fist on the table, compelling Greta to scamper into the front room.

Hans looked to his mother for support, but she was staring at her plate. The palms of her hands were on the table with her fingers splayed, as if she were trying to will things to settle down.

After several minutes of silence, his father, in a calmer voice now, asked Hans, "Do you have plans to go out this weekend?" Hans shook his head. "You can't spend your whole life at home listening to music and reading books. At some point, you need to go out with boys your age."

Hans didn't respond. While he understood his father's perspective regarding his social life, the fact of the matter was that Hans thought the boys his age were idiots.

After dinner, Hans went to his room, closed the door, and sat on the side of his bed, leaning forward so he wouldn't hit his head on the sloped ceiling. He looked at the bookcase his dad had built for him when he was little, filled with books about Dresden's architecture. The two of them shared an interest in this topic, and back then, they'd often go on walks through the city, with his dad pointing out interesting buildings and explaining how they were constructed.

On top of the bookcase sat a cardboard model of the Frauenkirche, or Church of Our Lady—Dresden's iconic Lutheran church with the bell-shaped dome. His dad had given him the kit as a Christmas present when he was ten, and Hans remembered those wonderful days after he received it, when he didn't have school, his dad didn't have work, and it was snowing and cold outside. The two of them had sat by the fireplace for hours, assembling and painting the model. It made him wistful to know they could never return to those days.

Hans's room was at the back of the house, so the wind chimes were directly below his open window. A slight breeze now caused the chimes to produce a series of solitary notes as he thought about the conversation they'd had over dinner. Was his father right that the war would get worse? Although Hans wasn't enamored with his dull life in Dresden, it was cer-tainly better than standing in mud-filled trenches for months on end while being shot at, bombed, and gassed. Surely this would end before he was required to fight.

He decided to stop thinking about the war and his father.

Instead, he lay down on his bed and turned his mind to contemplating more important matters. As far as Hans was concerned, Hitler could conquer whatever far-off country he wanted.

His conquest would be Elise.

CHAPTER 4

The next evening, August, disappointed in himself for show-ing up late and drunk to dinner the night before, skipped his usual postwork pub ritual and instead took the tram straight home. Whenever he went to the pub, he made a commitment to himself that he'd stay for either three beers or one hour, whichever came first. The three beers almost always came first, and after the three beers, the commitment was inevitably forgotten. He knew this commitment process was flawed, per-haps fatally, but his faith in his own good intentions compelled him to continue to utilize it.

Sitting on the tram, he rubbed his aching muscles and thought about how much sorer he got now than he had in his youth. When he was Hans's age, he'd already been out of school for three years, working ten-hour days as an apprentice mason while also helping out on his family's farm. And when he hadn't been working, he'd been out drinking with friends. How had he ended up with a son like Hans? Hans was a bad kid—not in the sense of being a troublemaker, but in the sense of being bad at being a kid.

As he looked out the window at the shops and restaurants, he wondered if it was Hans's city upbringing that had made them so different. The tram passed some teenage boys hang-ing out on a street corner. August thought it was unlikely they knew anything about manual labor. These city boys were soft, but they'd toughen up soon enough after they joined the military and, given the direction things appeared to be headed, fought in a war. He hated the thought that that's what it would take. Especially for Hans.

He had tried different approaches to get Hans out of his shell, such as having him work at his construction sites. Though the boy was quiet there, at least he was doing something physical and masculine. August wasn't sure if that helped with the boy's shyness, but Hans seemed to enjoy it, and he had a knack for construction and architecture. Hans was smart, much smarter than him. August figured Hans would ultimately do something with his brain rather than his strength, and as he rubbed his sore legs, he concluded that was a good thing.

A young couple boarded the tram and sat down in front of him. The man leaned over and whispered something in the woman's ear, and she giggled and kissed him on the cheek. He pretended to wipe it off and she giggled again and kissed him once more. They were absolutely adorable, and all August could think about was that he'd like to knock their skulls together.

Had he and Olga ever been that happy? Perhaps, but they certainly weren't anymore. He thought back to when they were that age, having just moved to Dresden from their village. Maybe that's where he'd gone wrong. He'd known that she didn't like the city and that she missed her family, but he'd assumed she'd eventually adjust. He was still waiting for that day to come. When he left the village, he'd been convinced he'd make his fortune in the big city, but he was still waiting for that day too.

The tram arrived at his stop, and August used the back of the seat in front of him to help him stand up. When had he become one of those people who always got up slowly? An autumn chill greeted him as he stepped off the tram and began his walk home.

When he reached the house, he stopped and stared at it

for several minutes. Hans was right—it didn't look nice. He had bought it shortly after Hans was born, and he knew Olga had been relieved to get out of their cramped apartment. He'd devoted most of his free time since then to renovating it, and while it was never going to look like one of the nicer houses in the neighborhood, he had made good progress with the structural issues. He vowed to work on the house's aesthetics as soon as he finished his other project. With that decided, he walked up the steps, careful not to grab the wobbly handrail.

Greta met him at the front door and seemed disappointed that his pants didn't have any of the customary tobacco or alcohol smells that so intrigued her. Going for the next best alternative, she rolled over for a belly rub.

After changing clothes, August came back downstairs, and then he and his family sat down for dinner. He looked at Hans and said, "I'm sorry I lost my temper last night." Hans nodded. "It's just that I don't think you're getting the full story at school, on the radio, and certainly not at your idiotic Hitler Youth meetings. I know you don't want a lecture from a crabby old man, but I've seen many things in my life, and I just want to make sure you're prepared to face the world."

Hans continued eating.

"This country is being led by bad men doing bad things, and it's going to get worse. You need to understand that, and I've got an idea about how you can learn things from a different perspective. I think we should buy a new radio."

Olga sat up straight and frowned at him. "What are you talking about?"

"We need a new one anyway. That People's Receiver was a piece of junk to begin with, and now it barely works. Plus, we can't get international broadcasts on it. I think it would be good for the boy to see Hitler as the world sees Hitler, not as Hitler wants you to see Hitler."

"That sounds great!" said Hans. He lowered his voice and said, "Can we listen to broadcasts from London?"

"Wait, wait, wait," Olga interrupted quietly. "You know we can't listen to international broadcasts. What are you thinking?"

"We'll be careful. See how excited the boy is? You're not going to ruin his fun, are you?"

Olga said, "You know you'll be arrested if you get caught listening to a foreign broadcast."

"That's why I said we'd be careful."

"Between the radio and the pub and not flying the flag on Nazi holidays, sometimes I think you want to be denounced."

"Fine. As a compromise, I'll fly the flag on Nazi holidays."

"That doesn't feel like much of a compromise."

"We're getting the radio."

Olga glared at him for several seconds and then stood up to clear the dishes.

CHAPTER 5

Hans's alarm clock jingled, and as he reached to turn it off, he remembered it was Sunday and he had a Hitler Youth meeting. He lay back down and listened to the rain on his window, a sound he enjoyed when he had the option of staying warm under his blanket.

He tried to convince himself to get up, but all he could think about was how much he dreaded going. When he was younger, he'd enjoyed being a Boy Scout, but that organization was banned after Hitler Youth membership became mandatory. At first, many of the activities were similar to those in Boy Scouts, but as time went on, the meetings had become increasingly militaristic. Competition and struggle, heroism and leadership, discipline and sacrifice. Much less bird watching and basketry these days, much more boxing and shooting.

He rolled out of bed, got dressed, and went to survey himself in the bathroom mirror. His uniform consisted of a brown shirt, black shorts, black neckerchief, and a swastika armband. The silver belt buckle featured an eagle and the Hitler Youth motto "Blood and Honor." Some boys wore patches on their sleeves that represented their various achievements in furthering the goals of National Socialism, but to date, Hans hadn't accomplished any of those achievements or even attempted them.

As he put his side cap on his head, he realized he looked

almost like a perfect German. Tall, fair skin, light brown hair, blue eyes—Hans could be viewed as the personification of a Nazified Aryan ideal if it were not for his introversion, absence of athletic ability, and lack of self-confidence. He knew these were all red flags for the Nazis.

Because he had grown so much in the prior year, the uniform no longer fit and his shirt continually came untucked in the back. He didn't want to ask his parents to buy a replacement, though, because in less than a year, he'd be required to transition from the Hitler Youth to the Hitler grown-ups, which would require a new uniform anyway.

Hans took a tram to the city's outskirts and then walked a kilometer to the parade grounds. The grounds, a simple clearing in the woods, consisted of a pole flying a Nazi flag, a small pavilion, and a makeshift boxing ring. Other sleepy-eyed boys were already there, silently milling about in the foggy drizzle.

Not far from Hans, a small group huddled around a boy named Gerhard Wolff. Gerhard was of slightly less than average height and significantly less than average intelligence. While Gerhard couldn't do much about his intelligence, he compensated for his lack of height by diligently training to strengthen his upper body. He was built like an inverted pyramid, and his shoulders were so well developed that their tops were the same height as his chin, all but concealing his neck. He had dark hair, and several months earlier had begun a heroic but seemingly doomed attempt at growing a Hitler-style mustache. Hans thought it looked like soot that had escaped from Gerhard's nostrils.

Gerhard was talking quietly, which was suspicious because he always talked loudly, despite having nothing interesting to say. As Hans watched, Gerhard took pills from a blue bottle and handed them to the other boys, who all snickered as they swallowed them. Hans moved slightly to get a better view of the bottle and saw it was the methamphetamine Pervitin. He remembered seeing advertisements targeted at housewives when he was younger, positioning the drug as a stimulant that would help the women complete their chores. He knew the German military had since repurposed it as a stimulant for the troops. Pervitin didn't just keep people awake, it also gave them feelings of aggressiveness and invincibility, which, as far as Hans was concerned, weren't traits that needed to be amplified in Gerhard.

The boys' leader, Herr Ziegler, arrived and ordered them into formation. He was a great ape of a man, burly and muscular, but rendered less fit-looking by the onset of a middle-aged belly. His face had a base level of ruddiness, but when he yelled, which was often, it became crimson. His lectures were vile and inane, and Hans had decided long before that if this man and his utterances represented the Nazi ideal that German boys should aspire to, he'd much prefer to take a pass.

The boys lined up and recited the Hitler Youth oath: "In the presence of this blood banner, which represents our Führer, I swear to devote all my energies and my strength to the savior of our country, Adolf Hitler. I am willing and ready to give up my life for him, so help me God." Whenever they recited the oath, Hans glanced at the other boys. Did they believe the words they were saying? He had no intention of giving up his life for Hitler, and he assumed most of the other boys felt the same way. But perhaps he was wrong.

Herr Ziegler announced that their first activity would be a five-kilometer hike, and shortly thereafter the long line of soggy aspiring Nazis disappeared one by one into the woods. A hundred meters later, Hans felt a push in his back as his right foot was tripped. He landed in the mud and looked up to see Gerhard laughing as he swaggered past.

After he'd gotten back up, Hans wiped his hands on his shorts, picked the wet leaves off his knees, and began walking again. He could see Gerhard about ten meters ahead but, as usual, chose not to confront him. The dynamics between them had been fixed for as long as Hans could remember. Gerhard was a perfect archetype of the young men who were celebrated and rewarded in the new Germany. Even if this hadn't been the case, Gerhard's father was a Gestapo agent, and people prudently tried to stay on the good side of the Gestapo. Gerhard wasn't exactly Hans's rival, since rivals are people who compete for the same things. While Gerhard was competing for glory, victory, and the Reich, Hans wasn't competing for much of anything at all.

It was still drizzling when the boys returned from their hike, but Herr Ziegler instructed them to sit on the ground in the rain rather than in the pavilion. It would help toughen them up, he said. Hans knew that toughening up young men for their future service to the Reich was an essential aspect of the Hitler Youth mission.

Herr Ziegler began the indoctrination portion of the meeting, covering the same material about the wonders of National Socialism and Hitler and the evils of Communism and the international Jewish conspiracy that Hans had heard for the last seven years. Behind Herr Ziegler in the pavilion was an easel that held a portrait of Hitler in shiny armor, riding a horse while carrying a Nazi flag. Herr Ziegler often displayed this portrait during his screeds, and every time Hans saw it, he had to stop himself from laughing. Did nobody else see how ridiculous this was?

Hans slumped on the wet ground and thought about how much time he had wasted in these lectures. He had been only ten when the Nazis came to power, and back then he had thought that much of the propaganda, such as newsreels of the Nuremberg rallies, was exciting. But as he got older, the endless repetition in school, music, movies, books, and, well, everywhere had become boring.

He briefly tuned back in to Herr Ziegler. "Our Führer is the only thing preventing Bolshevism from spreading throughout Europe," the man was saying. "Do you realize what will happen if Communism takes root here?"

Hans glanced at the other boys. To his left was Karl, who used to play marbles with Hans and was always the smallest kid in their class. Karl had struggled with the physical activities of the Hitler Youth when they first joined, and he and Hans had made fun of much of it. But Karl had bought into the message over the years, and he and Hans had drifted apart. Karl was now staring at Herr Ziegler with rapt attention. To Hans's right was Ernst, who had been in Boy Scouts with Hans. They had liked to build model airplanes together, but Ernst lost interest in that hobby as he became more committed to the Nazis. His sleeve was covered with patches, and it was rumored that Ernst had had a falling-out with his parents over his enthusiastic embrace of Nazism.

Hans shook his head slightly and let his thoughts drift to Elise. Where was she at that moment? Was she practicing the oboe? Doing homework? At a League of German Girls meeting? Whatever she was doing, maybe, just maybe, she was thinking of him? Probably not, but he smiled at the thought of it. "Becker! Answer the question!" Herr Ziegler's roar shattered Hans's musings. He didn't know how long he had been lost in his fantasy, but going from the dream of Elise to the nightmare of Herr Ziegler was distressing.

Hans clambered to his feet and proclaimed, "Heil Hitler!" Even standing at attention, he held himself slightly stooped, as if trying to appear less conspicuous. He realized with alarm that his shirt had come untucked in the back, but he was unable to rectify that while standing at attention.

"Answer the question!" barked Herr Ziegler.

"Sir, I didn't hear the question," Hans said in a tone that he hoped would sound heroic and forceful but realized sounded squeaky and weak.

Herr Ziegler lumbered toward Hans so that they were nose to nose, or as close to that as he could get, given that he was significantly shorter. "The information you're receiving here is a matter of life and death, not just for you, not just for Germany, but for the world." The spittle that landed on Hans's cheek disgusted him, but fortunately, it was diluted by the rain. As Herr Ziegler continued his rant, Hans realized the man must've eaten a snack while the boys were on their hike. Hans could identify hints of sauerkraut and schnapps, but there were other scents in the bouquet as well. The smell was overpowering, and Hans arched his back in an attempt to evade the stench and spit. It probably wasn't his intent, but Herr Ziegler had finally made Hans stand up straight. "Do you understand?"

"Yes, sir!"

"Fortunately, we're near the end of this lesson and are about to move to our next activity. Do you know what that activity is?"

"No, sir."

"It's boxing. You like boxing, right?"

"Yes, sir."

Herr Ziegler backed off from Hans. "Herr Becker apparently doesn't think the information you're learning is important. Would someone like to teach him a lesson?" Every boy knew that the correct response was to raise his hand, and that's what every boy did.

Herr Ziegler looked around before locking his gaze on Gerhard. "Herr Wolff. Why don't you teach Herr Becker a lesson?"

Gerhard sprang to his feet. "Heil Hitler! Sir, I would be honored and proud!"

Hans's heart sank. Gerhard was universally acknowledged as the best boxer in their unit, as well as the dirtiest.

Hans, Gerhard, and the other boys walked to the boxing ring, four posts stuck in the ground with ropes tied to each. Hans and Gerhard took off their uniform shirts but left on their undershirts. Several boys helped the boxers put on their gloves, and as usual, Hans was surprised by how heavy they were. The other boys crowded excitedly around the ring in anticipation of violence.

Hans and Gerhard went to their respective corners, and Herr Ziegler blew a whistle for them to start. Gerhard strode quickly and confidently to Hans's corner, propelled by a combination of Fascism, barbarism, and methamphetamine. He began to throw punches at Hans's midsection since their height differential made it challenging to land a shot to his head.

Hans tried to protect himself by keeping his gloves up near his face, but the body shots took their toll. Herr Ziegler yelled at him to fight back, but he knew that even if he hit Gerhard in the face, it probably wouldn't hurt him. As the body shots became unbearable, Hans lowered his gloves, which enabled Gerhard to unleash a left uppercut that caught Hans square on the chin. His knees buckled, and as he was falling to the ground, Gerhard nailed him with a right hook on the nose.

Hans collapsed into the mud, seeing stars and tasting the blood leaking from his nose. The other boys cheered wildly, as nothing got the Hitler Youth more excited than the sight of blood. Encouraged by their enthusiasm, Gerhard Wolff kicked Hans in the ribs and yelled, "If you're not a wolf, then you're a sheep!"—a play on words on his last name that he had used more than once and that he apparently thought was clever.

Herr Ziegler clapped and said, "That was a wonderful lesson, Herr Wolff! Herr Becker, has this helped you understand why listening is important?"

Still wallowing in muck and misery, Hans said, "Yes, sir."

He was confident this was not something that would've happened in Boy Scouts.

CHAPTER 6

When she heard the front door open, Olga left the kitchen to greet Hans. She stopped when she saw him in the doorway, soaking wet and holding a bloody handkerchief to his nose. He looked so sad and pathetic that she wanted to hug him, but she resisted the urge because August had told her that she babied their son too much.

She stared at the skinny, bloody boy standing in front of her. The thought that in less than a year he could be a soldier was not only frightening but also absurd. She remembered August coming home on leave in the last war, self-confident and ruggedly handsome in his uniform. She tried to picture Hans in similar circumstances, but it was impossible.

This wasn't the first time he had come home bloody from a Hitler Youth meeting, and she didn't bother to ask what happened. Instead, she just told him to change clothes and bring the bloody ones to her so she could wash them.

What were they teaching these children?

Hans brought down the clothes, gave them to her, and went back upstairs. He didn't seem upset by whatever had happened that morning, and she soon heard him practicing his violin. She filled a basin with cold water and began to scrub the clothes on the washboard.

The morning's events were just one more thing to worry

about. In addition to being responsible for nearly everything else in the house, she was by unspoken agreement also in charge of worrying, and she did enough for all three of them.

Her habit of constantly worrying had begun when August left to fight in the last war. During that time, she received frequent, usually upbeat letters from him, and for a brief period after each one, she would be able to stop worrying. She reread them often, but the nonworrying period shortened with each successive reading. The worrying would then recommence, intensifying until she received the next letter.

She and August were married shortly after the war, and then for several years, she worried because she was unable to get pregnant. When she finally did, she worried about the pregnancy, and then Hans came along, a development that naturally led to worrying about Hans. She and Hans were similar in many ways, both favoring quiet nights at home reading or listening to music. When he was young, she had treasured these moments, but as he got older, she worried that he was different from the other boys. He didn't enjoy sports or competition, and when Hitler came to power, the gap between Hans and the boys who tried to emulate the Nazified heroic ideal seemed to widen. Her worrying only got worse.

Sometimes, she even worried about bad things that could've happened but didn't. Once, at her family's farm, Hans had fallen out of a hayloft. He was fine afterward, but he could've landed on his head or broken his neck, and she often thought about how terrible that would've been. Her mother used to tell her, "Don't worry about things you can control, because you can control them, and don't worry about things you can't control, because you can't control them." While this theory made a certain amount of sense to Olga, its limitations had become clear to her when her mother died after getting kicked in the head by a horse. Sometimes, she thought, a little worrying wasn't such a bad idea.

In an effort to keep her mother's advice in mind, Olga regularly compiled mental lists of things to worry about, sorted by whether or not she could control them. It seemed that not that long ago, the controllable list had been longer than the noncontrollable list, and she'd been able to aggressively and enthusiastically attack those items.

As she stood at the wash basin now, though, she realized the relative balance of the lists had been inverted. The noncontrollable list had come to include the Hitler Youth; August's drinking and risk of denunciation; Hans's social awkwardness; August's increasingly frequent episodes of anxiety; the possibility of Dresden being bombed, which August had convinced her was very real; food shortages; Hans joining the military; and, of course, the war.

At that particular moment, the only item on the controllable list was eradicating the blood from Hans's clothes. So she continued scrubbing, with an intensity that bordered on violence.

CHAPTER 7

Several weeks after first making eye contact with Elise, Hans was finally prepared to implement his plan. He had learned to play Beethoven's "Für Elise," a song written for the piano, on the violin. He would play it as she walked by during warm-ups in hopes that she'd realize he had learned it for her. Elise was an old-fashioned, uncommon name, so it was possible her parents named her after the song. Maybe she liked Beethoven as much as he did, which could lead to the start of a conversation. They could discuss why Beethoven's odd-numbered symphonies were better than the even-numbered ones, or maybe even debate who "Für Elise" was written for, since nobody was sure. He knew it would be easier to simply talk to her rather than go to all this trouble, but he hoped she would think his efforts were charming. The worst-case scenario was that she wouldn't recognize the song or would think it was just a coincidence that he was playing it. The best case, of course, was that they would live happily ever after.

The night before rehearsal, as he tried to sleep, he fantasized about someday being Elise's hero. He didn't really see himself as the heroic sort and was pretty sure nobody else did either, but he imagined one day proving his love by sacrificing his life for her. He suspected this was an unusual fantasy to have, especially about someone he had never actually met, but for some reason, these thoughts comforted him. Other boys could be heroes for the Reich; he would be a hero for Elise.

The next morning, Hans arrived early to rehearsal, withdrew his worn secondhand violin from its case, and applied rosin to the bow. As other musicians took their seats and began practicing, tuning, and warming up, he felt his nerves calmed by the jumbled mishmash of notes and instruments, a sound he always enjoyed. The conductor approached the podium and began studying the day's agenda, but there was no sign of Elise.

Finally, the door opened and she entered the auditorium, listening to a friend as she talked animatedly. They walked toward Hans to get to the coatroom, and his heart raced as he worried he'd botch the song. As soon as she was within earshot, he placed the violin under his chin and began to play. The girls neared his chair, but the friend wouldn't stop yapping, and he wasn't sure Elise would be able to identify his song amid all the other music. As she reached his chair, though, she hesitated and appeared to have a moment of recognition. She glanced at Hans and gave him a quick, somewhat quizzical smile, but walked on.

Minutes later, she returned from the coatroom, sat in her chair, and took out her oboe, all without looking at him. The conductor tapped the podium with his baton and outlined the rehearsal schedule. As usual, it was all Wagner, Hitler's favorite composer. Hans's heart was pounding and his cheeks were tingling. On the list of traits that he disliked about himself, his tendency to blush was near the top. He had never understood the evolutionary purpose of blushing. How could someone's face turning red increase their chances of survival? It was such a pointless reflex.

What a disaster this had become. His best-case scenario of beginning a romance with Elise hadn't happened, and his worst-case scenario of her not recognizing the song hadn't happened either. Instead, this was worse than his assumed worst case: She recognized the song and understood he had learned it for her, but either didn't care or else thought his doing so was silly. He had spent hours contemplating the plan, yet the possibility of this outcome hadn't occurred to him.

The rest of the rehearsal was torture, and he steadfastly avoided looking in her direction. The realization that she might laugh at him was unbearable. As he replayed all their interactions over the past few weeks, he began to worry that she thought he was creepy and that his gesture was just another example of his creepiness. And what if she told her friends and they all laughed at him too?

Hans remained seated when rehearsal ended. He put the sheet music in his lap and hunched over, pretending to study it to avoid any risk of eye contact as Elise walked by. He intended to remain in that position until he was sure she was past, the rest of the day if necessary.

But then, right next to his chair, he saw a pair of black leather shoes, white ankle socks folded over with a bit of lace on them, two calves, and the hem of a dress. After weeks of watching, he knew to whom those shoes, socks, calves, and dress belonged.

He kept his head down and watched as her feet fidgeted and her shoes rolled onto their outer edges. Then he felt a hand on his shoulder.

When he looked up, Elise said, "That was lovely."

CHAPTER 8

The school day was a blur as alternating waves of euphoria and terror washed over Hans. He knew the first step in his plan for eternal bliss was to play "Für Elise" for Elise. He also knew the final step: living happily ever after. What he hadn't considered was what came in between. He needed time to think. Fortunately, it was Friday and he wouldn't see her again until rehearsal on Monday morning. He had taken weeks to devise and implement the first step of his plan, but he hoped to carry out the next step more quickly.

Hans had agreed to work with his father at a construction site after school, so he took the tram to the east side of town. He looked forward to a distraction from his thoughts of Elise and also to burning off the adrenaline that had been generated at rehearsal.

He got off the tram, and as he neared the site, several workers called out, "Herr Becker! Where have you been? We need your help!" Hans grinned modestly and blushed. The workers all seemed to like him, but he knew this was mostly because they liked his father. Before he began working, he examined the progress that had been made on the building. He always found it fascinating to see how buildings came together and how much had changed since the last time he was there.

The rest of the afternoon went quickly. The other workers liked to kid with Hans, and while their language was coarse and some of the topics were vile, several of the men were quite funny. He also liked seeing his father in this setting, which seemed to be a more natural habitat for him. Given his father's language at work, Hans was amazed that he had never heard him curse around his mother.

After they'd finished for the day, Hans's father told him he was going to the pub for an hour or so and that Hans should head home. Hans walked to the tram, boarded, and sat near the rear of the car with his back facing the window. He smiled as he thought about the day's triumph. She'd touched his shoulder! This time it was finally going to happen.

The tram proceeded along its route, filling with Friday evening commuters, and soon all the seats were taken. Hans watched people board at the next stop and was stunned when he saw Elise. They made eye contact, and he froze. Why the hell was she here? Lots of musicians could improvise, but he was a classical-music guy, not a jazz guy. He needed structure and a plan. The clump of new passengers shuffled toward the back of the tram, and Elise stopped directly in front of him, holding a bag from a bakery. He looked up at her, and for a moment they were both speechless. Then he stood, gestured toward his seat, and said, "Für Elise?"

As soon as the words left his mouth, he realized how ridiculous he sounded. That was perhaps the stupidest thing a boy ever said to a girl he was trying to win over, or in any other situation for that matter. Even if the "Für Elise" gimmick had worked in orchestra rehearsal, he was foolish to think he could use it again. She would almost certainly conclude he was a dolt or a creep, and perhaps she was right.

Instead, she smiled guardedly, sat down, and said, "Thank you."

As the bell clanged and the tram whirred forward, they remained silent, with him standing while holding on to a post and her sitting in front of him with the bag in her lap. He knew he should say something, but he hated when people could overhear his conversations. Was he going to blow this again? After several tram stops, she solved his problem for him. She looked up and said, "That was a beautiful version of 'Für Elise.' Where did you learn it?"

He knew he would need to strike the appropriate balance between three conflicting factors: She had to be able to hear him, other passengers had to be unable to hear him, and he needed not to be so close that he made her uncomfortable. While trying to determine this balance, he neglected to think about what he was going to say, and his default position of honesty took control. He leaned over, close but not too close, and said, "I learned it for you."

She blushed and looked down, but then lifted her head, smiled, and said, "Thank you."

Hans straightened back up. He didn't know what to do next but was reasonably certain that admitting he'd learned the song for her was a mistake. Once again, she saved him. "A group of my friends are going to Oktoberfest tomorrow night. Would you like to meet us there?"

This was all happening too fast and didn't seem real. "Sure," he said.

"Let's meet at the Martin Luther statue at seven o'clock, okay?"

"Sure," he repeated. *Say something besides "sure," you fool.*

"Okay. This is my stop, but I'll see you tomorrow."

"Okay, bye."

The tram stopped, and Hans watched her get off. He couldn't believe it.

Despite his complete ineptitude, he was going on something that resembled a date with the girl of his dreams.

CHAPTER 9

During the first block of her walk home, Elise felt exhilarated. A tall and handsome boy had learned a song for her! She was proud of herself for initiating the conversation; boldness was not in her nature.

As she continued walking, though, she began to have second thoughts. She steadfastly avoided situations that could cause her embarrassment, yet she had just created one that had the potential for a massive amount of it. She knew nothing about Hans but had invited him to join her at a group activity. What if his shyness prevented him from carrying on a conversation, and instead he just made low guttural noises when people tried to speak to him?

Further doubts arose as she replayed their interaction and realized he hadn't seemed excited about her invitation. Perhaps he was playing it cool, but from everything she had seen of Hans, she felt confident that "playing it cool" wasn't something he could pull off and likely wouldn't even try. By the time she reached her home, she was sure she had made a mistake.

Her mother, Maria, sitting in the parlor just off the foyer, set down her *Modenschau* fashion magazine and rose to greet her. She wore a blue satin dress and pearl necklace, which suggested to Elise that she had gone to a Prager Strasse restaurant for lunch, and perhaps a glass of wine or two, with her friends.

While the war and its accompanying constraints had curtailed such opportunities, they still existed for people in her family's social circle.

Her mother glided into the foyer and said, "Welcome home! Were you able to pick up the Sandkuchen?"

"Yes, it's right here." Elise handed her the bag from the bakery.

"Wonderful! Thank you so much. I know it was a headache for you to go to the bakery across town, but I think it's worth it. If you have time, why don't we sit and talk for a minute." Because Elise's brother was in the army and her father worked long hours at the hospital, she often had her mother's undivided attention, which was usually, but not always, a good thing.

They sat in the parlor across from each other, the bakery bag on the coffee table between them. As usual, her mother did most of the talking, recapping that day's neighborhood news and gossip. The butcher said he wouldn't be able to get beef sirloin again for a while . . . their tailor's apprentice had been drafted . . . production delays meant the Hoffmann family wouldn't be able to get their new BMW for at least six months. After several minutes, she paused and said, "You look worried. Is everything all right?"

Elise hesitated, unsure whether to talk about Hans. She realized, though, that her mother was the most socially gifted person she knew, so she decided to ask her for advice. "I met a boy," she said, without making eye contact.

Her mother stiffened and was uncharacteristically silent for a moment but then said, "That's wonderful. Tell me about him."

Elise took a deep breath. "His name is Hans, and he's in the orchestra."

"I see. How old is he?"

"I'm not sure. Probably seventeen."

"What does he look like?"

"Well, he's tall and has blue eyes."

"You've always liked tall boys, haven't you?" Her mother smiled. Elise blushed and looked down, beginning to regret confiding in her. "Do you sit near each other?"

"No, he plays the violin, so we're not that close." Elise wasn't sure how much to tell her. While she thought Hans's learning "Für Elise" was charming, she didn't know if her mother would agree, and she was quite sure her father would think it was bizarre. "We just started talking one day. He seems nice, but he's quiet."

"Well, there's nothing wrong with being quiet, is there. For goodness' sake, I've been married to a quiet man for twenty years."

"Yes, I suppose that's true. So many boys are arrogant and obnoxious, and he seems to be the opposite of that."

"Well, that sounds wonderful. Why do you look worried?"

"I think I told you I'm going to Oktoberfest with friends tomorrow night? Well, I sort of invited Hans to meet us there. It's not a date or anything. But like I said, I don't really know him, and I'm nervous he'll embarrass me. I'm afraid people will be mad at me for inviting him."

"I'm sure it'll be fine. I've somehow managed to attend all sorts of social events with your father for all these years."

"Yes, but you can do enough talking for both of you, and I don't have that skill."

"I'm sure it'll work out. If it's awkward or you decide you don't like him, you can tell him your mother said you need to be home by a certain hour."

"I guess," she said, looking down at the table. "I just wish I hadn't invited him."

"It'll be fine. Should we have a slice of this Sandkuchen?"

Sweets were her mother's answer to most of life's problems, and Elise firmly believed in their effectiveness.

After eating the cake and talking with her mother a while longer, Elise went upstairs to her bedroom. As she turned on the light, she was suddenly struck by how pink her room was. Wallpaper with alternating vertical stripes of dark pink and light pink, pink bedspread, pink curtains. She'd loved pink when she was five, and her mother had gone overboard to make her happy. But now she was sixteen and abruptly decided she hated it.

She took off her shoes and walked to the mirror mounted on the wall above her dresser. Her pink ballet shoes from when she was little hung from the top of the mirror, and she wondered how long her mother would make her keep them.

She leaned toward the mirror for a quick evaluation. A few stray hairs had escaped from her pigtails, and as she rotated her face, she noticed a nascent pimple on her cheek. Overall, though, given that it was the end of the day and she hadn't expected to see Hans, she concluded that her appearance had been satisfactory.

She walked to her four-poster bed, relocated her doll from the pillow to her nightstand, and lay down. Her mother's words and the accompanying sweets had been comforting, but she was still worried.

After exchanging glances with Hans for several weeks, she had begun to wonder how two shy people would ever meet. And then today, she'd managed to initiate two separate interactions, although she wasn't sure if she was proud of herself or mad at herself for doing so. She'd approached him after rehearsal to thank him for the song, but when he hadn't raised his head, she'd begun to panic as she realized how foolish she must have appeared just standing there. She'd looked at what he was studying so intently and had seen that his sheet music was upside down. The awkwardness was unbearable, so she'd reflexively touched his shoulder to get his attention and make it end.

And then, the tram. She'd been relieved when he offered her his seat because that was her first evidence that he possessed some social skills. While she didn't know if his "Für Elise" line had been charming, funny, or ridiculous, at least they were words. She'd been glad to finally hear his voice, and while she hadn't been sure what to expect, it was rather deep. It was also soft, perhaps because it was so rarely used.

She stared at the ceiling and thought about how strangely this had developed. Many girls her age were boy crazy, but she wasn't one of them. She still enjoyed spending time with her family and wasn't in a hurry to cut those ties. The fact that some of her friends already had boyfriends, though, made her worry that she was falling behind.

She knew she should be excited about meeting up with Hans, but instead she was focused on what could go wrong. Whenever she was anxious about an upcoming event, she liked to think about how long it would be until it was over, and she did this again now.

Elise told herself that maybe she'd have fun at Oktoberfest. But even if she didn't, it would be over in thirty hours.

CHAPTER 10

That night, Hans lay in bed and replayed his interactions with Elise. By his count, he had spoken a total of eleven words to her on the tram yet had somehow managed to arrange a date.

But was it a date? "A group of my friends." What did that mean? Would it be all girls, a mixture of girls and boys, or a group of couples, of which his pairing with Elise would be the most awkward? Why did it have to be a group? He hated speaking in groups because he worried people were listening to and judging him.

He went to sleep thrilled with how things had transpired but also terrified by the prospect of what the next day held. Now that Elise was real, he wondered if he would've preferred her to remain a fantasy. There was no risk of failure in a fantasy.

Hans awoke the next morning to the sound of dull thuds coming from the backyard. He peeked out the window and saw his father unloading bricks from a wheelbarrow and piling them next to the piece of steel in the middle of the yard. Apparently, today was going to be another day of working on his ridiculous project.

He got dressed and went downstairs, where his mother was wiping down the counters. Greta was right beside her, hoping for a crumb or two to come her way. His mother said,

"Your father wants you to help him when you're finished with breakfast."

Hans sighed and looked out the open window. Birds were chirping, and he could hear his dad rustling around in his toolshed. The piece of metal in the middle of the yard had been moved to the side, revealing a hole in the ground. But it wasn't an ordinary piece of metal—it was a hatch. And it wasn't an ordinary hole in the ground—it was the entrance to an air-raid shelter.

For the past year, construction of the shelter had taken up most of his father's time when he wasn't working or drinking, and sometimes even when he *was* drinking. He and Hans had spent weeks digging the hole, and afterward some construction buddies had helped pour the concrete for the floor. His father had laid the bricks for the walls, and then he and Hans had installed the concrete roof, which was supported by heavy wooden beams. His father was proud of how the project was progressing, but when Hans looked at it, all he saw was a big box in the ground and a colossal waste of time.

Hans's father emerged from the toolshed, wearing overalls laden with tools, many of which Hans didn't know the names of, much less what they were used for. The older man grabbed the wheelbarrow, and as he headed toward the front of the house, Hans could hear him whistling, which he always did when he worked, at least when he wasn't talking or cursing. He was an excellent whistler, and while it wasn't a skill that generated any commercial value, Hans liked to listen to it. He, of course, would never admit that. Once his father started on a song, he'd usually stick with it for the entire day, so Hans braced himself for a hundred renditions of "Lili Marleen."

Hans's mother gave him a piece of black bread and jam, and he sat down to eat. Greta sat politely next to him, eternally optimistic about the possibility of receiving table scraps.

When Hans was nearly finished, she put her head on his lap and made a noise that she might have intended to sound like a growl, but was actually more like a purr. She was the gentlest dog Hans knew, and she had never mastered the art of growling. Hans gave her the last bite, and after two quick chomps it was gone. She gave him a look that Hans interpreted as appreciation for the food combined with disappointment over the absence of protein.

After twenty minutes, he could dawdle no longer, so he put on his jacket and went outside. Next to the stack of bricks, there was now a pile of conduit, pipes, and scrap metal. As he tried to deduce what that day's tasks could be, he heard the approaching strains of "Lili Marleen" and saw his father turn the corner with another wheelbarrow full of metal. "Hello, young man. I'm glad you could finally join me."

"Why are you moving all this metal from the front porch?"

"The metal drives are getting more aggressive. I don't want your crazy Hitler Youth buddies taking my stuff, so I'm going to store it in the shelter. We should also start concealing the hatch when it's not open. If one of those morons saw a big piece of steel like that, he'd probably have an orgasm." Hans blushed but smiled. "Why don't you go into the shelter, and I'll hand you everything."

Hans climbed down the rickety wooden ladder, and for the next half hour, his father handed him pieces of metal to stack in the rear of the shelter. "Okay," his father said, "that's it for the metal. Now I'll hand you the bricks. Today we're going to build steps so we can get rid of this ladder. We can't have your mother stumbling down it in the dark. Plus, the less wood we have in here, the better, in case there's a fire." Hans nodded and began taking the bricks and piling them near the entrance.

"All right, genius, you have a real job today," his father said once that was done. "I don't want the steps to protrude more than a meter into the shelter, but they need to reach the lip of the hatch. While I mix the mortar, I want you to figure out how many bricks and half bricks we need and then mark their location on the floor and wall." Like a magician, he swiftly produced a pencil, paper, chalk, measuring tape, and level from various hiding places in his pockets and tool belt and handed them all to Hans. Hans usually just served as manual labor on these projects, so he was happy to perform a task that contributed more value. He sat down, did his calculations, and made his marks.

By the time Hans was finished, his father had prepared the mortar, and after double-checking Hans's calculations and measurements ("Measure twice and cut once," he always said), he split some bricks with a chisel and hammer. When he had all the bricks and half bricks he needed, he stirred the bucket of mortar, spread some on a mortar board, and went to work. Hans was fascinated by craftsmen who could take nothing and turn it into something, and he considered his dad to be an artist with bricks, mortar, and a trowel.

As his father worked, he said, "It's coming along well, don't you think?" Hans had to admit the shelter was impressive. It was five meters square, big enough to hold four people comfortably, or in his family's case, three people and a dog. Eventually, there would be an electric light, but for now, it was illuminated by a kerosene lamp. Although the ceiling was high enough for Hans to stand up inside, he had learned from experience that he needed to duck when he passed under the wooden beams.

"Yes, but I'm still not sure why we need this when English planes can't reach here."

"Wars have a way of accelerating technology. When the last war started, armies still had cavalry units, but by the time it was over, they had tanks. Nothing motivates governments more than the prospect of killing people more efficiently, and nothing motivates companies more than making money by helping them."

"Why can't we just reinforce our cellar, like other people are doing?"

"Well, for one thing, our cellar is too shallow—we can't even stand up in it. Also, what happens if the house catches fire? Then the coal in the cellar would start burning, and before you knew it, the entire house would burn and collapse. A separate shelter is the only way to go."

"We're the only ones in the neighborhood doing this. It's embarrassing."

"When you know you're right, you need to act on your beliefs. Mark my words, at some point, in some form, the war will come to Dresden." He wiped the last bit of excess mortar from the top layer of bricks and stepped back to admire his handiwork. "Looks good, right?" He didn't wait for an answer. "Our next task will be ventilation shafts."

"I thought the next step was going to be electricity."

"The air sometimes gets thin down here, so we need to do the shafts next. Let's mark where they'll go." He whistled as he picked up the chalk and tape measure, walked to the right wall of the shelter, took some measurements, and drew a fist-sized circle near the ceiling. Then, as he moved to the left side of the shelter, he abruptly stopped whistling, right in the middle of the chorus of "Lili Marleen." Hans watched as his father stood motionless and stared at the wall. After about twenty seconds, he dropped the chalk and tape measure and bounded up the newly constructed steps. Hans heard the back door open and close.

This was the second time in several months Hans had seen something like this happen. The first incident had occurred shortly after the roof was installed. He sat on the floor and waited an hour for his father to return, but then concluded they were finished for the day.

CHAPTER 11

When Hans ate dinner with his parents that night, nobody mentioned his father's abrupt departure from the shelter. Afterward, he went upstairs to prepare for his date, or whatever it was. He didn't know what to wear since all his clothes were too small, worn out, or both, but he eventually settled on a snug long-sleeved shirt, jacket, and slightly short corduroy pants.

He rode a crowded tram to Dresden's Altstadt, or Old Town, and as he got off, he heard a polka band and the buzz of people talking and laughing. He walked to the meeting point near the Frauenkirche, a statue of Martin Luther holding a Bible and wearing long robes and a grim expression. To ensure he didn't make Elise wait, he had arrived fifteen minutes early, and as he expected, she wasn't there. But when seven o'clock came and went and she still hadn't appeared, he began to wonder if there was another Martin Luther statue in Dresden and he was waiting at the wrong one.

Hans watched the revelers stroll about as the minutes rolled by, but there was no sign of Elise or her ill-defined "group of friends." He had nothing to lean or sit on, so he stood awkwardly in front of the statue. He put his hands in his jacket pockets, took them out, put them in his pants pockets, and then took them out again. He couldn't decide where they looked least ridiculous. He continually tugged at the sleeves of his shirt and jacket in a futile effort to make them longer. With all the seemingly involuntary movements of his hands and arms, he realized a passerby might think he had some sort of neurological ailment.

Finally, he saw her, leading a gaggle of seven or eight teenagers as they weaved toward him through the crowd. She wore a plaid skirt, a white blouse with a lace collar, and a brown leather jacket. Her hair, freed from its braided pigtails, hung loosely around her shoulders, constrained only by a red bow on the side. She also appeared to be wearing lipstick and some blush.

His height enabled him to see her before she saw him, and he stared as she scanned the crowd and made her way forward. She was almost to the statue before she saw him, and for the briefest of moments, she raised her eyebrows and smiled, causing her green eyes to sparkle. But an instant later, her glow vanished when a voice behind her said, "No! This is the guy you're meeting?" It was Gerhard. Hans's heart sank.

"We left the band to come and get this guy?" Gerhard said as he elbowed his way to the front of the group. His glassy eyes and slurred speech told Hans he had been drinking, and he wondered if it was possible that alcohol would make him even more obnoxious. Gerhard turned to Elise and said, "You're way too pretty for this clown. What are you thinking?"

The petite girl who appeared to be with Gerhard hit him playfully on the arm, giggled, and said, "Be nice!" She looked at Hans and said, "Hi, I'm Ruth. And I guess you know Gerhard?"

Not waiting for Hans to answer, Gerhard said, "He's the worst guy in my Hitler Youth troop. In fact, he's probably the worst guy in the entire Hitler Youth."

Hans realized he should respond with either violence or humor, but he knew that if he attempted the former, it would probably lead to the latter, and if he attempted the latter, it would probably lead to the former. So he remained frozen, which was his usual defense mechanism when faced with threats. As defense mechanisms went, it wasn't very effective, but it was the only one he had in his arsenal.

Fortunately, Ruth said, "Come on, let's go back to the band." She turned, grabbed Gerhard's hand, and led the way. Hans couldn't imagine a worse start to the evening.

Since Elise had been at the front of the group, when they turned to retrace their steps, she and Hans were now at the rear. Hans had developed a list of clever and charming conversation starters, but he couldn't think of any of them. In fact, he couldn't think of anything at all; his mind, which was usually buzzing with thoughts and ideas, had shut down.

When he saw Elise glance at her watch, he panicked and blurted out the only thing he could think of. "Did I look like the statue?"

Elise furrowed her brow. "What?"

"When I was standing there and Gerhard was being Gerhard, all I could think was that I was as frozen as the statue."

Hans looked at Elise, was relieved to see her smile, and was even happier when she said, "Now that you mention it, yeah, a little bit. You just needed some robes and a Bible."

"That's what I was afraid of, although I suspect the statue was more likely to think of a clever comeback than I was."

They walked for several minutes, allowing the leading group to get out of earshot. Elise said, "Sorry about Gerhard. He recently started dating my friend Ruth. He seems a bit . . . abrasive."

"Yes, 'abrasive' is one adjective for him, but I can think of others. I've known him almost my whole life, and I can tell you that his personality isn't just something he's pretending to be because of the new Germany—that's the real him."

"I guess it's good that he's authentic."

"Yes, he's completely authentic. I won't say an authentic what, but he is authentic."

"I don't understand what Ruth sees in him. She seems to like cocky boys."

"Then he's perfect for her." Unsure of whether to share this particular story but also not wanting the conversation to stall, he said, "We boxed each other a few weeks ago at our Hitler Youth meeting."

"How did it go?"

"Do you know how marionettes are sometimes out of proportion—their legs, arms, and torsos are too long? Well, picture me as a marionette making movements that resemble boxing, but then imagine someone cutting all the strings. That's what I looked like." He glanced at Elise, and she looked up at him and smiled.

They made it back to the small square where the band was playing and revelers were dancing. Gerhard turned to the others and shouted, "Who wants beer?"

Everyone in the group enthusiastically raised their hands except Elise and Hans. Fortunately, Gerhard was so focused on beer that he missed the opportunity to bully Hans about not drinking. Hans said to Elise, "Sorry, but I don't drink."

"That's all right, I don't either."

"My dad sometimes drinks too much and does foolish things," Hans said, immediately regretting sharing something so personal. Elise didn't respond, and Hans looked for a way to extricate himself from the topic. He saw a nearby booth and asked, "Can I buy you an apple cider?" She nodded and Hans was relieved to have found an escape from the larger group.

After getting their cider, they stood and watched the partiers drink and dance as the music from the polka band echoed off the walls and narrow lanes of the ancient Altstadt. To Hans's surprise and relief, their conversation flowed reasonably well. They had enough to talk about regarding orchestra and people from their neighborhood that there were only a few gaps, and in those moments it was easy for Hans to pretend he was simply taking a break from the conversation to listen to the music.

At one point, Elise's friends went out to dance. "Come with us!" a drunken Ruth shouted to Elise. Elise didn't respond, so Ruth bounced toward her and stood on her tiptoes to whisper in her ear. The music was too loud for Elise to hear her, and when she asked Ruth to repeat herself, Ruth yelled, "He's cute!" She laughed, twirled away, and started dancing with Gerhard. Gerhard had lost interest in Hans and was entirely focused on Ruth.

Hans grinned bashfully and looked down at Elise, who smiled up at him. He was pleased to get support from this unexpected source but moved past his moment of triumph to say, "I'm sorry, but I don't know how to dance."

"That's all right. I don't like dancing when there are a bunch of people around."

They continued talking for nearly two hours, but then Elise looked at her watch and said, "It's later than I thought. Would you like to walk me home?"

Hans took that as a sign that he hadn't ruined everything yet but also recognized there was still time for that to happen. "Yes, I'd like that."

They said goodbye to her friends and made the twenty-minute walk to Elise's house. As they strolled, Elise asked him questions about his family, school, and music, and at one point Hans was surprised to realize he was doing most of the talking. About halfway home, Elise said, "It's chilly tonight," and began to button her jacket.

As she reached the top button, Hans said, "I have a theory that when you're cold, you should always leave one button unbuttoned." She looked at him quizzically. "If you button every button, then you know you can't get any warmer, so your mind starts to think it's colder than it actually is. As long as you leave one button unbuttoned, you can tell yourself there's a way to get warmer if you really need to. You've always got something to fall back on."

Elise furrowed her brow but also smiled. "That's . . . an interesting theory." She left the top button unbuttoned.

They arrived at her house and stopped outside the gate. She turned to him and said, "I had a nice time. Thank you for walking me home."

"I did too." He hesitated and looked into her eyes. "So I guess I'll see you Monday?"

"Yes, see you then." After a moment of awkwardness, Hans took a step back, shook her hand, and said goodbye.

As he walked away he muttered, "A handshake? I'm so stupid." He shook his head but smiled the whole way home.

A Bach concerto greeted Elise when she entered the house, and she looked to the parlor where her mother was knitting and her father, Max, was reading a medical journal. "How was the festival?" her mother asked before Elise had even closed the door.

"It was nice. Lots of good music."

Her father looked up from his journal and asked, "Why are you smiling so much? Have you been drinking?"

Elise hadn't realized she was smiling, and she quickly swallowed it. "No, I just had a nice night. I'm going to bed now. Good night." She hurried up the stairs, embarrassed. Perhaps she liked Hans more than she thought she did. He was a bit odd but also smart and interesting. And Ruth was right—he was cute.

After she left, Max said, "I think she was drinking."

Maria replied, "I think she met a boy."

He looked at his wife for a few seconds and then said, "I'd prefer it if she were drinking."

He returned to his journal, and it was several moments

before he realized that Maria was still talking. He hated to admit it, but sometimes, especially after a long day of work, her words turned into background noise for him. He was amazed by her ability to talk and was convinced that she felt compelled to speak a certain number of words every day. If it was late in the evening, she would talk about almost anything in order to meet her quota, and he was often relieved to hear she had spoken to her mother, sister, or friends because that meant she had gone a long way toward meeting her daily goal.

He occasionally wondered what would happen if he added up all the words the two of them had said to each other over the course of their lives together. He estimated that she had spoken about ninety percent of them, and that was only if "uh-huh" counted as a word. If it didn't, her percentage would be significantly higher.

As he tuned back in, he employed a trick he had learned years before, of replaying her several prior sentences in his mind to catch up to what she was talking about. In so doing, he realized she was discussing the possibility that Elise would start dating soon. She monologued for five more minutes and then finally asked, "Don't you agree?"

He said, "Uh-huh."

CHAPTER 12

Two weeks later, Hans walked to Elise's house to meet her parents as a prelude to their first real date. During those weeks, they had gotten into the habit of arriving early to orchestra rehearsal each day so they could chat for a few minutes. At first, Elise had stood next to his chair while they visited, but by the second week, she was sitting in the chair next to his.

He'd been nervous when Elise mentioned he'd have to meet her parents, so she'd given him a suggestion. Her father had once told her that the best conversational tactic for people who didn't like to talk about themselves was to ask questions. She'd assured Hans that if he asked her mother a question, she'd talk for hours.

As Hans neared Elise's house, he reminded himself to follow her advice, the genius of which had become clear to him the more he thought about it. Most people loved themselves and were desperate for others to know how wonderful they were. Hans, though, had at best a lukewarm relationship with himself and didn't think anyone would be interested in him. If he asked questions, everyone would get what they wanted.

As he arrived at the wrought iron gate he observed that Elise's house was immense, at least compared to his family's shack. When he'd walked her home after Oktoberfest, he'd been too nervous to notice the house, but now he realized it was a stately villa, not quite a mansion, but definitely upscale. Both the porch and the stone walkway that led to it were brightly illuminated. Multicolored chrysanthemums overflowed from flower boxes at every windowsill, and ivy crept up the tan stone walls.

He walked through the gate, up the steps to the porch, and to the front door. As he reached for and rang the doorbell, he noticed his hand was trembling. After a few seconds, Elise pulled aside the lace front-door curtain and peeked out, causing Hans's heart to skip a beat. She opened the door, looking more nervous than excited, and said, "Hi. Please come in."

As Hans entered, he was greeted by the smell of freshly baked cookies and a feeling of warmth and security. Elise's parents rose from chairs in the parlor, and he realized that perhaps he should've brought a small gift or flowers or something. What was the etiquette? He knew he needed to refocus as her parents walked toward him but was concerned he had already made a mistake. His parents hadn't taught him anything about social mores, which were as foreign to them as they were to him.

Elise said, "Hans, this is my father, Dr. Max Engel, and my mother, Maria Engel."

With a wooden smile, Dr. Engel extended his hand, and Hans, after furtively wiping his sweaty palm on his pants, shook it. The doctor's handshake was firm to the point that it was slightly painful, and even though Hans was taller than Dr. Engel, he got the strange feeling he was looking up at him. The doctor had strong, patrician features, dark slicked-back hair that was beginning to gray at the temples, and a five o'clock shadow that looked as if it might be permanent. He had removed his suit coat but still wore a vest, and his tie was knotted stiffly beneath his high starched collar. If Hans had encountered Dr. Engel as a patient, he thought, the man's appearance and demeanor would have filled him with confidence. But

Hans was meeting him as his daughter's suitor, and so he was instead filled with terror.

"Hello, Dr. Engel," Hans said, his voice cracking on the word "Hello." And then, "Hello, Frau Engel." As he shook her hand he noticed that she had the same perfect posture and green eyes as her daughter.

They walked to the parlor and Hans and Elise sat on a small couch while Elise's parents sat facing them in parlor chairs. The cookies Hans had smelled were cooling on a silver platter that sat on a lace doily on the coffee table between the four of them. They looked delicious, but Hans was once again bewildered by etiquette. Would it be rude to take one without anyone else taking one first, or would it be rude not to when they had apparently been baked for him? He decided it was safer not to take one.

Hans looked around the high-ceilinged room and noticed all the lovely decor, things he would never see in his house. Oil paintings hung on the walls, and fresh flowers bloomed in gold-rimmed vases. In the adjacent room, he could see a piano as well as a lighted display case that housed a porcelain collection. The wood floors, wood walls, and wood furniture were all dark, giving the house an aura of nobility and permanence.

Hans had prepared and memorized a list of questions. He began with, "This is a beautiful house. How long have you lived here?"

Frau Engel glanced at a silent Dr. Engel but then looked back to Hans and said, "We moved here shortly after Elise's brother was born but before Elise was born. Before this house, we lived in an apartment while Dr. Engel was in medical school."

"I see," said Hans. He looked at Dr. Engel and asked, "Elise tells me you're a doctor. What hospital do you work in?" He knew the answer but was firing off questions to keep the conversation going and limit the amount of time available to ask questions of him.

"The Friedrichstadt," Dr. Engel replied, without elaboration. Hans noted that both Engels had perfect High German accents, making him self-conscious of the rural accent he had acquired from his parents.

The terseness of the man's answer surprised Hans and resulted in a brief lull in the conversation, but then the piano caught his eye again. "That's a lovely baby grand. Do either of you play?"

This time Frau Engel didn't give her husband an opportunity to answer. "I used to play often, but I don't seem to get around to it anymore. Elise tells me you're in the orchestra. What do you play?"

"I play the violin," Hans said and then volleyed a question right back. "Do you play anything?" he asked Dr. Engel.

"No," he replied.

Frau Engel said, "Dr. Engel is being modest. He used to play the piano too and was quite good at it. Do you have a favorite composer, Hans?"

Hans couldn't believe his luck. She had asked him a question, but it wasn't about himself, which was his least favorite topic. "Yes, I like Beethoven." He knew from Elise that her parents were admirers as well, so it was a perfect way to ingratiate himself with them and had the added advantage of being true.

"Oh my, that's wonderful!" Frau Engel said. "That's Dr. Engel's and my favorite too. We named Elise for 'Für Elise,' and her brother is named Ludwig for Beethoven." Hans already knew all of this but feigned surprise. She continued, "What would you say is your favorite Beethoven piece?"

He thought saying "Für Elise" would sound phony, so instead said, "That's a difficult question. 'Moonlight Sonata' and 'Pathétique' are two of my favorites. I also like the Seventh and Ninth Symphonies."

"Wonderful. Have you ever seen the Ninth Symphony performed in person?"

Hans lowered his eyes and then said, "No, I've never seen a real concert before," quickly regretting that he had shared more information than necessary. He recovered, though, with "If I saw a concert, the Ninth Symphony is what I'd want to see."

"We saw the Ninth performed by the Dresden Philharmonic a few years ago, and it was amazing. Wasn't it amazing, dear?" she asked Dr. Engel.

"Yes, amazing," he replied. Frau Engel briefly glared at him.

Hans, not wanting to abandon the topic yet, said, "Sometimes I wonder what a tenth symphony would've sounded like."

"What do you mean?"

"Well, when Beethoven died after composing the Ninth, he was only fifty-six years old. What if he had lived to sixty and composed a tenth? Would it have been even better than the Ninth? It's sad to think about."

Frau Engel said, "That's an interesting thought," and then looked down at the floor. Hans immediately regretted pushing the conversation to the point where he had exposed the inner workings of his brain. He was relieved when she looked up and said, "I prefer to think of it the other way around. What if he had died before writing the Ninth? I think we should be thankful for what we have instead of worrying about what we don't."

Elise and Dr. Engel were silent as the Beethoven dialogue continued for several more minutes. Elise wore the hint of a smile on her face, while Dr. Engel looked as if he had taken a bite of spoiled fish. Eventually, the conversation reached the point where both participants recognized the topic had fizzled out, but neither was sure what the next one should be. After a few awkward seconds, Hans remembered the display case and said, "That looks like a beautiful porcelain collection."

Frau Engel said, "Oh yes, it's my pride and joy, after Elise and her brother, of course," which elicited a blush from Elise. "Would you like to see it?"

"Of course," said Hans.

Frau Engel, Hans, and Elise walked to the display case. Frau Engel looked at Dr. Engel with raised eyebrows, but he remained seated and said, "I've already seen the porcelain."

Other than in museums, Hans had never viewed a porcelain collection like this. It included delicate tea and coffee sets, dinnerware settings, and vases, as well as figurines of courting couples, noblemen on horses, and ballerinas. Each piece was shiny, and every color was bright and vibrant. Frau Engel pointed out her favorites and explained how each one had been acquired. Some had been purchased, some inherited, and others received as wedding gifts. Hans guessed that a traditional wedding gift in his parents' village was probably something like a pitchfork or a pig.

Frau Engel carefully opened the case and said, "This is the only part of the house I don't let the maid touch. I clean all of this myself." She reached in and carefully removed a ballerina. "This is my favorite. See how the dress looks like it's lace? Do you know how they do that?" Hans shook his head. "They make a dress out of actual lace, dip it in porcelain, and when they put it in the kiln, the lace burns off and leaves the porcelain. So they start with lace, the most delicate thing you can imagine, and after the fire, all that's left is the hard stuff. Isn't she beautiful?"

She held it out to Hans, but he was unsure what she wanted him to do. He had no intention of ruining the evening by breaking something, so he just leaned forward to examine it while keeping his hands clasped behind his back.

Frau Engel continued, "Doesn't it look like Elise? She used to do ballet, and I always thought this piece looked just like her." For the second time that evening, Hans saw Elise blush. He studied the delicate figurine in the pink tutu with yellow hair and green eyes, and all he could do was nod. It looked exactly like Elise.

As she returned the ballerina to the case, Frau Engel said, "Elise, I know you need to leave soon for your movie, but can you help me in the kitchen for a few minutes? Hans, why don't you sit with Dr. Engel so you two can get to know each other better."

As Frau Engel left for the kitchen, the energy in the room followed in her wake, leaving a social and conversational vacuum. Hans avoided eye contact with the doctor as he returned to the couch and sat down quietly, in a vain hope that Dr. Engel wouldn't notice him. The only sound was the ticking of the grandfather clock, which to Hans seemed remarkably loud in the otherwise silent parlor. He looked idly around the room with his hands in his lap, digging the fingernails of one hand into the palm of the other.

Noticing that Dr. Engel wasn't wearing a Nazi lapel pin, Hans wondered about his politics. He certainly wouldn't be the first doctor living in a house like this who was a Nazi, which would make for an awkward conversation if he ever met Hans's father. But before that potential meeting could take place, Hans would first need to survive this night.

Dr. Engel took his watch out of his vest pocket, compared the time to the time on the grandfather clock, and then put it back again. Next he picked up a brierwood pipe from the side table, emptied the ashes into an ashtray, and used a pipe cleaner to remove the remaining debris. He poured the contents of a tobacco pouch into the bowl of the pipe, packed it down with a tamper, and then topped it off with more tobacco. Hans assumed that Dr. Engel was trying to make him uncomfortable, but in fact he was thrilled—every second Dr. Engel spent messing with his watch and pipe was a second he wasn't talking to Hans.

Finally, without looking at Hans, he said, "So, Hans." He

put the pipe in his mouth, lit a match, touched it to the top of the tobacco, and took several big puffs. He removed the pipe from his mouth and said, "What does your father do for a living?"

"Oh, um . . . he does construction."

"So he's an engineer or an architect?"

"No. He . . . he's a mason." Dr. Engel nodded, and Hans elaborated. "A master mason."

Dr. Engel tilted his head, like a confused dog. "I see. Is he originally from Dresden?"

"No, he grew up on a farm about fifty kilometers from here."

"Ah yes, I thought so. It's difficult to hide that accent, isn't it."

Hans wondered what Dr. Engel would think of his parents' accents, which were significantly thicker than his.

By this point, Hans had abandoned the idea of asking questions and simply wanted the nightmare to end. Just then, Elise and Frau Engel returned from the kitchen, and Hans jumped up from the couch. They said their goodbyes and left.

Once they were gone, Maria poured two glasses of wine and handed one to her husband. "Well, he seems like a nice boy."

Max took a drink. "She could do better. And that accent—how far out in the country is his family from?"

"Don't be such a snob. He's all right. And don't worry—first boyfriends never last."

CHAPTER 13

Hans and Elise arrived at the theater and settled into their seats. Hans said, "The movies have always been one of my favorite things to do."

"Me too. My brother and I used to come here on Sunday afternoons, and I always loved when they showed Mickey Mouse. I hate that we can't see those cartoons anymore."

"He was one of my favorites too. I suppose other people have sacrificed more for the Nazi cause than not being able to watch Mickey Mouse, but I miss him." He looked around to make sure nobody had heard him.

The lights dimmed, and triumphal music filled the theater as the newsreel began. It showcased the heroic and victorious German military, and when a downed British bomber appeared, several audience members cheered.

As the main feature, a romantic comedy, began, Hans debated whether or not to hold Elise's hand. It was on the armrest between them, just sitting there, minding its own business. In the flickering light of the film, he stared at the delicate, long, ringless fingers and neatly trimmed, unpainted nails. It was just a hand, but it was so alluring he could hardly take his eyes off it.

Before making his move, he had to consider what could go wrong. His hands were often sweaty, and sometimes even thinking about them getting sweaty was enough to make them sweaty. Would she be disgusted? What if they held hands for a few minutes, then she pulled hers away and wiped it on her skirt? While he considered his options, he lost track of the movie's plot. Thankfully it wasn't difficult to catch up in this type of film.

Hans decided to wait until the movie was nearly over and then hold her hand for the last few minutes. Just as it was wrapping up, as if she were reading his mind, she put her hand on top of his. This was perfect! She was touching the back of his hand, so she couldn't tell how sweaty his palm was. A chill went through his body.

After the movie, they meandered through the neighborhood, moving in the general direction of her house, before eventually sitting on a bench. Across the street was a boarded-up storefront. "That used to be a jeweler," Elise said. "My mom would buy gifts for herself there, and I remember she was upset when it closed."

"The Greenberg family owned that, right? I wonder what happened to them." They glanced at each other briefly, but then Elise shrugged and looked away. Changing the subject, Hans said, "Your mom mentioned your brother, and I know he's in the army, but you haven't said much about him."

"He's stationed in France and appears to be enjoying himself. He sent us a picture of him in front of the Eiffel Tower a few weeks ago."

"Maybe this will all be over soon, and he can just be a tourist for however long he's in the army. Is he more like your mom or your dad?"

"He's outgoing and social like my mom. I'm more like my dad. By the way, I apologize for his behavior earlier tonight."

"I guess that's how dads protect their daughters."

"Yes, he was always tough on my brother, but he always spoiled me."

"Are you still a daddy's girl?"

"I don't know. He works all the time so we don't see him much anymore. It's like he's trying to save the lives of everyone in Dresden all by himself. His dad was a doctor too, so I guess medicine is in his blood, and he takes it very seriously."

"He asked me if my father was from Dresden. Is his family from here?"

"Yes, they've been here for generations and are kind of snobs about it. My mom comes from old Dresden money too. Her parents and my dad's parents ran in the same social circles and knew each other before the two of them were even born. She went away to finishing school, and when she came home, they started dating and then got married."

Hans hesitated and then said, "Sorry, but I don't know what finishing school is."

"Oh, it's a school where they teach rich girls about etiquette, the arts, languages, and how to manage a household. They also learn how to socialize, entertain, and dance. You should see my mom dance—she's amazing."

"I can't picture your dad dancing with her. Do they still go out dancing together?"

"No, it's sad. They used to go out all the time, drinking and dancing, but now she mostly stays home, only going out to lunches with friends. You should see her with her friends, though. It's hilarious. Most of them are just like her, and they talk, talk, talk. I'm not even sure they hear each other. It's different with my parents—she does all the talking, and he does all the listening. At least, I think he's listening. Sometimes I'm not sure."

Hans paused and then said, "All right, I should probably tell you that I have theories about things."

"Like leaving one button of your coat unbuttoned?"

"Well, yes, that's one of them. I spend too much time

thinking about stuff, so these theories periodically come into my head."

"Give me an example."

"Well, this one applies to your parents."

"I'm not sure I like the sound of that."

"No, it's fine. This theory proposes that there are only two types of people in the world: high-strung and low-key. High-strung people get wound up easily, and low-key people settle things down. And by the way, being high-strung or low-key is neither a good thing nor a bad thing, it's just a thing. So the theory is that high-strung people need to be partnered with low-key people or else there will be problems. When two high-strung people are with each other, they wind each other up, and there's no one to calm things down."

"I think I see where this is going."

"Yes. In your case, your mom is high-strung, but your dad is low-key, or at least that's my take on the situation after spending a half hour with them."

"Very perceptive, given that my mom was bouncing off the walls and my dad just sat there."

He smiled. "Yes, I'm very perceptive. And by the way, it can go in either direction. For example, my parents' roles are flipped compared to yours, but it still works."

She thought about it for a moment and then asked, "So what are we?"

"Well, I'm low-key, and I think you are too."

"Do relationships between two low-key people work?"

"Absolutely. Sometimes they might be a little boring, but they can definitely work."

"So that's the kind of stuff that's spinning around in your head when you're not talking?"

"Yes, that's one example, but there are more."

"I'll have to hear them sometime."

For a few moments, they were silent and simply watched people strolling on the sidewalk. Then Hans asked, "Can I see you tomorrow?"

Elise furrowed her brow for a second but said, "Um, okay. What do you want to do?"

"I want to show you Dresden."

"I think I've mentioned this, but I've lived here my entire life."

"I know, but I believe I can show you stuff you're not aware of. When you visit a new town, you notice all sorts of things, but when it's something you've been around your whole life, you stop noticing. A tourist seeing Dresden for the first time could probably describe the Frauenkirche better than a native who's seen it a thousand times. It becomes part of the background if you see it every day."

"I have to admit I'm intrigued. I need to check with my parents, so can you call me in the morning to set up a time?"

Hans looked down and said, "We don't have a phone."

"Oh. A lot of people don't have phones. We only have one because my dad gets calls from the hospital."

Hans shook off the embarrassment and asked, "Can we set up a time now?"

"Sure, how about ten o'clock?"

"Perfect."

They walked to her house and stopped at the gate. She turned to face him, but then, apparently deciding not to wait for an awkward moment to develop, she stood on her toes and kissed him on the cheek.

CHAPTER 14

Hans awoke the next morning brimming with energy. He hadn't been comfortable with either Oktoberfest or meeting Elise's parents, but a tour of Dresden? That was something he could do. He got dressed, ate breakfast, and walked to her house.

As they rode the tram to the city center, he periodically glanced at her, still hardly believing she was with him. The tram rolled through the stirring city as fastidious shopkeepers swept sidewalks in front of their establishments to prepare for the day's commerce and café owners set up tables and chairs in hopes that it would be warm enough for alfresco dining. Rather than exploring individual buildings, Hans said they should start the tour by getting a view of the entire city. They therefore stayed on the tram as it crossed from the south side of the Elbe to the north, where they disembarked.

They walked to a meadow that sloped gently to the riverbank, and Hans took off his jacket and laid it on the ground for Elise to sit on. Later in the day, picnickers would spread their blankets and children would frolic across the meadow and down to the river, but on this chilly October morning, Hans and Elise had the area to themselves. Through a soft mist rising from the two-hundred-meter-wide stream, they could see the Altstadt directly across from them. The morning sun created a silhouette of the city, profiling castles and steeples and spires, fountains and statues and clock towers, with the entire scene dominated by the proud Frauenkirche.

Church bells chimed, signaling the half hour. When they finished, Hans said, "This is my favorite place to view the city. Doesn't it look like an illustration from a fairy tale? It's fascinating that everything was constructed in different eras, yet when it's all put together it looks perfect. Some of it was built five hundred years ago, and some just a hundred years ago. Some buildings are Renaissance, some are baroque, and some even medieval, but it looks like one person designed it so that all the pieces make an integrated whole." He realized he was talking too much and paused. "Do you know what I mean?"

"I think so. It looks—harmonious."

"Yes! That's the right word. I should've thought of that. I'll have to include that word the next time I give a tour to a girl." Elise smiled. "This isn't a skyline like they have in America. The Frauenkirche is the tallest building, and it's less than a hundred meters. It would only go up to the kneecap of the Empire State Building. This skyline is subtle and elegant, while the American ones are garish." He paused again and glanced at Elise to see if she looked bored. She seemed to be paying attention, or at least not falling asleep, so he forged ahead. "It's also interesting that Dresden wasn't part of Germany when most of this was built. It was first in the Holy Roman Empire, then it was in Poland, and then it was in the Kingdom of Saxony. It wasn't part of what we know as Germany until seventy years ago."

"But everything has been leading toward this, right? Everything here feels so German. It's hard to imagine it being anything else."

"I don't know. Everyone thinks the current situation will stay the same forever, but in reality, things are always changing."

Elise was silent for a moment and then said, "So you don't

believe Hitler when he says this is going to be a thousand-year Reich?"

"Nothing has ever lasted for a thousand years. Nothing is permanent, is it?"

"I never thought about it, but I guess not."

"Even these buildings. This skyline was basically the same two hundred years ago, and I hope it'll still be here two hundred years from now, but you never know." He paused. "Anyway, I'm sure it'll be here for at least the rest of today so that we can do our tour. Are you ready to start?"

"Yes! Let me see this mysterious Dresden you say I've been missing for the past sixteen years."

"Good, because I'm cold and I need my jacket back." Elise smiled as Hans stood and held her hands to help her up. As he put on his jacket he said, "By the way, it's going to feel like we're walking in circles, but I think it's the best route."

"Okay, you're the tour guide."

They walked across the Augustus Bridge to the south bank and approached Dresden's main Catholic church, the Hofkirche. They craned their necks to view its exceptionally tall belfry and its roof lined by statues that appeared to be keeping watch over the city. Hans said, "My favorite part is the statues. There are seventy-eight of them, each representing different histori-cal and religious figures."

"Can you name all seventy-eight?" Elise teased.

Hans returned her smile and said, "I'm not that much of a loser that I'd memorize all seventy-eight statues atop the Hofkirche." Actually, he indeed was that much of a loser that he would memorize all seventy-eight statues atop the Hofkirche, but he didn't think she needed to know that at this point. "Let's go inside."

They climbed the stone steps, and Hans opened the

massive oak door for Elise. They walked quietly through the vestibule and halfway to the altar before sitting in a pew. The nearly white walls and the sunlight streaming through the stained glass windows made the nave bright and airy.

He leaned toward Elise and whispered, "The architects put a lot of the interesting features and sources of light toward the top in order to draw the eye upward. When people walk into a church, the first thing they do is look toward heaven, but it's not because of God, it's because of the architects."

They eventually left the church and walked next door to the historic Dresden Castle, before continuing westward to the vast Theater Square. It had recently been renamed Adolf Hitler Square, and Hans grimaced at the sight of the countless black-white-and-bloodred Nazi banners that hung from every building and lamppost. At the far end of the square stood the Semper Opera House, and as they approached it, Elise said, "I was hoping we'd stop here. I love this place."

Hans said, "I've never been inside, but it looks nice."

"My family and I have seen several operas here, and it's beautiful inside. Maybe you and I can go sometime." Hans grinned at the thought of a fancy grown-up date with Elise.

They didn't go in the opera house and instead walked south across the square to the Zwinger Palace and Gardens, entering through the onion-domed front gate. They wandered through the peaceful, well-manicured gardens, admiring the elaborately decorated pavilions, intricately carved statues, and ornamented fountains. Hans had been there hundreds of times, but it had never looked more beautiful than it did today. He had expected Elise to see Dresden differently with him, but he was surprised to find that he was seeing it differently too.

Happy couples strolled arm in arm through the gardens, and while Hans knew he and Elise weren't arm in arm, and he wasn't sure if they were a couple, he did know that he was happy. They spent over an hour roaming the grounds, and

Hans realized that the pace of the tour had slowed, causing them to fall behind his planned schedule. He didn't object.

They left the gardens and walked a kilometer east before stopping in front of a vacant lot containing the remnants of some blackened walls. "This is where the synagogue used to be," Hans said quietly. "Do you remember it?"

"Yes, but I never paid it much attention."

"It was designed by Semper, the same architect who did the opera house, and it was one of the most beautiful buildings in Dresden." He lowered his voice further. "And now it's gone—burned to the ground on Kristallnacht. There's such a finality to burning something down. Couldn't they have just thrown some rocks or broken some windows? They're such fools." Hans stopped speaking and looked at Elise.

She furrowed her brow and then looked around to see if anyone had heard him. "We should probably keep going."

They walked back westward along Brühl's Terrace, which overlooked the river, and eventually arrived at Neumarkt Square. Looking across the square, they could see the Martin Luther statue where they'd met at Oktoberfest, and behind it, the Frauenkirche. The church, constructed of golden sandstone, was twice as tall as it was wide. It was crowned by a massive bell-shaped dome, which was in turn topped by a cupola, a gilded orb, and a gilded cross.

They walked toward the church, and Hans said, "The architects had limited space, so they built it as an octagon instead of a rectangle. There are towers at each corner so it looks the same from any direction." Hans realized he was becoming hoarse, and hoped he wasn't talking too much.

As they approached the entrance, Hans steered Elise away from the door and led her to the wall beside it. "Sometimes when I visit old buildings, I like to feel the stones. The architects get all the credit, but individual craftsmen did the actual construction. Here." He held her wrist and put her hand on the stone and then put his hand on the back of hers.

"The person who carved this lived over two hundred years ago. What was his life like? How long did it take him to craft it? Was he happy with how it turned out, or were there imperfections in his work that only he could see? If that did happen, did he go home that night and tell his wife he messed up at work? It took seventeen years to build this church—did he live long enough to see it finished?" Hans paused and looked at Elise. "I'm being weird. Sorry."

She smiled as she touched the stone and said, "I've never thought about it like that. But yes, you're weird. Let's go inside." She took his hand as they walked through the entrance.

As they entered the nave, Elise looked up at the frescoes high above them on the ceiling and whispered, "You're right— when I walked in, I looked up. I never noticed myself doing that before." The nave was circular and compact, and the pews gently curved around the altar. Four stories of galleries rose above them, and everything was elaborately decorated and brightly painted in pastel pinks and blues.

The tall windows admitted an abundance of light, and Hans said, "Do you see how the walls sort of glow?" Elise nodded. "They used huge numbers of eggs to get that effect when they painted it."

They walked several rows forward and then sat down. A middle-aged woman rose from a nearby pew and walked back toward the exit, her high heels clicking on the stone floor and echoing off the walls.

Hans whispered, "Do you hear how loud that echo is? The acoustics are perfect, and Bach even played his 'Christmas Oratorio' here. But the acoustics are designed for a church full of people. The people absorb the sound, but when it's empty like now, the echoes bounce all over the place." The woman left the church, and the clang of the closing door echoed off the walls. But then there was silence.

Hans looked up at the dome and whispered, "I used to think that when people died, they went to heaven through that dome. Sort of like a portal. Whenever I see it, I think of people going to heaven."

"That's very sweet."

Hans shrugged, realizing he was probably sharing too much again.

After a few minutes, they left the church and sat down on the steps outside. Hans said, "You can hear the tiniest noise in there, and I used to think that the architects designed it that way so that God could hear all the prayers, even the quietest ones."

"Do you not think that anymore?"

"I don't know. It seems like lots of people aren't getting their prayers answered these days." Hans looked at her and said, "But other people are."

Elise didn't know if he was talking about himself, but she blushed anyway, just in case.

CHAPTER 15

The day had flown by for Elise, and even though it was getting late, she suggested they walk home rather than take the tram. Before they left, Hans bought her a rose from one of the flower stalls lining the Altmarkt. As they began their walk, Elise said, "You were right—I learned some interesting things today. Where did you get all this information?"

"I read a lot—probably too much. Also, my father likes architecture, so he's taught me some stuff. It's why I want to be an architect."

"That sounds perfect for you."

"Unfortunately, with how things are going, I'll probably be a soldier instead."

"I think the war will be over soon, don't you?"

"It seems like it should be. What's the point of bombing each other's cities?"

"Exactly! If it does end soon, there should be a lot of work for architects. I saw a magazine with drawings of the gigantic buildings Albert Speer plans to construct in Berlin. Have you seen that?"

"Yes, but I don't like it. Everything they do has to be the biggest thing in the world." He lowered his voice and said, "It seems like they're compensating for shortcomings in other areas, doesn't it?" She felt herself blush, and then he blushed and said, "Sorry, that's something my father said. It's probably inappropriate."

"That's okay."

"So I told you I want to be an architect. What do you want to be?"

"I had some good teachers when I was little, and that's what I always thought I'd do, but now I don't know." She looked over her shoulder and spoke more quietly. "It seems we don't spend much time learning things anymore. It's all Nazi stuff."

"I think teachers are afraid to teach what they want, so they just say whatever will keep them out of trouble."

"Plus, all the teachers are so old now. The young ones are either in the army or else they got fed up and quit."

"So if that doesn't work out, what would your second choice be?"

"I don't know. I love my mom, but I don't want to follow her path and just learn how to cook and sew and dance and be a housewife. But I might not have a choice."

"You know what your Führer wants for you, right?"

"Yes, stay home, make babies, and keep your husband happy."

"Exactly."

Just then, Elise saw a group of five Hitler Youth teenagers walking toward them. She glanced at Hans and saw that he was looking down, apparently trying to avoid eye contact. The boys were rowdy and spirited, and they swaggered five abreast, blocking most of the sidewalk. Even though Hans and Elise squeezed in single file between the boys and a building, one of them bumped shoulders with Hans. Hans didn't break stride at this provocation, and Elise continued to follow him. The boy who bumped him turned and said, "You must be in a hurry to get her home and get that pretty dress off. I guess I'd do the same if I were you!" The other boys whooped and hollered.

When Elise looked at Hans, he shook his head, his eyes still lowered.

Elise glanced over her shoulder to ensure they weren't being followed, and when she turned around again, she saw a man sprawled on the sidewalk thirty meters in front of them. She watched as he dragged himself into a sitting position with his back against a wall.

Hans and Elise stopped when they reached him. His coat was torn and splattered with spit, blood oozed from a cut lip, and his left eye was swollen and well on its way to becoming a shiner. He clutched his left ribs with his right hand, and his breaths were shallow wheezes. A yarmulke lay on the ground next to him.

Elise leaned over and said, "Can we help?"

He retrieved his yarmulke and clambered to his feet. His eyes danced between the two of them but settled on Elise. He scowled at her for several seconds, and she wasn't sure what she saw in his eyes. Hate? Accusation? Perhaps just resignation. Whatever it was, she had never felt more uncomfortable. He said, "You can, but you won't."

The man spat blood onto the sidewalk and wobbled away as they remained frozen. Elise looked at Hans, whose face was expressionless. His arms were by his side, but his hands were horizontal, and his long fingers were splayed. They began walking again but didn't speak of what they had seen, or anything else.

Elise began to feel more secure only after they reached her neighborhood. The autumn sun was setting, and a lamplighter on a bicycle pedaled past them before stopping at a streetlamp. He lifted a wick at the end of a long pole to light the lamp and then pedaled to the next one to repeat the process. While many neighborhoods had electric streetlamps, Elise liked that hers still had gas. The fire in the lamps gave the impression of producing not just light but warmth.

They arrived at her house and shared a hug at the gate. Hans left, and Elise entered, concealing the rose in her jacket. She tried to sneak up to her room without being noticed, but when she got to the base of the stairs, her mother came out of the kitchen. "Well, you were certainly gone longer than I expected," she said, without a trace of her usual affability.

"I'm sorry. I lost track of time."

"I don't like you being gone all day with someone we don't know. Quite frankly, you don't know him either."

Elise had never been in any sort of trouble, so she wasn't sure if that's what this was. "I know. I'm sorry."

She took two steps up the stairs, but her mother asked, "Aren't you going to leave your jacket down here?" Like a criminal accepting that she'd been caught red handed, she took off her jacket, revealing the rose. "Did Hans buy that for you?" Elise nodded. "Your father is at work, so perhaps you and I can chat for a bit." They sat down in the parlor, and Elise set the rose on the coffee table between them. "It seems like things are going well with Hans, but it's moving awfully quickly."

"We've only gone out a couple of times. I don't think it's a big deal."

"Well, you had your date last night and spent all day together today, and then you came home with a rose. You must really like him."

"I don't know. He's odd but interesting. And funny. He's definitely not like the other boys." She thought about what she had witnessed with the Hitler Youth gang but decided not to recount that story.

"Just remember that we don't know anything about him or his family. You're new at this, so please listen to me when I say it's best if you take things slowly. The flame that burns brightest burns shortest."

Elise remained silent.

"All right, wait here a minute." She left the parlor and went into the kitchen, returning with a small porcelain vase filled with water. "Put the flower in here and leave it in your room so your father doesn't see it. And please think about what I told you."

Elise put the flower in the vase and hurried upstairs, smiling and feeling confident that her mother didn't know what she was talking about.

CHAPTER 16

The following Saturday, August sluggishly ate breakfast and drank several cups of ersatz coffee, trying to clear his head of the lingering effects of the previous night's alcohol. He then went outside to work on the shelter. The week before, he'd installed hinges on the hatch, making it possible for it to be swung open rather than lifted off. It squeaked now as he opened it, and he made a mental note to oil the hinges.

He walked down the steps and struck a match to light the kerosene lamp. Everything had taken longer than he'd hoped, but as he looked around, he was satisfied with how it was turning out. The next task was to install the ventilation shafts, and after that, an escape hatch, a small tunnel opposite the main entrance that would serve as an exit if the main entrance became blocked. Eventually, there would be an electric light, two cisterns of water, and enough canned food for three people to survive for a week. Gas masks would hang from hooks on the wall, and buckets of sand would be available in case of fire.

He knew the value of a good shelter from his experience in the previous war. The German fortifications were built exceptionally well and withstood even the most intense bombardments. Whenever they captured British trenches, August and his comrades would mock their shoddy construction.

His only concern with this bunker was the ventilation. Shortly after installing the roof, he'd experienced an episode of being unable to breathe, and had been compelled to scramble out. This episode had repeated itself several times since then, including twice when Hans was with him. While there seemed to be enough oxygen in the shelter, the moment he thought about the issue, he would immediately need to get out. He was embarrassed that Hans had witnessed this, especially since Hans didn't seem to have the same problem with breathing. Perhaps it was because he was younger and didn't smoke. Whatever the reason, August was sure everything would be fine once he installed the ventilation shafts.

As he plucked the necessary vents, ducts, and hardware from the pile at the back of the shelter, Hans descended the steps. August said, "Glad you could finally make it, because we need to finish the shafts today. I've already marked the spots where I'll chisel holes in the walls on opposite sides of the shelter. From those holes, I'll dig horizontally outward for one meter. Meanwhile, you'll go into the yard and dig vertically for one meter to the point where my horizontal tunnel will end. We'll then install duct covers so rain doesn't get in. It's important to have two shafts for cross-ventilation, and in case one of them gets blocked by debris."

"What if they both get blocked?" Hans asked.

"Well, that's unlikely because they'll be spaced far apart, and even if—"

Several seconds passed and then Hans asked, "Even if what?"

A flash. *1916 Battle of the Somme. Bunker entrance collapsed. Trapped. Panic.* He shook his head and it was gone. "Nothing. Stop asking so many questions." He picked up a tape measure, a piece of paper, and a spade and handed them to Hans. "That paper has the measurements of the duct placement. Make sure you dig in exactly the right spot so the horizontal and vertical shafts connect properly." Hans nodded and disappeared.

August took a deep breath, relieved that he had avoided another episode. He thought of his war memories as being like a high-pressure water pipe with a small hole in it. As long as he covered the hole with his hand, only a few drops would leak out here and there. He'd see tree branches on the ground after an ice storm, and they would remind him of the aftermath of an artillery barrage. Or he'd view lightning in the distance and think of the poor suckers who were getting bombarded. He could deal with a couple of drops here and there, and he found that alcohol helped him keep his hand on the pipe.

But when he loosened his grip, the water would gush out, and the memories would flood back. Lately, either the hole was getting larger or his hand was getting weaker, and he knew he would have to either toughen up or drink more. He shook his head again and walked to the side of the shelter to begin work on the first shaft. He placed a chisel on the brick, but as he raised his hammer, his mind returned to the Somme.

The British artillery barrage was in its fifth day, or maybe its fifth night; it was impossible to tell in the bunker. The air was fetid, the noise was deafening, and the ground shook with every explosion.

A couple of days before, men, even veterans, had begun to crack under the strain of the barrage. One man, a corporal, had started screaming and tried to flee, to go outside and get some air. A sergeant tackled him, and other men held him down. The sergeant ordered August to tie him up, and after he had done so, the man started to vomit. They dragged him to a corner of the bunker and left him there. Over the next two days, August had occasionally looked at the pathetic corporal, tied up and lying in a puddle of vomit. Sometimes the man slept, but he usually just lay there with eyes that were open, glassy, and dead. August wondered how a man could live with himself after behaving like that in front of his comrades. Death would be preferable to that humiliation.

The bad thoughts were coming again. He closed his eyes and told himself to press on the pipe more firmly, but the water was already squirting out. His chest was tightening and he could see his heartbeats on the back of his eyelids and hear them pounding in his ears. He couldn't hold the pipe any longer, and it burst open. The explosions, the darkness, the bound soldier in the puddle of vomit . . .

From somewhere he heard the word "Papa," but he didn't react. He wasn't there. When the voice again said "Papa," he opened his eyes.

A wall was directly in front of him, and when he looked left he saw a wall, and when he looked right he saw a wall, and when he looked up he saw the roof, mere centimeters from his head. The shelter, which had seemed spacious just a few minutes earlier, suddenly felt like a coffin. He dropped his tools, wheeled around, and almost knocked Hans off the steps as he dashed out of the shelter and into the house.

Late that afternoon, Hans's father went to meet his buddies at the pub, so it was only Hans and his mother for dinner. They didn't say anything for a while, but then Hans asked, "What's going on with Papa? That's the third time he's left the shelter like that."

She looked down, stirred her potato soup, and said, "Your father has some unpleasant memories from the last war."

"What does that have to do with building a shelter more than twenty years later?"

"I think maybe being in that shelter reminds him of some of his experiences. He hasn't said anything to me, so I don't know if that's what it is, but it's what I suspect. Please be considerate of his feelings."

Hans had always assumed his father didn't have any feelings other than confidence and drunkenness, and he wasn't sure drunkenness counted as a feeling. "But then why is he building a shelter? Why doesn't he just fix up the house?" She didn't answer.

Hans tried to process what his mother had told him. He was, of course, concerned, but a part of him was pleased that his dad was afraid of something. There was finally a situation where Hans was tougher than his old man. What he couldn't understand was why his father kept wasting his time on that stupid shelter if it caused him so much anxiety. He wished his dad would repair the porch handrail instead.

What if Elise came over?

CHAPTER 17

Three weeks later, Elise did come over, for a Saturday-evening dinner. As Hans waited for her on the front porch, he noticed the handrail was freshly painted, and when he grabbed it, he realized it no longer wobbled. His father hadn't said anything but must've repaired it earlier that day. He also saw that his father had kept his commitment to fly the Nazi flag on national holidays, in this case the anniversary of Hitler's Beer Hall Putsch. He had taped a flag to the porch railing, but it wasn't much bigger than a page from a magazine.

He saw Elise when she was still a block away, her dress gently swaying as she walked. Had she always been able to make a dress sway like that? Little girls couldn't do that but women could. He was momentarily mesmerized as he wondered if this was a newfound skill, a show she was staging for him, or perhaps he just hadn't noticed it before. The last alternative seemed unlikely.

She carried a small bouquet of flowers, and he cursed himself for not bringing anything to the Engels on his first visit. As he met her at the base of the steps, they shared a brief kiss, something they had been practicing for the prior couple of weeks, and he asked, "Are you sure you're ready for this?"

"I think it'll be fun," she said.

"Ha! Don't get your hopes up."

They entered the house and were greeted by Greta, who

wagged her tail wildly when Elise bent down to pet her. As his parents walked into the front room from the kitchen, Hans looked at them in their shabby clothes in their shabby house and, for the first time in his life, was embarrassed by his family's social status. The Engels were so gracious and dignified, and his parents were—well, not that. He prayed they wouldn't humiliate him and hoped his father wouldn't drink too much or talk about politics.

Hans introduced Elise, and when she stood next to his mother, he realized how much heavier his mother was. Not fatter, just thicker. Elise and her mother had the same delicate build, but his mother was stout and sturdy. Elise handed her the flowers, but she didn't seem to know what to do with them.

They made small talk for several minutes while standing awkwardly in the front room, his mother holding the flowers, his father holding a beer, and Elise appearing as unsure about what to do with her hands as Hans was about his own. Then Elise said to Hans's father, "Hans tells me you've made a lot of improvements to this house. Can you show me what you've done?"

His face lit up. "Of course! Let's start upstairs." Hans was impressed that Elise had brought up a topic that would allow her to avoid talking but was terrified that his father now had control of the conversation. Following his father and Elise up the stairs, Hans glanced at his mother and saw her frowning as she and Greta walked to the kitchen. He guessed that she hadn't foreseen a tour of the house and was probably worried she hadn't cleaned upstairs.

As they inspected the bathroom and both bedrooms, Hans's father loudly shared a remarkable and, from Hans's perspective, excessive amount of detail about wiring, plumbing, and load-bearing walls. Hans was sure Elise was bored, but she feigned interest convincingly. After twenty minutes, his father led them back downstairs, where he pointed to one side of the room and said, "This is my proudest achievement. When we moved in, the house didn't have a fireplace, so I had to build it from scratch." The brickwork of the fireplace, chimney, and mantel was elaborate and ornate, beautiful even, but Hans thought it made the rest of the house look shoddy by comparison, like a hobo clothed in rags and wearing a fancy top hat.

His father rambled about it for too long, and Hans was relieved when he looked into the kitchen and saw his mother putting food on the table. His father was describing the challenges of constructing the multitiered mantel when Hans interrupted and said it was time to eat. The kitchen was even more cramped than usual because his mother had pulled the table away from the wall to accommodate a fourth chair, which Hans noticed didn't match the other three. He saw that his mother had put Elise's flowers in a glass of water and set it on the counter, and he realized they probably didn't own a vase.

Hans squeezed into the chair that was up against the wall, and Elise sat across from him. Before his father sat down, he asked Elise, "Would you like a glass of wine?"

"No, thank you."

"Schnapps?"

"Thank you, but I'm fine with water."

"Suit yourself," he said, grabbing a beer for himself and sitting down. His mother had attempted to be classy by preparing beef rouladen, which Hans was sure had exhausted a large portion of their monthly meat ration.

His father took a swig of beer and said, "So Hans tells me you're in the orchestra. What do you play?"

"I play the oboe. Do the two of you play any instruments?" Hans realized this could turn into a replay of his innocuous conversation with the Engels, and he was content with that.

His mother shook her head, but his father said, "Well, I

don't play an instrument unless you count my voice as an instrument. Has Hans told you what a great singer I am?"

Oh God, no, Hans thought. Where was this going?

Elise glanced at Hans and said, "Um, no, he didn't say anything about that."

The older man took another swig of beer, and Hans wondered how much he'd already had to drink. His accent was getting thicker as his tongue seemed to swell. "I've got a great story about singing. Young Hans here loves Beethoven. Hey, I just realized that your name is Elise, and a few weeks ago, Hans was practicing 'Für Elise' on his violin. He played it over and over and over again."

Hans blushed but realized his father was on too much of a roll to make the connection. His mother, though, gave Hans a quick, quizzical look.

"When Hans was little, he'd play 'Ode to Joy' on the gramophone and sing along. His voice hadn't changed yet, so he couldn't do the tenor or bass parts. He did all right with the alto but was amazing with the soprano." He laughed and took another gulp of beer.

Elise laughed too. Hans's hands were resting on his legs under the table, and he was digging his fingernails into his thighs. He glanced at his mother and saw she wasn't laughing and seemed to be as uncomfortable as he was. He felt sorry for her for a moment—had he ever seen her laugh? But his mind quickly returned to his own concerns.

His father continued. "Maybe after dinner, we can play the old 'Ode to Joy' record. There are four of us and four vocal parts, so we can all sing along. Hans probably can't do the soprano part anymore, but I'm sure we can make it work. What do you think?" he asked Elise.

"I'm not much of a singer, but I'd love to hear Hans sing." She smiled at Hans and tapped his foot with hers under the table. Hans glared at her but realized she was just humoring his father. He could see how this would be funny in different circumstances, but he wasn't in different circumstances.

His mother rescued him. "Maybe we should save that for another time."

His father relented and said, "All right, fine. You people aren't any fun."

The crisis was averted. Elise asked about his father's job, and he spent most of the rest of dinner describing various construction projects around Dresden. Hans's heart was still racing, and he remained on edge, but the remainder of the evening passed without further embarrassment.

As Hans walked Elise back to her house, he said, "Sorry my dad was so annoying."

"Not at all! I thought he was funny. He actually talks, as opposed to my dad."

"But the problem is he never stops talking. He'll talk to anyone about anything for any length of time. It's embarrassing."

"Maybe you're jealous?"

Hans was quiet for a few seconds and then said, "I don't know. Maybe."

"How well do your parents get along? They seem so different."

"Pretty well, I guess. She never criticizes anything he does, even though he deserves it. He makes a big deal about being in charge of the house, yet she does all the work."

"Does she have time to go out with friends?"

"I guess I never thought about it, but I don't think she has any friends, at least not here. Everybody she's close to is back in her village, but she doesn't go back very often, just a few times a year. Every summer since I was a little kid, I've spent a week or two there, and I've got lots of good memories, especially about food. Fresh milk, real butter, eggs, honey, and my aunt bakes wonderful apple strudel. It's like going back in time—hardly anybody has cars, and everything is a lot quieter and cleaner."

"Does your dad like to go back?"

"No, not at all. It's sad because I think my mom would prefer to live there permanently, but he'd never do that. His ego won't let him."

They arrived at her house and when they reached the porch, Elise walked toward the swing rather than the front door. She sat down and patted the seat, inviting Hans to join her. He stared as she swung gently back and forth, her feet dangling and an enigmatic smile on her face. In the porch light her hair glistened and her eyes sparkled. She was so beautiful it was almost painful for Hans to look at her.

He sat down, nearly, but not quite, touching her, but she scooted closer and said, "It's cold." He put his arm around her shoulders and leaned in for a kiss. It began gentle and sweet but quickly turned passionate and intense.

Twenty minutes later, a car door closed across the street, but neither of them paid any attention. They didn't hear the gate opening and closing either. They did, however, notice the footfalls on the porch steps and separated just in time to see Dr. Engel reach the porch. They hastily disentangled themselves from one another, and Hans's heart, which had been racing because of passion, now raced because of terror.

"Time to go home, Herr Becker," Dr. Engel said as he crossed the porch, opened the front door, and walked inside. He barely looked at them.

Elise, her face crimson, stood up, straightened her dress, and said, "I'll see you Monday." She smiled at Hans as she disappeared into the house.

Hans remained on the swing for several minutes to regain his composure and then began his trek home. He felt like running or skipping or jumping or even doing a cartwheel, but instead just walked briskly, grinning the whole way.

CHAPTER 18

Hans awoke the next morning in his freezing, unheated bedroom as the wind outside compelled the chimes to compose not a song but a discordant mess. The thought of emerging from under the blanket to go to his Hitler Youth meeting paralyzed him, so instead he remained in bed, thinking about the previous night. He hoped for a moment that the fire in his heart would keep him warm throughout the cold morning but quickly realized that was just a stupid expression and his feelings wouldn't help him at all. He eventually forced himself out of bed and took the tram to the meeting.

As he waited for their hike to begin, Hans thought to himself that the worst possible weather was when it was just above freezing, windy, and rainy. Ten degrees colder and snowing was preferable to that. Fortunately, only two of those three factors were at play this morning.

After they finished reciting the oath, Herr Ziegler said it was a perfect day to toughen them up, so that day's hike would be coatless. Hans stared at him in disbelief. He was already cold and probably had the least amount of body fat of anyone in the troop. The boys obediently removed their coats, piled them next to the flagpole, and set off on their hike. Halfway through, it began to rain, and Hans silently blamed himself for his musings about the worst kind of weather. As expected, his thoughts of Elise didn't help keep him warm, but they were a pleasant distraction from his miseries nonetheless.

They returned to the parade grounds, and Herr Ziegler began his lecture, in which he exulted in the German bombing that had destroyed the ancient English town of Coventry. Hans had read about the bombing and the ensuing fire and he thought celebrating the destruction of something so beautiful was demented. He looked at the other boys and was disappointed but not surprised that they appeared delighted with Herr Ziegler's description of the carnage.

Herr Ziegler said, "All right, after Coventry, I feel happy, and I'd like to make you all happy too, so I will let you choose our next activity. Suggestions?"

Everyone, Hans included, raised their hands. In this situation, you didn't dare not raise your hand. It would show a lack of leadership or something. Herr Ziegler pointed to a boy and said, "Bauer, what do you think?"

The boy jumped up, stood at attention, and exclaimed, "Boxing!"

Herr Ziegler said, "All right, boxing. What has been our best boxing match this autumn?"

Hans's stomach fell as he realized where this was going. He raised his hand, just like everyone else, hoping to forestall the inevitable. The Hitler Youth wanted blood, and there had been no match with more blood than when he'd fought Gerhard.

Herr Ziegler called on a boy, who leaped to his feet and shouted, "Hans versus Gerhard!"

Herr Ziegler said, "I think you're right! That was a great fight. Let's do that one again." Hans wondered how his circumstances could have deteriorated so badly in just twelve hours.

Hans once again trudged to the boxing ring, but as he put on the gloves, he realized he felt different than he had during the previous fight. He had Elise now, and his confidence had never been higher. His confidence hadn't been high to begin with, so this surge left him well short of the mean, but still, it was something.

He looked across the ring as he waited for the fight to begin. He hated Gerhard with the white-hot passion of a thousand suns, and the humiliation from the last time they'd boxed was still raw. Herr Ziegler blew his whistle, and Gerhard once again rushed toward Hans's corner, looking to replicate the carnage of their first fight. Hans covered up as his opponent approached, but when Gerhard got within striking distance, Hans smacked him on the nose with a left jab. Gerhard was stunned and took a step back, but after regaining his composure, he came forward again. Hans jabbed his nose again, which backed him up a second time. The ridiculous Hitler mustache was a perfect target.

His face crimson, Gerhard stormed forward once more, not giving Hans time to use his extra reach to get in another jab. But Gerhard was all offense and no defense, and as he got close, Hans bent down and unleashed an uppercut with all the energy available to him. Because of his long arms, the leverage on the blow was significant, even though the punch itself wasn't that powerful.

The shot wobbled Gerhard, but he remained unsteadily on his feet. Hans then unloaded with a right hook to his face. Blood poured from Gerhard's nose, drenching his mustache, but he still didn't go down. He stumbled forward and got into a clinch with Hans. Hans's adrenaline flowed, his heart pounded, and after a few seconds, he separated himself and threw one more punch to Gerhard's jaw. Gerhard crumpled to the ground as Hans remained upright, towering over his vanquished foe. He wished he had something clever to say, but he hadn't expected to be in this situation and was therefore unprepared.

Hans's victory was greeted with silence from the assembled Hitler Youth. Although the blood was much appreciated, nobody was going to cheer the pummeling of the son of a Gestapo agent. As the adrenaline wore off, Hans started shivering, and after removing his gloves he left the ring to retrieve his shirt and coat. When Gerhard came to his senses and saw Hans walking away, he staggered out of the ring and tripped him. As Hans lay on the ground, Gerhard kicked him in the ribs, with the blood from his nose dripping onto Hans.

Hans smiled, knowing that this time the blood on his clothes wasn't his.

CHAPTER 19

That afternoon, Elise lay in bed, still wearing the uniform from her League of German Girls meeting. She was attempting to write a diary entry but had been staring at a blank page for ten minutes. Her feelings, both emotional and physical, were new to her, and she didn't know how to describe them. She also didn't know the right word to describe the look on her father's face when he'd discovered Hans and her on the porch the night before. It seemed like it should've been anger or disappointment, but it had looked more like sorrow.

The doorbell rang, and since nobody else was home, she put her diary in the nightstand drawer and went downstairs. She peeked through the lace curtain, saw Hans standing there grinning, and opened the door. "Hi. Is everything all right?"

"Yes, everything is great. I just wanted to tell you something."

She let him in, but before closing the door, she scanned the street to ensure her parents weren't around.

Hans took off his coat, and they sat down on the couch. He said, "First of all, did you get in trouble with your dad last night?"

"He didn't say anything, but I think he told my mom because she was acting weird this morning. It'll be fine. So what did you want to tell me?"

"I knocked down Gerhard in boxing today!"

A chill went through Elise. "Oh. Are you sure that was a good idea?"

Hans furrowed his brow and said, "What was I supposed to do, let him beat me up again?"

"I don't know—maybe. I don't think he's a guy you want to have as an enemy." Hans looked down at the floor. Elise smiled and leaned over to hug him. "I'm sorry I'm not more excited— it just makes me nervous. Tell me what happened."

Hans described the fight but had clearly lost the enthusiasm he'd had when he arrived. As he told her about the other boys' silence after the knockout, he said, "Now that I think about it, maybe you're right."

"Don't worry. It's a great story, and now everybody's going to think you're the toughest guy in town."

"Or else the stupidest."

"I'm sure it'll be fine. Sometimes bullies need to get knocked down."

Hans looked her over and said, "I was so excited about my story that I didn't notice you're in your uniform. I've never seen you wear that before."

She stood up and spun around, showing off her long navy blue skirt, white short-sleeved blouse, and black neckerchief. She faced him, curtsied, and said, "Do you like it?"

"You might be the only girl in the world who could look gorgeous in that thing." She smiled and sat back down, tucking her bare feet beneath her. "So what do you do in those meetings?" he asked.

"Well, there's not as much violence as the Hitler Youth, so that's good. We mostly learn about the wonders of making babies and raising future soldiers for the Reich. In the past few years, there's been more physical fitness stuff and some lessons that could be useful in war, like nursing. Today we learned about air defense, which wasn't nice to think about. And of course, lots and lots of political lectures."

"I can't stand their lectures. They repeat the same stuff we've been hearing for the past seven years, but when I look around, most of the boys seem enthralled. Even if they believe it all, isn't it just boring at this point?"

"It's certainly repetitive."

"I don't believe these boys I've known my whole life are bad people. I think they're idiots, but teenage boys have been idiots for all eternity. The Nazis reward them for acting tough and being obnoxious, so that's what they do, but I don't think they're evil. All this hatred that everybody's spewing is mostly just for show, don't you think?"

"Maybe, but then things like Kristallnacht happen."

"That's true, but I sometimes wonder how many people were actually involved in that." He paused and then said, "So . . . what do you think about what's going on?"

Elise squirmed on the couch. "What do you mean?"

"What do you think about what's happening in Germany? We've never really talked about it."

"I don't remember much about the time before Hitler, and I'm sure you're the same way. It's basically—it's all I know. I remember being eight years old and having school assemblies where we'd listen to Hitler's speeches on a loudspeaker. I never knew what he was talking about."

"I don't think he knows what he's talking about either."

Elise smiled briefly but then frowned. "You shouldn't say stuff like that."

"You sound like my mom. She's always telling my dad to be careful, but he doesn't listen. He was friends with some Jews in his army unit in the last war, and he says they were great soldiers and were as patriotic as anybody, so he can't understand why they're such villains now. You were lucky he didn't go on one of his rants about the evil Nazis and the coming apocalypse when you were over last night." He paused and then said, "I'm sort of wondering—is your father a Nazi?"

Elise took her feet out from underneath her and put them on the floor. She said quietly, "I don't know. I vaguely remember him being a Nazi supporter when I was younger, and we'd always listen to Hitler's speeches, but it's not like we had pictures of Hitler on our walls or anything. But lately I don't get to talk to him very often, and he has a strict rule about not having political discussions at the dinner table."

"I wish my dad had that rule. What about your mom?"

"I think she just wants the war to end so Ludwig can come home and she can return to her regular life."

"What do you personally think about . . . the other stuff?"

"You mean the Jews?" she asked. Hans nodded. "I can't say I ever knew many of them. There was one family in our neighborhood, but they moved away a few years ago. But to answer your question, I don't understand all the hatred and violence. For example, why did those boys beat up the man we saw on the sidewalk?"

"I don't understand either," he admitted. They were quiet for a few minutes, and then Hans said, "Did you hear about Coventry? Herr Ziegler was elated about it today."

"Yes, that looked bad." She thought about it for a few seconds and then said, "But don't you think the bombing will make England give up? I'm in favor of anything that will shorten the war."

"I know that's the theory, but I listened to a speech Churchill made after Coventry, and he didn't sound like he was close to surrendering. He said, 'They have sown the wind; they shall reap the whirlwind.' It sounded ominous."

Elise looked at him quizzically. "Where did you hear a Churchill speech?"

"My dad and I heard it on the BBC."

Elise recoiled. "You listen to the BBC?"

Hans sat up straight and suddenly looked uncomfortable. "Well, yes, sometimes. Please don't tell your father."

"Of course not. I just . . . I didn't know you did that."

"Doesn't it seem like we should be *allowed* to do that? This whole thing is absurd, and I don't understand the point. We're supposed to sacrifice, spy on our parents, get wounded, and sometimes die, and for what? Isn't life supposed to be fun sometimes? All this struggle and sacrifice will supposedly lead to something amazing, but I've never understood what it is."

Elise shrugged and said, "I guess I've always trusted that the government knows what it's doing, and so far it seems like it does."

"If my dad were here, he'd say that the key part of your sentence was 'so far.' I hope he's proven wrong, or at least that the war ends before the British figure out how to make their planes fly this far. But if not, I'm sure we could fit you into my dad's shelter."

"Let's hope it doesn't come to that."

Hans smiled and said, "So . . . that's probably enough politics for one day. Should we pick up where we left off last night?" He grabbed the end of her neckerchief and gently tugged her toward him.

Elise looked out the window and then back at Hans. "I don't know when my dad is getting home, so you should probably leave. He'd be mad if he found us here alone."

Hans left, and Elise watched him walk away, still unsure what to write in her diary.

CHAPTER 20

On a cold December evening, Hans and Elise walked hand in hand to the Dresden Christmas market, the Striezelmarkt, delighting in the candles and Christmas decorations that adorned the windows of nearly every house they passed. As they neared the festival, they saw families with young children who appeared to be headed home. The children carried wooden toys and were animated no doubt by an overabundance of sugar, while the parents looked exhausted after several hours of corralling their kids and perhaps a mug or two of mulled wine.

Before they could see, hear, or smell the festival, they could feel it. Their paths began to merge with other Dresdeners, all headed in the same direction, and the sense of anticipation caused them to unconsciously walk faster. The first sound they heard was a low hum, which eventually separated into its component parts: carolers, a trumpeter, an accordion or two, and the voices of revelers intermixed with eruptions of laughter.

As they turned the last corner, they finally saw the festival, a shimmering sea of lights, nativity scenes, elf cottages, musicians, Moravian stars, and Christmas trees, all crammed into the Neumarkt Square. The Frauenkirche stood as an indomitable sentinel over the festivities, and the glow from the celebration reached high into the nighttime sky. Gleeful children darted across straw-covered cobblestones, mostly ignored by parents who preferred to eat, drink, and forget about the war for an evening.

The smell reminded Hans of Christmases past, a blend of sweets, sausage, gingerbread, cinnamon, roasting nuts, freshly cut pines, incense, and, of course, beer. As Elise and Hans waded into the crowd, the overall feeling was one of warmth, partly because of the many bodies packed close together but primarily because of the sense of community the festival engendered. The fact that Dresden's citizens had participated in this ritual for five hundred years provided assurance that regardless of what else was happening in the world, there would always be a Dresden.

They strolled from stall to stall, admiring the array of handcrafted pottery, glass ornaments, lace, and linen. However, the primary attraction, especially for children, was the wooden handiwork, including marionettes, ornaments, toys, and nutcrackers, as well as Räuchermann, carved figures of men with incense burning inside, a design that made the figures appear to be smoking.

After an hour, Hans bought two mugs of hot chocolate and slices of Christstollen, and they sat down on the steps of the Frauenkirche. Elise asked, "Do you come here every year?"

"I've never missed it. This is my favorite thing about Dresden."

"Mine too. I remember begging my dad one year for a little wooden horse. He could never say no to me, so he eventually bought it."

"Do you still have it?"

"It's probably in our basement. My mom never wants to throw anything away, so when my dad tells her to get rid of stuff, she puts it in the basement and hopes he doesn't notice. It's extra crowded down there now because the air-raid warden made us move everything out of the attic. A few weeks ago I was helping my mom bring up Christmas decorations and saw that she'd hidden my dollhouse from when I was little in the back corner behind a mountain of boxes. She had promised my dad she'd get rid of it." She was quiet for a moment and then said, "It's strange to be here without my parents. My mom tells stories about coming here with my grandparents, and my grandma tells stories about coming here with my great-grandparents."

"Given how long your family has lived in Dresden, you could probably go back ten or fifteen generations of ancestors coming here. Maybe someday we'll come here with our—"

Just then the bells of the Frauenkirche began to chime the half hour. They looked at each other while they waited for the bells to finish and then Elise asked, "What were you saying?"

Hans looked away and said, "Oh, I was just going to say that maybe someday you'll come here with your kids and you can tell them about your ancestors coming here." He finished his hot chocolate, stood up, and said, "Let's keep looking around."

They resumed their stroll and came across a stall selling music boxes. The craftsman was a stereotypical Bavarian artisan, with a bushy white beard, lederhosen, and a Tyrolean hat. It wasn't clear whether this was his everyday attire or if he just opportunistically donned it to try to sell his wares to the city folk. The spirit of the evening compelled Hans to overcome his usual shyness around strangers and ask, "What songs do these play?"

"All sorts. Here's one of my favorites." The man picked up a box, wound it, and handed it to Elise.

She held it to her ear. "'Eine kleine Nachtmusik,' right?"

The craftsman nodded. "So you know your music, eh?"

"Do any of these play Beethoven?" asked Hans.

"Ah—a perfect evening for Beethoven. It's his birthday you know." Hans nodded confidently, as if that were a fact that every good German should know. "Let's see what I have." The craftsman picked up an elaborately decorated box, wound it, and handed that one to Elise too.

She put it up to her ear. "'Moonlight Sonata.' Pretty." While she was still listening, the craftsman wound another. She set one down as he handed her the next. "'Ode to Joy.'" She gave it to Hans, who listened intently and then set it down.

"And then there's this one," the craftsman said as he picked up a rather plain box. "It plays 'Für Elise.'"

Hans and Elise smiled at each other, and Hans blurted out, "We'll take it." Elise stepped back from the stall and held the box to her ear. When Hans turned back to the craftsman, he felt his smile disappear and his face redden. His father loved to negotiate, but Hans found the experience stressful, and he was pretty sure that agreeing to buy something before knowing the price didn't put a person in a strong bargaining position. "How much?" he asked, his voice cracking.

"Thirty marks."

Hans's heart sank. He had come to the festival with thirteen marks but had already spent one on the Christstollen and hot chocolate. He took out his wallet, withdrew the twelve marks, and showed the money to the craftsman. The pathetic look on Hans's face was met by a frustrated one on the craftsman's.

Hans turned to Elise, whose head bobbed rhythmically as she held the box to her ear. Her face was framed by a red wool stocking cap and matching scarf, and her smile made her green eyes sparkle. The craftsman looked at her too and seemed pleased that his creation was producing so much happiness.

Hans turned back to the craftsman and said, "Her name is Elise."

The craftsman seemed to recognize the look on Hans's face; perhaps he had been young and in love once too. "Just give me five. Go enjoy yourself."

Hans gave him the money, his hands trembling and his eyes welling up with tears. *Sometimes you find good people,* he thought. "Thank you," he said as he stepped toward Elise.

"I'm going to treasure this forever," she said, hugging it to her chest. As they left the stall, Hans looked over his shoulder and nodded toward the craftsman. With a modest smile, the man nodded back and then turned to speak to other customers.

They walked to her house holding hands, and it occurred to Hans that he had never before been so happy. When he glanced at Elise and saw her smiling while clutching the music box tightly, he dared to think she might feel the same way.

At that very moment, five hundred kilometers away, the city of Mannheim was being bombed by the Royal Air Force. For the British, the raid represented a change in strategy. From that night on, rather than trying to hit specific military targets, which their bombers' inaccuracy made nearly impossible, they would instead focus on "area bombing," a diplomatic way of saying burning entire cities to the ground. The raid was only moderately successful, and Mannheim did not burn to the ground. But, unbeknownst to Hans, Elise, the Striezelmarkt revelers, and even the British airmen, the war was just getting started. The British still had ample time to improve their technique.

CHAPTER 21

The following Saturday, four days before Christmas, Hans was working with his father in the shelter when he heard a man's voice at the top of the steps call out, "Hello?" It was Herr Schmidt, his father's best friend. Hans always liked it when Herr Schmidt was around; he brought out a lighthearted side of his father that was often absent, and had been so especially since the start of the war. Schmidt always wore a look on his face that made him appear as if he had just said something funny, was about to say something funny, or was simply thinking about something funny.

"Hello, Schmidt!" said his father as he walked to the base of the steps. "What are you doing here on a cold Saturday afternoon?"

"I came to see how this crazy project is going. Hey, where did this hatch come from? Don't you know that steel is a valuable commodity now?"

"I just found it on the street one day," Hans's father said, smiling.

"That's strange because it looks like something that would've been used at one of your construction sites. You didn't accidentally bring it home with you one night after work, did you? Maybe it slipped into your pocket or something?"

"Of course not! I would never take steel that could be

better utilized in the Führer's tanks or planes. Why don't you come down and see how it's progressing."

Schmidt walked down the steps and said, "This is nice, very nice indeed, but I think you may have neglected something. How high are the ceilings?"

"Two meters. High enough for me and the boy to be comfortable as long as I don't jump in the air and as long as the boy doesn't stand on his toes."

"Ah, but you forgot something. How are the occupants supposed to give the Nazi salute? I'm not as tall as you, but look what happens if I try." He raised his right arm in a mock salute, and his hand hit the ceiling. "See! You need to either raise the ceiling or lower the floor."

Hans's father laughed loudly. Nobody could make him laugh like Herr Schmidt.

"That's it!" continued Herr Schmidt. "Either rebuild this shelter, or I'm going to denounce you!"

"We don't have to worry about any of that, Schmidt, because I'm going to forbid the Nazi salute in this shelter. You're lucky I'm letting you stay down here after that stunt."

"All right, all right."

"So, do you have any jokes?" This in itself was a joke—Herr Schmidt always had a joke, and Hans's father always asked if he had one.

"It just so happens that I do. Have you heard about the new German greeting that's replacing the one-armed salute?"

"No, what is it?"

"Whenever two Germans meet, before they say anything, they both look over their shoulders to make sure nobody is listening." With that, Herr Schmidt roared with laughter. Part of the effectiveness of his jokes was that he always laughed at them himself, making it difficult not to laugh along with him.

"That's a good one. Should we get out of here and grab a beer to toast the thousand-year Reich and total victory?"

The three of them left the shelter and went into the house, Schmidt limping due to an injury he'd suffered in the last war. He somehow seemed to have a bounce in his step despite the limp.

As they walked into the kitchen, Greta awoke from a nap and shook her head. Schmidt said, "Good afternoon, Greta. Hey, August, that reminds me—I meant to give you a piece of advice. You remember last Friday when we were at the tavern a bit too late?"

"That was a wild one. I remember saying to myself the next day, *I don't know how things went off the rails last night, but I think I had a lot to do with it.*"

"Indeed you did. Well, when I woke up the next day, my head was pounding, and I wondered if there was a way to fix it. So I decided to shake my head like dogs do when they wake up. My theory was that they've had thousands of years to evolve and figure out the best way to wake up, so if it works for them, it could work for me."

"How did it go?"

"Let's just say that Greta has probably never been drunk, so she isn't a good authority on the best way to cure a hangover." Both men laughed.

Herr Schmidt patted Greta on the head, and then he and Hans sat at the kitchen table. Hans's father opened two beers, handed one to Schmidt, and sat down. Schmidt took a big swig, faced Hans, and said, "So are you ready to go to war?"

"To be honest, I'd prefer not to."

"Good for you. I'm amazed how many young men are attracted to its supposed glamour."

"We were like that in 1914," said Hans's father.

"Yes, I guess we were. Now we know better, don't we, old friend?"

"I suppose every generation has to learn the lesson the hard way."

Schmidt said, "Hey—what about young Hans? Doesn't he get a beer? I don't see his mother, and we won't tell."

"Olga is out, probably waiting in a line somewhere, but Hans doesn't drink."

"Doesn't drink? Do you have a health problem or something?"

His father didn't wait for Hans to respond, a habit he had developed over the years. "He just doesn't like it."

Schmidt looked at Hans. "You don't know what you're missing, young man. Someday you'll understand."

"He does have a girlfriend, though."

Hans blushed.

"A girlfriend! Wonderful! You got a girlfriend before you started drinking? It usually goes the other way around. Tell me all about her. And August, you need to shut up and let your son speak." Herr Schmidt took a gulp of beer.

"Well, her name is Elise Engel, and she lives a few blocks from here."

"I think I know that family. Is her father a doctor?"

"Yes, his name is Max."

"Yes! I don't know him, but I know of him. He's a Nazi, right? All those doctors are Nazis."

Hans furrowed his brow and said, "I don't know."

"That's a beautiful house they live in, unlike this shack your father has supposedly been renovating for decades. Hey August, while the boy is telling me about his love life, why don't you get me another beer."

Hans had seen this play out before and knew that if the two of them had one more beer, they'd switch to schnapps, and once that happened, the work on the shelter would be done for the day.

"Where did you meet?" asked Herr Schmidt.

"In the orchestra."

"The orchestra! Wonderful. What does she play?"

"She plays the oboe."

A wry smile came across Herr Schmidt's face, and he said, "Oh, so she likes to have things in her mouth?" The two men burst into laughter as Hans turned beet red.

"I'm sorry," said Schmidt, regaining his composure. "That was inappropriate. Your father is a bad influence on me. So how long have you been seeing her?"

"It's been a couple of months now."

"I see. Have you met her, August?"

"Yes, she's been over here several times. She seems nice. And she's very pretty."

Hans blushed again. His father was so annoying sometimes.

"What was your opening move to win her over?"

Hans froze. His parents hadn't asked him this question, and he had no intention of telling Herr Schmidt. He hesitated, but in the meantime noticed that both men were almost done with their second beers.

"Uh, we just started talking one day."

"I'm afraid I'm going to need more details than that. I don't know much about music, but I know that violin players don't sit next to oboe players. Did the two of you make googly eyes at each other from across the orchestra?"

Hans's father made things worse by saying, "Yeah, I've never heard this story. I need to know how a goofy kid like you got a girl like that."

Hans remained frozen, and Herr Schmidt seemed to sense his discomfort. "That's all right. You don't have to tell us your secrets. I'm sure you were charming and cool, and whatever you did worked, so congratulations. And by the way, the next time you want to meet a girl in the woodwind section, you can say, 'So it appears that you like to have things in your mouth.'"

The two men laughed again as Hans's father went to the cabinet to get a bottle of schnapps. Hans excused himself and made his escape.

CHAPTER 22

In January, Hans and Elise ice-skated while Hitler's Luftwaffe gained air superiority over the Mediterranean. In February, Hans and Elise delighted in Dresden's Fasching festivities while Hitler sent troops to North Africa. In March, Hans bought Elise a bracelet for her birthday while Hitler gave orders to expand Auschwitz. In early April, Hans and Elise attended the Dresden Philharmonic while Hitler invaded Yugoslavia and Greece.

By the middle of April, Hans, feeling courageous and invincible, began secretly making grand plans for the bright future that he envisioned. Hitler did the same.

Their six-month anniversary fell on a perfect spring Saturday. Hans, standing in front of his house, watched as a sleek, shiny black Mercedes Cabriolet with its top down approached and then stopped at the curb. Elise, wearing sunglasses, a red beret, and a gingham dress, sat in the driver's seat behind a steering wheel that appeared much too large for her.

Hans got in and ran his hand across the leather seats while scanning the lavish interior. All he could say was, "Wow."

"Do you like it?"

"Of course! Perhaps this can be the start of a tradition where on all our future anniversaries, you'll chauffeur me around in a Mercedes."

"I wouldn't get used to it. My father was nervous about my taking his car since I'm still so new at this." After several unsuccessful attempts, she put the car in first gear and they lurched forward. Soon they were driving over the river and into the hills north of the city.

Hans studied the Mercedes's gauges, buttons, and dials but, being unfamiliar with cars, could only positively identify the dashboard clock. His eyes were continually drawn to Elise, and she was so focused on her driving that she didn't notice him staring. Her hair fluttered in the wind and occasionally got caught on her sunglasses, forcing her to temporarily take one hand off the wheel. Her calves, peeking out from below the hem of her dress, flexed whenever she pushed the pedals. When she changed gears, Hans watched as her delicate hand and long fingers manipulated the knob at the top of the stick shift. He knew many boys in this situation would be fascinated by the car, but he was fascinated by the driver.

She parked at the top of a hill near a verdant meadow dotted with blossoming daffodils and tulips. Hans lifted the picnic basket from the back seat, Elise grabbed the blanket, and they walked to a spot with an expansive view of Dresden and the Elbe. Elise unrolled the blanket, sat down, and took off her shoes and socks, exposing feet that were as white as her mother's porcelain.

As she opened the basket and began unpacking the apple cider, cheese, sausage, and crackers, Hans asked, "How are you always able to get all this food? My mom can never seem to find anything."

"I don't know how the system works, but we always have enough. My mom bought all this stuff yesterday, and then this morning she didn't like how I was packing it, so she did it herself." She poured two glasses of cider, and then said "Prost" as they clinked glasses.

After taking a sip, Hans said, "I was thinking we should tell each other our favorite things from the past six months."

Elise set her glass on top of the picnic basket and leaned back on her elbows, the sun reflecting off her sunglasses and a gentle breeze tousling her hair. "Interesting idea. I'd say the Striezelmarkt. And, of course, the tour of Dresden."

"Those are good choices. I also liked the Fasching parade. I know we were too old to wear costumes like that, but you looked cute with your princess tiara and scepter."

"I didn't want to say anything at the time, but you looked ridiculous in the hat and bandanna from Ludwig's cowboy costume. That was probably the only time I regretted that my mom never throws anything away. Actually, that costume might fall into the category of my least favorite things," she said with a smile.

"Any other least favorite things?"

"Well, there's the obvious one of the war."

"When we started dating, I was sure it would be over by now, and it was hard to picture my having to participate in it. But now it's real, and instead of the war ending, it's expanding. I don't see any way it will be over in three months when I leave for training or nine months when I have to go off to fight. And the thought of combat in the desert is awful. I'd rather have it be too cold than too hot, and I don't think my skin is particularly well suited for the African sun."

"Yes. I wish we would stop invading new places. Is there anything else that you didn't like?"

"Well, it was nice to meet your brother when he was home for Christmas, but I wish we would've gotten along better."

"I think you overreacted to that. He liked you, he was just watching out for me. He was also unhappy about his transfer from France to Poland. I don't understand why he had to go there."

Hans hesitated and then said, "I also wish I got along better with your dad. I can't figure him out."

Elise looked off in the distance and said, "Sometimes I can't either."

Hans decided not to pursue the topic and instead said, "And of course, there's Gerhard. The other day he was droning on about how we'd easily defeat the British in the desert and in the sea. A few months ago, he said we'd easily beat them in the air. He's been making incorrect predictions for as long as I've known him."

"My father uses the phrase 'Sometimes wrong but never in doubt.'"

"I like that. He's definitely in category four."

"What's category four?"

"Well, I have a theory that there are four types of people."

"How many theories do you have?"

"I don't know. More than most people, I guess."

"Clearly. But I thought there were only two types of people."

"Who told you that?"

"You did. It's your high-strung and low-key theory."

"Oh, right. There are only two types of people, but there are also only four types of people."

"I'm confused. Are the original two types included in the four types?"

"No, this is a different classification system. Please try to keep up," Hans joked. "In this system, there are four types. First, there are those who know and know that they know, and you should congratulate them. Second, there are those who don't know and know that they don't know, and you should teach them. Third, there are those who know but don't know that they know, and you should wake them up. Lastly, there are those who don't know and don't know that they don't know. Gerhard is definitely category four."

"And what are you supposed to do with category fours?"

"My first thought is that you should kill them because you

can't fix them, but that's not a nice thing to say. I don't think there's anything you can do with them."

"I believe everybody eventually gets what they deserve. Retribution will someday come for Gerhard Wolff."

"I hope you're right, and I hope I'm there to see it. Anyway, let's not talk about Gerhard anymore. Or the war either. Let's just enjoy our picnic."

CHAPTER 23

Hans trudged to Elise's house on a warm late-June evening, a week after Hitler's invasion of the Soviet Union, knowing it would be the last time he'd make this trek for several months. He rang the doorbell, and as usual, Elise peeked out through the lace curtain. She opened the door with a weak smile, and they walked into the parlor, where her parents were waiting. Hans and Elise sat on the couch opposite Dr. and Frau Engel, just like they had nine months earlier after they'd first met.

Frau Engel asked, "So you're leaving tomorrow, Hans?" While she was her usual polite and gracious self, her voice contained more than a hint of worry.

"Yes, my train is tomorrow morning."

"Well, Elise is going to miss you, and we will too. We enjoy having you around here."

Hans blushed and said, "I'm going to miss all of you as well."

"Let's hope the war is over by the time you finish your training."

"Yes, I feel strongly that it would be in the best interests of both me and the Reich if this wraps up quickly." He meant it as a joke, but nobody laughed.

Frau Engel said, "Oh dear, I forgot the cookies. Excuse me." She went to the kitchen, brought back slightly burned short-bread cookies, and placed them on the coffee table. Hans had overcome his unease about eating in front of the Engels, and as he grabbed a cookie, Frau Engel said, "I don't know if Elise told you, but Ludwig is now part of Army Group North. We obviously don't know his exact location, but it sounds like things are going well. Is that what you've heard, Hans?"

Hans noticed that she was talking even faster than usual. "Yes, based on what I've heard on the radio and read in the papers, the Russians are surrendering by the tens of thousands."

Frau Engel nodded and said, "Anyway, enough about the war. So you're leaving tomorrow?"

Hans furrowed his brow briefly at the uncharacteristic repetition of a question. "Yes, my train is tomorrow morning," he repeated.

After a few more minutes of small talk, Elise said it was time for them to go to the café. Frau Engel hugged Hans, and Dr. Engel shook his hand and wished him luck.

Hans and Elise held hands as they walked silently to the café. They passed groups of men clustered around newsstands, so anxious for information about the war that they read the newspapers immediately rather than taking them home first. Newscasts blared from the open doors and windows of Prager Strasse pubs and restaurants, trumpeting the latest Wehrmacht triumphs. In summers past, the district would have been abuzz with cheerful diners, shoppers, and revelers, but since the invasion, the level of anxiety had increased in proportion to the scope of the war.

They reached the café and sat across from each other at an outdoor table. Elise broke the silence. "I'm sorry my mom was being so weird. She's worried sick about Ludwig. Of course, she's also worried about you."

"Well, if it helps, I'm worried about me too."

Elise smiled and said, "She's grown quite fond of you."

"That's understandable. What's not to like?"

"I agree," she said with a smile.

"It's just three months of labor service and then three months of military training. At the pace our armies are moving, the war will be over before I have to join the fight."

"Do you truly believe that?"

"I think so." He lowered his voice. "For once, what my dad and I hear on the BBC is the same as what we hear from Goebbels. The Wehrmacht appears to be unstoppable." Elise leaned back in her chair, seemingly relieved. Then Hans said quietly, "But I'm not sure. My dad told me a joke the other day. A German general is bragging to his mistress about the exploits of his army. He shows her a world map, and she studies it for a minute and then asks, 'What is this tiny gray area?' 'Oh, that's Germany,' he answers. 'I see. And what is this gigantic red area?' 'That's the Soviet Union,' he explains. She appears confused and then worried, and then she looks at the general and asks, 'Has the Führer seen this map?'"

Elise smiled and said softly, "I guess that's funny unless you think about the implications." Hans nodded. "So, how are your parents doing with your leaving?"

"Well, as you can guess, my mom is worried. Her baseline level of anxiety is already high, so when you add this on top of it, she's barely able to function."

"Oh, that's so sad. Make sure you do something nice for her before you leave. How about your dad?"

"For years, he's been saying that Hitler would eventually pick a fight with the wrong country and disaster would follow, so I think there's a part of him that wants to be able to say 'I told you so.' But because I might be caught up in the fighting, he's concerned. Plus, at this point, it doesn't look like Hitler picked the wrong fight."

Their food arrived, and they ate mostly in silence. Eventually, Hans said, "I know I've brought up 'Für Elise' too many times in the past nine months, but I was listening to it the other day and thought of an analogy. Do you want to hear it?"

"Um, sure. But you're right, you've definitely overused it," she said with a smile.

"The song starts with a fairly basic tune, simple but pretty. Then it turns into something exciting, and then it's back to the simple-but-pretty part. But then it turns into something that sounds troubling and dark before concluding with the simple-and-pretty part. It's amazing that he could fit all those emotions into three minutes. Anyway, here's the analogy. Before I met you, my life was simple and pleasant, and I think that's equivalent to the first part of the song. Then we've had these special months together, and that's equivalent to the exciting part of the song. Then it goes back to simple, which I hope is my training and your return to school. But then there's the troubling part. In the song, that part is only about thirty seconds, and then it goes back to simple and pretty. So I was thinking—we can handle thirty seconds of trouble, right?"

"Yes, but what if the troubling part is more troubling than you think, or longer than you think? What if it lasts for a year or even two?"

He reached across the table and grabbed her hands. "I know this sounds corny, but I believe we're meant for each other. At the same time, I sometimes wonder why you're even with me. You're perfect, and I'm, well, me."

"I never thought about it in those terms, but you're right. I should probably reconsider this whole thing." She smiled, squeezed his hands, and said quietly, "The whole country has been overrun with arrogant jerks. You might be the last nice guy here."

"You make a good point. Maybe I'm the one who should reconsider this whole thing," he said with a smile.

After dinner, they returned to her house and sat on the porch swing. Even though it was late, it was still warm, and Elise said, "I always loved summer when I was a kid. We'd rent a house on the Baltic coast, and my brother and I would go to the beach every day. I wish you and I could have a whole summer together."

"We'll have lots of summers together, just not this one. And I'll be home before Christmas, and maybe the war will be over by then."

"So we'll go to the Striezelmarkt?" she asked, tears welling up in her eyes.

"Of course. We'll go this year and every year after that. I promise."

CHAPTER 24

Six months later, Hans's train chugged slowly into the Dresden station on a sunny but cold December afternoon. He scanned the platform and eventually saw Elise, illuminated by the sunlight that streamed through the glass roof. She was looking up and down the length of the train, and when their eyes finally met, she beamed and waved.

The train hissed to a stop, and he pushed his way past the other passengers to get to the exit. When he stepped off, she was waiting for him, and they embraced, kissed, and then embraced again. As they separated, she eyed his Wehrmacht uniform and said, "You look quite dashing! And you're bigger than when you left. What do they feed you?"

"They apparently don't like to have skinny little men in the army, so we eat pretty well. Of course, they might just be fattening us up like pigs for the slaughter." Elise frowned, and Hans said, "Sorry, that humor probably isn't appropriate here."

She surveyed his uniform again and said, "You look like a different person."

"I sort of feel like a different person too. But I'm not sure that's a good thing."

As they exited the station, Elise nearly skipped with excitement as she told him about everything she had planned for his leave. Halfway to his house, they passed an elderly couple with yellow stars sewn on their coats. Hans asked quietly, "When did they start wearing those?"

Elise replied, just as quietly, "The Judenstern? They became mandatory in September."

"The government keeps making it worse for them. I don't understand why they don't leave."

"That's the other change—they're not allowed to emigrate anymore."

"They've been encouraged to leave for years, and now it's not allowed? That doesn't make any sense."

Elise shrugged, and they kept walking.

When Hans opened the door to his house, Greta bounded toward him and nearly knocked him over. He squatted down to pet her and she licked his face. His father entered from the kitchen, and Hans stood up to shake his hand. "Your mother isn't back from the market yet. Those damn lines keep getting worse, and I swear she spends half her life there."

The front door, which Elise had just closed, opened and his mother entered, carrying a bag of groceries. She set the bag on the floor and hugged Hans. After a few seconds, he tried to pull away, but she continued to squeeze him, sniffling quietly into his chest.

When she finally let him go, she said through her tears, "I wanted to make you a special dinner, and I went all over town but couldn't find a store that had any meat. I'm so sorry."

"It's fine. I'm sure it'll be great."

He made eye contact with Elise, whose eyes had welled up with tears too. "I'll go home so the three of you can catch up. I'll see you later, right?" she asked Hans.

"Yes, I'll come over in a few hours." They hugged, and Elise left.

His father said, "We can't get enough coal to heat this room, so we need to go into the kitchen." Hans hadn't noticed it when he walked in but now realized that the front room wasn't much warmer than outside.

They sat at the table, with Greta lying on his mother's feet. His father said, "So tell us what you've been doing."

"Well, in the Reich Labor Service, we mostly drained swamps, which wasn't especially fun, and after that, I did basic training. I also did extra training to be a communications specialist, so I guess all that time I spent tinkering with our radio paid off."

"See—I knew that radio was a good idea."

"I hoped all this training would allow the Russians enough time to surrender, but unfortunately, that didn't happen."

"No, it didn't. How much do you know about what's going on?"

"I know we got stopped outside Moscow, and I also heard that the Japanese bombed Pearl Harbor, so now we're fighting the Americans too."

"I heard on the BBC that the situation in Russia is a disaster. We didn't have winter coats for the army because we thought the war would be over by now, so all those poor soldiers are freezing to death. And Hitler saying he's happy to be fighting the Americans? The man's a lunatic."

His mother squirmed in her chair and asked, "How long will you be home?"

"Three weeks. I report right after the New Year."

She said, "You've told us what you've been doing, but you haven't said if you enjoy it."

Hans looked down at his hands. "Well, I've never been good at making decisions, so I guess I like that they make all of them for me. Overall, I'd say I don't have a great personality for soldiering, but they're able to fit a square peg into a round hole. It turns out you can fit any shaped peg into any shaped hole if you hammer it hard enough. I know how to do all the army stuff, I just don't feel that I'm a natural-born killer."

"Well, I think that's a good thing," she said.

His father scowled at her and said to Hans, "Unfortunately, you're not going to have a choice. I hate to say this, but if you don't kill, you're going to get killed."

"Yes, they've explained that thoroughly. I'm sure I'll be fine once I get there."

His mother frowned and got up to finish preparing dinner while his father shared reminiscences of his own military training from twenty-five years earlier. After a while, she brought a pot of cabbage stew to the table and when she ladled it into his father's bowl, it splashed onto his shirt. He glared at her as she filled Hans's bowl and asked him what he wanted to drink. When he requested a beer, his father said, "So you've started drinking?"

"Yes, everybody does in the army."

"Well, I guess it was bound to happen eventually. Good for you."

His mother got beers for both men and sat down. "Prost," said his father, and they tapped their bottles.

They ate quietly for a few minutes, and then his father said, "So your mother thinks we should go back to the village and move in with her father. She says it's dangerous here. Somewhere she got the idea that Dresden is going to be bombed."

"Huh, I wonder where she heard that," Hans said.

His father continued talking as if his mother weren't there. "I explained to her that my work is here, and I'd have no way to make a living there."

Hans said, "But isn't there a shortage of farmworkers because all the young men are in the army or working in armaments factories?"

"Yes, but I'm not a farmer. My work is here," he repeated. "And by the way, there's a shortage of construction workers for the same reason."

She said, "But there's less and less construction going on because of the shortages of materials. Lots of people are leaving the cities and moving to the country and—"

"There will always be work for craftsmen like me. Plus, if we left, what would happen to the house?" Hans didn't know whether his father was concerned about the house or if he just wanted to stay in Dresden so he could say "I told you so" if the bombs started raining down. Or maybe he thought going back would be an admission that he hadn't been successful in the big city.

Uncharacteristically, she continued to push. "They have food in the country. The rationing here is going to starve us to death."

"We're not going anywhere now. Perhaps we'll reconsider later."

For the rest of dinner, Hans and his father talked about what was happening in the neighborhood and which boys were fighting in which units. Hans watched his mother as she ate in silence. He knew she was probably right about moving back to the village, and he knew that in his heart, his dad probably agreed with her.

But he also knew that his father would never leave Dresden.

CHAPTER 25

After dinner, Hans, still dressed in his uniform, walked to Elise's house on snowy sidewalks darkened by blackout restrictions. The headlights of passing cars were partially masked and looked like squinting eyes. The streetlamps, which a year earlier would've illuminated a festive wintry landscape, had been extinguished, and Hans wondered what had happened to the lamplighters who had been put out of business. They were probably in the army, he thought. Maybe even frozen to death in Russia.

Hans flinched at the sound of his jackboots clicking on the stone steps that led to the Engels' darkened porch and tried to tread more softly. As Elise opened the door and Hans stepped in from the cold, it was like entering a different world. The home was bright and warm, and he was greeted by the smell of Christstollen, candles, and pine needles. It felt like a sanctuary where everything was still good and happy and safe. The blackout curtains on every window added to the impression that this house was isolated from and immune to the horrors of the outside world.

As he took off his Wehrmacht coat and cap, he looked around the room. An Advent wreath containing pine cones, berries, dried flowers, and candles sat on the dining room table. Stockings hung above the fireplace, and angels and wooden nutcrackers adorned nearly every shelf and table.

Hans thought back to the prior year's Christmas Eve when he had helped decorate the Engels' tree. Everything was the same now, except instead of Christmas music playing on the gramophone, he heard a news broadcast on the radio.

Frau and Dr. Engel entered the parlor. Dr. Engel's hair had grayed since the summer, and dark circles framed his eyes. Frau Engel was thinner, and her eyes danced around the room as if watching out for danger. She said, "Welcome home, Hans. Oh my goodness, you look so handsome in your uniform! Please sit down." The days of conversation about Beethoven and porcelain were past, and she immediately began to ask questions. "How long will you be home?"

"Just three weeks."

"Do you know where you're being sent?"

"I'll be in the Sixth Army, which is one of the most successful armies in the Wehrmacht. Last summer, they made great progress—"

"Shh!" Frau Engel said as she held up a finger and looked over her shoulder at the radio, from which martial music signaled a victory news bulletin. The announcer reported that the Wehrmacht was consolidating its positions around Moscow and was taking action to straighten its lines. To Hans, that sounded like retreating. The bulletin concluded, and Frau Engel said, "Sorry to interrupt. Ludwig is near Leningrad, and I was hoping they'd have an update about the fighting there. Please continue."

"I was saying that the Sixth Army did well in France in 1940 and then also last summer in Russia."

"What do you know about Leningrad? We haven't heard from Ludwig in weeks."

"It sounds like the city won't be able to hold out much longer. The Russians are surrounded and will all starve to death if they don't surrender."

"Yes, that's what I heard too. I know this is a difficult question, but when do you think this will all be over?"

"I can't imagine it will go on much longer. I feel that if we make one more big push, Russia will collapse. We've already captured and killed millions of their soldiers, and they have to run out at some point, right?"

"Yes, exactly. One more big push. We've been doing everything we can to help. We contributed all our extra coats to the coat drive." She continued at a frantic pace, "I think 1942 will be the last year of the war. Have you heard what it will be like when it's over?"

"They told us that all the land we're capturing in Ukraine and western Russia will be divided into farms and given to German soldiers. Young couples will move there and be encouraged to have lots of babies." He looked at Elise, but she didn't meet his eyes.

Frau Engel jumped from one worry to another. "We sometimes hear air-raid sirens and go to the basement, but they're always false alarms. It's quite a nuisance. Did you see any bomb damage during your trip back from training?"

"No, not at all. The British bombers are taking huge losses, so maybe they'll give up on this strategy at some point."

"I hope so, but it worries me that the Americans might start bombing too. Do you think the British or Americans will eventually bomb Dresden?"

"I don't think so. British bombers can't make it this far, and I doubt the American ones are any better. Plus, I really think the British and Americans believe Dresden is different from other German cities."

"Yes, I've thought that too. This isn't a military or industrial city, it's a cultural city. I remember reading about the Grand Tour of Europe that rich English people used to take, and Dresden was part of it. Many British and Americans used to live here—how many German cities have a British quarter?"

"I agree. What would be the point of bombing us?"

"Exactly. Are you familiar with the American author Washington Irving? He lived here for a while."

"He wrote 'Rip Van Winkle,' right?"

"Yes. That was based on a German folktale. And the Duke of Windsor visited here just a few years ago." Frau Engel was clearly trying to convince someone that Dresden was safe, but it appeared to Hans that the person she was trying to convince was herself.

She took a sip of wine and leaned back in her chair. "Maybe this will turn out all right after all. One more big push and it'll be over, and things can go back to normal."

CHAPTER 26

After Hans and Elise left, Max retired to his refuge from the world, the library at the back of the house. He lit a fire, poured a single malt scotch, and sat down on the leather wingback chair as the flame sputtered to life. The sight of Hans in a uniform had rattled him, even more than seeing his own son in one. Hans seemed like such a child, and now he was leaving to fight in a war.

He shook his head. How had they gotten here? He'd supported the Nazis when they'd first come to power, mostly because he craved order, and the chaos in Germany, with competing groups of rabble-rousers fighting in the streets, had been unsustainable. Hitler had promised to put an end to it, and he had. Max had initially believed that much of Hitler's vitriol was just talk, but because of his profession, he'd quickly learned he was mistaken. At first, doctors were simply required to submit the names of people with certain hereditary conditions, but then came the forced sterilizations and special camps. He didn't know what happened in the camps, but he could guess. The fact that many of his fellow physicians approved of these actions appalled him, and he had quickly realized that his acquiescence to the rise of the Nazis had been a mistake, probably the biggest of his life.

Since he wasn't able to voice his dissent, he had decided several years earlier to heal as many people as he could to make amends for his earlier complicity. It was too late to stop the Nazis, but his profession provided him a unique opportunity to offset the bad with some good. The Nazis took lives; he would save them. The overall ledger would still be negative, but he was committed to doing his share to make things better. Perhaps even more than his share.

He knew Maria was frustrated with his workload and that he should explain his motivations to her. His futile attempts to save the world forced him to make sacrifices, but at least he had consciously chosen to make them. His absence forced Maria to make sacrifices too, but she had never agreed to his moral bargain and, in fact, didn't even know it existed. He believed that if he explained his reasoning to her, she'd understand and be supportive. He just had to find the right words and the right moment, and to date, neither of those things had become apparent. He sighed and took another sip of scotch.

Maria entered the library, refilled his glass, poured herself more wine, and sat down in the chair next to his. In years past, this was when she would've talked about what had happened that evening, what she liked and what she didn't, where she thought Hans and Elise's relationship was going, and anything else that popped into her head. Sometimes her rehashing of an event took longer than the event itself. Tonight, though, she sat quietly, sipping her wine and staring into the crackling fire. She had either met her quota of words for the day, or else the quota had been reduced due to anxiety and weariness. He considered taking this opportunity to explain his rationale for working so much, but she already seemed so stressed. He could always tell her tomorrow. Or the next day.

Max spoke English fluently and had studied English-language poetry at university. Among his favorite poems was one by Yeats that he'd thought about often in the years since Hitler's rise:

Turning and turning in the widening gyre
The falcon cannot hear the falconer;
Things fall apart; the centre cannot hold;
Mere anarchy is loosed upon the world,
The blood-dimmed tide is loosed, and
    everywhere
The ceremony of innocence is drowned;
The best lack all conviction, while the
    worst
Are full of passionate intensity.

Many lines in the poem reminded him of the past eight years, especially, "Things fall apart; the centre cannot hold" and "The best lack all conviction, while the worst / Are full of passionate intensity." He, and so many others, lacked all conviction, while the worst Germans were full of passionate intensity. He'd gone along with it, and having the best people go along with the worst was how they had ended up here.

Given the events of the previous weeks, he didn't believe Germany could win the war. Russia's vastness had swallowed the Wehrmacht, America was now an adversary, and Germany hadn't even been able to knock out puny England. Moreover, he had begun to talk to wounded soldiers returning from Russia, and if even half their stories of atrocities were true, there was going to be a day of reckoning for Germany. He didn't know how his beloved country had come to this point, but as he stared into the fire, he wondered if the only remedy for Germany's disease was to burn the country down.

He took another sip. The image of Hans and Elise on the couch evoked other lines from the poem, "The blood-dimmed tide is loosed, and everywhere / The ceremony of innocence is drowned." When he looked at Elise, he saw an innocent girl in love, full of sweetness and optimism. He felt that he and Maria had done everything they could to give her the best possible start in life, but the ceremony of innocence was being drowned. He also realized that this era would probably not end well for her, and almost certainly not for Hans, and there was nothing anyone could do about it. "Mere anarchy is loosed upon the world."

CHAPTER 27

For Hans, the length of each day of his leave seemed to shorten in proportion to the number of days he had left. He increasingly wasted time brooding about the war, and by his last day at home, it was all he could think about. He and Elise had dinner plans for that evening, but before he could leave the house, his father asked him to visit the shelter. Up until then, Hans had avoided it because it depressed him to realize that if they ever needed it, his parents would have to face the peril without him.

His father grabbed two beers, and Hans followed him outside into the early-evening winter darkness. After lifting the hatch, his father bent down to flip a switch at the top of the steps, and light emanated from the opening. Hans entered the shelter and saw a bare bulb hanging from the ceiling, casting a harsh light in the cramped space. As his eyes adjusted, he saw the words "Beckers Bunker" painted in black Gothic script on the back wall. "What's that?"

"That was Schmidt's contribution to the project. He thought it was funny."

Hans smiled as he pictured Herr Schmidt showing up with a bucket of paint and convincing his father to give the shelter a name, laughing all the while.

Hans scanned the completed shelter, which appeared to be exactly as his father had designed it. It was equipped with buckets of sand, casks of water, gas masks, goggles, jars of preserves, canned food, a bottle of schnapps, and three cots. Hans got a lump in his throat as he pictured his parents cowering on their cots, with the third one empty. On the walls, his father had drawn outlines of what hung from each hook and rested on each shelf, as a craftsman would do in his workshop.

The only thing Hans saw that he didn't remember from the original plan was a coil of rope resting on a wooden chair in the corner. "What are the chair and rope for?" he asked.

His father ignored the question and instead said, "Why don't we get started on these beers?" He opened the bottles, gave one to Hans, and they sat down on a cot with their backs against the wall.

Hans said, "I'm impressed with how this turned out. I just hope you don't need it."

"Unfortunately, I think we will." He turned his head toward Hans. "I know I should give you encouragement on your last night here, but . . ." His voice trailed off as he faced forward again and took another swig. Hans took a drink too. "Your being gone is going to be hard on your mother. It's going to be hard on me too. I just want to tell you that I'm proud of you, and I'm going to miss you."

The two men turned to face each other again, and Hans cringed as the eyes of his unsentimental, unshakable, invincible father filled with tears. Hans had long ago developed a habit in awkward social situations of drinking things quickly, in part so he had something to do with his hands. But now the drink was alcohol, and as he finished his first bottle he said, "I'm going to get another beer. Do you want one?"

"Sure," his father said, turning his face away.

Hans returned to the cot with two more beers, and his father, facing forward, said, "I'm sorry to be so emotional." He turned to Hans and their eyes met. "It's just . . . I always thought this would end badly, but now I'm afraid that after to-morrow the three of us won't see each other again."

Hans knew he should embrace his father, tell him he loved him, or give him some sort of reassurance. Instead, he broke eye contact and took another drink.

CHAPTER 28

Elise flitted around her house, intermittently packing up Christmas decorations and sweeping up pine needles. She knew her mother would eventually perform these tasks, but she wanted to take her mind off the fact that it was Hans's last night at home and he was twenty minutes late.

She had always felt that the weeks before Christmas were the best time of the year but the weeks after were the worst. The anticipation and merriment of the holidays had passed, and she had nothing to look forward to except three months of bad weather. She knew this post-Christmas season would be the worst of all.

Hans finally arrived, and when they kissed, Elise smelled beer on his breath. They walked to the restaurant, sat down, and he ordered two beers. She knew he'd drink both of them, and as he started the first one, she said, "I have to admit I'm a bit surprised by how much you drink now."

"I find that a couple of beers make me much more charming. Plus, everyone in the army drinks—I'm just trying to be one of the guys."

"I don't want you to be one of the guys. I don't like the guys."

Hans shrugged. "Funny, I don't like the guys either." He reached across the table and grasped her hand. "I'm sorry these past few weeks haven't been more fun. It's my fault."

"Everything is just so hard now with all the restrictions. The Striezelmarkt is completely different when it's only open in the daytime." She squeezed his hand. "I'm not worried about my plans for your time here not working out perfectly—I'm worried about you. Are you okay?"

"I don't know. For the past two years, whenever I thought about the war, I'd feel an enormous weight settle over me—just an incredible sense of dread. Until recently, I could always push it to the back of my mind, but since I've been home, the weight is always there. I can't stop thinking about it."

She squeezed his hand again, and he gave her a feeble smile.

"Anyway, I apologize. I appreciate all the planning you did, but once I got past the halfway point of my leave, I started counting down the days and got increasingly angry that I wouldn't be able to do these things again for a long time. I promise I'll try to make tonight as fun as possible." He let go of her hand and took another swig.

After they got their food, Hans lowered his voice and said, "I didn't intend to talk about this, but I think I've been wrong about the Nazis. I used to think they were just obnoxious and boring and occasionally violent, but that the boys our age were mostly playacting. After the past six months, I think it's much worse than that." He paused. "Are we evil?"

"Is who evil?"

"Are Germans evil? Are the boys our age evil? If you saw how they behave at training, you might feel that way."

"I don't think you can vilify an entire generation like that. I'm sure some boys are bad, but probably not most of them."

Hans shook his head and said, "I don't know anymore."

"As long as we're talking about things we didn't intend to, I wanted to tell you more about the hospital. I mentioned that I was volunteering there, but I didn't give you details." She swallowed hard. "It's terrifying. I see boys our age coming back from Russia, and it's so horrible that I can't even describe it." Tears welled up in her eyes. "Please be careful."

"Trust me, I will, and I'm sorry you had to see all of that." They were silent for a moment and then he said, "It was interesting that your mom brought up Rip Van Winkle a couple of weeks ago. Do you know that story?"

"Is that the one where the guy falls asleep and wakes up years later to find that everything has changed?"

Hans started his second beer. "Yes. He goes into the hills to get away from his nagging wife and sees a dwarf and helps him carry a keg of liquor up the mountain. When he gets to the top, he has a drink and falls asleep, and when he wakes up, it's twenty years later. He returns to his village and discovers his wife is dead and his kids are grown. Also, the American Revolution happened, so he went to sleep in an English colony and woke up in the United States. I was thinking about it the other day because I wish I could go to sleep and then wake up and have Hitler be gone and have Germany be a different country. Then we could start our real lives." Hans said this too loudly, and Elise looked around to ensure nobody had heard him.

She looked back at him and said, "So in this scenario, am I the nagging wife who's dead when he comes back?"

"Of course not. You're the thing I'm excited to come back to."

"Well, I hope we don't have to wait twenty years to start our lives."

"I truly believe I'll be home soon. I guarantee you it'll be less than twenty years."

With a weak smile, she said, "I certainly hope so."

"My dad was gone for two years in the last war and that was the bloodiest war in history, so I've made that my worst case. I think we can handle two years, right?"

"That seems like forever, but I guess so."

They stayed for dessert, and Hans ordered a schnapps. And then another. As he stood up to leave, he bumped his thigh on the corner of the table, and as they left the restaurant, he stumbled on the threshold.

Hans suggested they walk to his house to see the completed shelter. Elise didn't like the fact that he was drunk but also didn't want to say goodbye, so she accompanied him to the backyard of his house. He opened the hatch, turned on the light, and lumbered down the steps. Elise reluctantly followed him. Her other visits to the shelter had been in the daytime, but now the light from the bare bulb emitted an eerie glow in the cold, dank air. She got a chill as she reached the bottom of the steps.

Hans turned to face her, and as he stepped backward, his head hit the light bulb, causing it to swing on its wire. He sat on a cot and when she sat beside him, he awkwardly put his arm around her shoulders. She suddenly realized where this might be headed and recoiled. "I think I should probably go. You're drunk—"

"Please stay. My parents are asleep, and nobody can hear us down here. My dad worked so hard on this shelter—we might as well get some use out of it," he said, grinning stupidly.

She started to get up, but he grabbed her wrists. "Please stay. I need you to stay."

She looked in his glassy eyes and recognized the sweet, innocent boy from the orchestra, but also saw a drunken soldier who had been transformed by alcohol and the military. "I'm sorry, but I have to go." She twisted away from his grip and walked to the steps.

"Please don't let this be our last night together. I don't know if I'm coming back."

She turned to face him as the swinging light bulb created dancing ghosts on the walls. "You're going to come back. I keep thinking about what you said about 'Für Elise.' You said we'll hit our troubled times, but then we'll get back to the simple times." Tears rolled down her cheeks. "I just want the simple times."

"Me too, but my train is tomorrow morning."

"I want this to be special, and you're drunk. I'm going to leave now, but I promise I'll wait for you. Maybe that'll make you extra careful, knowing you have something to look forward to when you get back." She tried to smile but failed.

"Please? My train leaves in less than twelve hours."

"No! And I don't think I can go with you to the station. This needs to be goodbye." She waited to see if he would get up to embrace her, but he remained seated. "I love you. Please be careful."

"I love you too," he slurred. "Can I ask you one favor? When I'm gone, can you make sure my parents are okay? I'm really worried about them."

She looked at him as he sat on the cot with tears in his eyes. "Yes, I'll make sure they're okay." And she left.

She walked home on the darkened streets, crying most of the way. Why did their last night have to be like this? She was prepared to sleep with him, but not while he was drunk. By the time she got home, she had regained her composure. She was confident she had made the right decision and looked forward to a special night with him when he returned, whenever that turned out to be.

CHAPTER 29

Olga was sitting in the cold, dark kitchen in her nightdress and a coat when she heard noises from the backyard. Greta, who had been asleep on her slippers, woke up and stared at the door. Olga stood up, looked out the window, and saw Hans and Elise enter the shelter. She considered going to see what they were doing but then thought better of it and sat back down. *Teenagers will do what they'll do,* she thought.

Her presence in the kitchen wasn't a coincidence; she was there nearly every night. August's snoring, especially when he was drunk, was overwhelming, so she usually waited for him to fall asleep and then came downstairs. Some nights she didn't sleep at all and just sat in the kitchen, gnawing at the remains of her fingernails.

She thought about the things that used to worry her and realized how trivial they were. Sometimes they hadn't been able to afford a nice birthday present for Hans, and sometimes food shortages had meant she couldn't prepare a particular meal. Silly, ridiculous stuff.

Now her baby was going off to war. To make matters worse, August was drinking more, and his refusal to even consider returning to their village infuriated her. Her life in the village was predictable, stable, and maybe even boring, but that's what she liked about it. They'd be poor in the village, but everybody was poor in the village so it didn't bother her. In

Dresden, it bothered her. For the first time in their marriage, she and August fought. It occurred to her that perhaps Hans had been the glue that held them together, and that when he'd gone away, the bonds of their marriage had gone too.

Hans. Poor, sweet Hans. What would he be like when he returned from the war? August had still been jovial when he came back from his war, but he had definitely changed. There was a darkness that hadn't been there before. And outbursts of anger and fits of anxiety. Hans—who knew what Hans would be like?

She was jolted from her thoughts by the sound of the back door opening. Hans entered, turned on the light, and grunted. "Is everything all right?" he asked.

She was embarrassed and realized she should've gone up- stairs when she saw Hans come home. She considered asking him what he was doing in the shelter and why he hadn't walked Elise home but decided against it. "I'm having trouble sleeping. Can I get you anything to eat or drink?"

"No, that's all right." Through years of experience, she knew the indications of drunkenness and saw all of them in Hans. He walked to the sink and picked up a glass. August's bottle of schnapps was on the counter, and for a moment, it wasn't clear if he'd fill the glass with schnapps or water. She was relieved when he chose water and sat down across from her in August's customary chair. Neither of them spoke as Hans sipped his water, staring at the glass.

She had so much she wanted to tell him, about herself, about August, about their marriage, but she didn't know where to begin. Maybe if she explained why she and August should return to the village, Hans could convince his dad that it was the sensible thing to do. But she knew Hans's concerns were bigger than hers, so she remained silent.

CHAPTER 30

After finishing his water, Hans stood up, kissed his mother on top of her head, and trudged upstairs. He lay down on his bed without changing out of his clothes, looked around his darkened room, and wondered if this would be the last night he'd ever spend in it. Despite the alcohol, he knew he wouldn't be able to sleep, and as the buzz waned, the despair rose.

An hour later, he heard his mother's lonely footsteps on the stairs. She sniffled as she walked past his room, and when she opened her bedroom door, he could hear his father snoring. Hans didn't even try to sleep but instead just lay on his back and stared at the ceiling, waiting to cross the dreadful line where drunkenness gives way to a hangover. The wind chimes occasionally produced solitary, forlorn notes, and he wondered if they were a portent, like in the poem: "Send not to know / For whom the bell tolls, / It tolls for thee."

Just before dawn, a chorus of birds began singing outside his window, as they always did at that time of the morning. Whenever he heard them, he knew he was up either too late or too early; in this case, he was both. He realized he wouldn't hear them again for months or even years. Would the same birds be there when he returned? How long did birds live? He had never thought about that before.

Shortly afterward, he heard his mother get up and walk downstairs, and he realized she probably hadn't slept either.

He listened to all the sounds of a routine morning. His mother went to the cellar, filled the coal scuttle, and then brought it to the kitchen to replenish the stove. Greta went outside and then came back in. His mother put food in Greta's bowl, and she wolfed it down. To Greta, this was a day just like any other day. Hans wished he could be her.

After breakfast, Hans's parents accompanied him to the station. During the walk, he watched for Elise, but she apparently had been serious when she told him goodbye the night before. At the platform, he hugged his parents and took one last look around, but there was no sign of Elise. He was dismayed that he wouldn't have the lasting image of her he had hoped for.

He took a seat and looked out the window at his parents standing on the platform. They appeared old, tired, and defeated. His mother was slouching and had heavy bags under her eyes. Had she looked like that the entire time he was home? He realized he was so focused on his own misery that he hadn't considered how difficult this was for his parents. He had a sudden urge to get off the train and tell them that he loved them, but it was already starting to move. So he waved, and they waved back. His mother smiled, but when they were nearly out of sight, he saw her bury her head in his father's chest.

As the train left the station, Hans could see the tops of some of the Dresden landmarks—the Hofkirche, the castle, and the Frauenkirche. He'd miss seeing them but was comforted by the knowledge that they'd be waiting for him when he returned. But would Elise? He was mortified by his behavior the night before, and he began to think about the letter he would write to apologize.

He looked forward to the day when he'd be able to tell her he was sorry in person. But when would that be? The two-year estimate he had given Elise seemed like an eternity. In two years, it would be 1944—surely he'd be home before then. As the train rolled eastward, he decided to set two years as his official expectation, believing it was always better to be surprised than disappointed. If his father could endure two years, then so could he. His head gradually began to nod and he fell into a deep sleep . . .

1942–1943

GERMANS ADVANCE TOWARD STALINGRAD

(*New York Chronicle*, August 24, 1942) The Soviet high command acknowledged that the German summer offensive is nearing the strategic Volga River, and that the great industrial city of Stalingrad is in peril.

GERMANS SURRENDER ALL REMAINING FORCES IN STALINGRAD

(*New York Chronicle*, February 1, 1943) Nearly 100,000 surrounded, frozen, and starving German soldiers were taken into captivity, bringing to an end six months of brutal fighting and resulting in the destruction of the famed German Sixth Army. Total German casualties (killed, wounded, and missing) during the battle are estimated at approximately one million men.

1945

DRESDEN IN RUINS

(*New York Chronicle*, February 15, 1945)
The great city of Dresden, known as "the German Florence" because of its architectural treasures, is in ruins today after being firebombed by multiple waves of Anglo-American bombers. Preliminary estimates are that tens of thousands have been killed and hundreds of thousands have fled in panic from what witnesses called "huge oceans of fire."

DRESDEN FALLS AS WAR ENDS

(*New York Chronicle*, May 9, 1945)
Dresden, the last great city in German hands, fell to the Soviets just as the German high command signed surrender documents bringing the European war to an end.

1955

SOVIETS TO RELEASE LAST GER-MAN PRISONERS

(*New York Chronicle*, December 25, 1955)
After years of negotiations, delays, and German anger and frustration, the Soviet Union has agreed to release the last of their German POWs early next year, more than a decade after the end of the war.

PART TWO

1956

CHAPTER 1

Elise and Hans contemplated each other silently, two rocks in the tide of travelers swirling across the railway station's platform. After a few seconds, he spoke the line he had thought of more than a decade earlier, "So, did I miss anything?" He meant it as a joke, and in his imagination, Elise had laughed and hugged and kissed him when he said it. But she didn't appear to think it was funny, and he quickly realized he didn't think it was funny either.

After another moment of silence, he said, "Thank you for meeting me. I'm not sure who I still know here."

"Yes, everything is different, but you'll soon see my mom."

"I'm looking forward to seeing her again. And I'm sorry to hear about your dad. And your brother." Hans wondered how many postwar reunions in the past eleven years had begun with some variation of "Sorry about your." Probably most of them.

He picked up his bag and slung it over his shoulder. "Do you have anything else?" she asked.

"No. I was thinking on the train that I'm thirty-two years old and all my worldly possessions are in this bag. Not exactly where I thought I'd be at this stage of my life."

Elise just nodded.

They started walking, maneuvering through the mothers, sisters, and wives who hoped to hear news of their sons, brothers, and husbands. Hans knew they were desperate for any tidbit of information that would help them learn what had happened to their loved ones and allow them to move on with their lives. He did his best to avoid eye contact with them.

They passed the concourse, which was lined with boarded-up storefronts, then walked out of the station and into the cold late-afternoon sunlight. Hans asked, "Do you mind if we stop by my parents' house?"

"We can, but as I told you in my letter, there's nothing there."

"I understand, but I need to see it."

Elise shrugged. "Okay, if you want to."

As they walked toward their old neighborhood, Hans felt a sensation akin to déjà vu. It was as if he had seen a city similar to this one before, but nothing was quite what it was supposed to be. Buildings that should've been white were black, trees that should've been thriving were charred stumps, and avenues that should've contained houses were empty. Even the street names had changed.

They reached his parents' block, which was now a parking lot half-filled with small boxy cars. Hans entered it and maneuvered around the cars, walking to where he estimated his house had stood. Elise trailed behind him. "If this was the front of the house," he said, "then if I keep walking this way, I'll get to the backyard." He took a few more steps and then stopped in front of a gray Wartburg coupe. "And right here would've been the shelter." He paused and then asked, "So you don't know what happened to them?"

Without looking at him she said, "I checked on them the morning after the bombing, and they were alive and in the shelter. When I came back the next day, they were gone."

"But the shelter survived?" Elise nodded. "That doesn't make sense. How do you know for sure that they died?"

"A list was published a few weeks later, and their names were on it."

"But someone had to put their names on the list, right? I want to find out what happened to them, and whoever put them on the list would have that information."

"Why does it matter?"

"I don't know anything about what happened here while I was gone, and I've spent all these years wondering." He paused, looked at her, and said, "I just want to know."

Elise turned her head.

Hans gazed blankly at the parking lot. "No graves, no house, no pictures, no possessions. Not a trace that they ever existed." He was quiet for several minutes, then he said, "These cars are hideous." Elise smiled briefly, and Hans took a deep breath and started back toward the sidewalk. "Was your house replaced by a parking lot too?"

"I don't know. We don't go down that street anymore."

CHAPTER 2

They walked in silence to Elise's new neighborhood, which was fifteen minutes farther from the city center than her previous one. Elise stopped outside the entrance to her apartment building, a dilapidated turn-of-the-century four-story structure, and said, "I should warn you that my mom hasn't done well with everything that's happened, either emotionally or physically."

Hans nodded.

They entered the building, and he followed her up the stairs to the third floor. As they walked down the long, dimly lit corridor, Hans heard a baby crying and flinched at the thought that it could be Elise's. He was relieved when they passed the apartment that was the source of the racket, but the scare only served to highlight how little he now knew about Elise, whose letters had been as devoid of information as they were infrequent.

Elise unlocked a door that had "3E" painted on it and entered. Hans followed. Maria was sitting on one of two chairs that faced the door and backed up against a wall. A couch sat opposite the chairs, with a coffee table in between. The furniture was much drabber and the room much smaller, but the layout reminded Hans of the parlor at the Engels' old house. The parlor, though, had been just one of many rooms in the house, while this appeared to be the only common room in the apartment. The kitchen, which held a wooden table and two chairs, adjoined the common room, and just off the kitchen was a hallway that presumably led to the bedrooms. The sole source of light was the setting sun, visible through a small window behind Maria.

Hans had always associated Maria with the aroma of baked goods, a freshly cut Christmas tree, and perfume, but all he could smell now was camphor oil, mustiness, and perhaps the sauerkraut from last night's dinner. She wore a faded housecoat, slippers, and thick eyeglasses, and she didn't stand up as Hans and Elise entered. She started to speak but had to stop and clear her throat before she could produce words. "Hello, Hans."

"Hello, Frau Engel." Hans and Elise sat down on the couch, and Hans grimaced as he bumped his shins on the coffee table. In the uncomfortable silence, he looked around the apartment, which was clean, orderly, functional, and charmless. He wondered if Elise hadn't tried to make it appear welcoming and attractive for his arrival, or if she had tried and failed.

The absence of decorations made it seem as if they didn't plan on living there for long, or perhaps they just didn't care. The only photograph he saw was a badly creased black-and-white one displayed on a side table in the corner. It captured the Engel family on the beach, and Hans guessed it had been taken a few summers before he met Elise. Max and Maria smiled as they sat cross-legged on either side of a sand castle. Ludwig and Elise stood behind the castle, Ludwig with a too-big smile, arms akimbo and flexing a bit, and Elise with a modest grin and the self-consciousness of a girl in her early teens, her arms crossed over her chest. Knowing their fate, it was difficult for Hans to look at the happy family in the picture.

He was startled when Elise asked, "How was the train ride?"

Ah yes, Hans thought, *the traditional conversation starter when nobody knows how to start the conversation.* "It was fine. It's nice to finally be back in Germany."

"Well, you're not in the Germany that you remember. You're in the German Democratic Republic, or GDR. It's also referred to as East Germany."

"Yes, I know, but I sometimes forget. It's so strange that when I left Dresden it was in one country, but now that I've returned it's in a different one."

"It was even worse for the German people who lived east of here. After the war, the borders of Germany, Poland, and the Soviet Union were shifted westward, so we're now at the eastern edge of Germany, almost to the Polish border. Large areas of the old Germany are now part of Poland."

Hans sat up straight and said, "Oh—it all makes sense now. We came through what I was sure was Breslau, but it had a Polish name. I thought I was losing my mind. What a relief."

Maria said, "It wasn't a relief for the Germans in Breslau."

Hans shrank back and said, "What happened to them?"

Elise said, "They mostly became refugees, and some of them are here now. Prussia had it even worse—it doesn't even exist anymore." Hans wondered how a centuries-old German state like Prussia could cease to exist but chose not to pursue the topic. Was there anything that hadn't changed?

After Elise prepared dinner, Hans followed Maria into the kitchen, carrying a third chair in from the living room. When Maria got to the table, she rearranged the silverware to put the forks on the left side of the plates, and Hans noticed that his plate didn't match the other two. Elise poured a glass of wine for her mother and offered one to Hans, but he declined. She then served a meal of cabbage and potatoes, and Hans realized he had finally found something that hadn't changed.

Fourteen years earlier, Hans would've used the tactic of asking questions to get a conversation started, but what was possible to ask now? How was the bombing? How did your husband and son die? He hesitated to ask about their old neighbors because he didn't know if they were alive. He realized that Elise and Maria probably didn't know how to start the conversation either. How was Stalingrad? How was prison camp for the past thirteen years? He recognized the absurdity of their situation, and it was all he could do not to laugh.

Hans had gotten in the habit of wolfing down his food, partly because he was always hungry, and partly because he feared his guards would take it away from him. When he finished and looked up from his plate, he realized that the Engels were only halfway done. As he waited for them to finish, he noticed scars on Elise's wrists and briefly panicked at the thought that they were from him drunkenly grabbing her on their last night together in 1942. But he had held her for only a few seconds—he couldn't have caused that. She had probably been burned in the bombing, and he wondered how many other scars she was hiding. She seemed to notice what he was looking at and pulled down her sleeves.

Elise finished eating and poured another glass of wine for her mother, who spent several minutes moving the last bits of food around her plate, as if trying to compensate for the meagerness of the meal by extending the time it took to eat it. Eventually, Hans could no longer tolerate the silence. "How long have you lived here?"

"After the war ended we lived in several temporary shelters and then a few apartments," Elise said. "We were able to get this apartment when the prior family escaped to the West." Hans thought "escaped" was a strange word to use. Why would anyone need to escape from Dresden?

He wanted to say the apartment was lovely but didn't want to lie so soon after being reacquainted. Several more minutes of silence followed, and then Maria said, "Elise tells me you're going to be staying here."

Hans looked at Elise and then Maria. "I was hoping to stay here just until I get a job. If that's too much trouble, we were told at the transition center that the government has a shelter for returning POWs."

Elise said, "You can stay for a while, but you should know that there's still a housing shortage, so it might be difficult to find a place. You should start looking right away."

"I will. I have an appointment with a government agency tomorrow, and I'm hoping they can help me find a job and a place to live. At the transition center, they told everybody going to the GDR that we're required to register with them."

Elise furrowed her brow and asked, "Which government agency?"

"I think it's called the Ministry for State Security or something like that. It's on Bautzner Strasse."

Elise and her mother looked at each other. "That organization is also known as the Stasi," Elise said. "Are you familiar with it?"

"I hadn't heard of it before yesterday."

Elise nodded. "They probably want to know where you're living, and it wouldn't surprise me if they want to monitor the returning POWs."

"Monitor," huffed Maria.

Elise shot her a glance and then looked back at Hans. "I'll make sure you're up before I go to work."

"Where do you work?" Hans asked, realizing he should've mined this vein of innocuous conversational material earlier.

Elise looked down and said, "In a textile mill."

"So you decided not to be a teacher?"

"I tried, but it didn't work out." She stood up and said, "I'm sure you're tired."

"Well, yes. It's been a strange day."

Maria said good night and shuffled down the hallway, her slippers *shushing* on the wood floor. Elise retrieved a thin pillow and threadbare blanket and handed them to Hans. "The couch is going to be too short for you."

"Compared to where I've been sleeping, this is wonderful. And like I said, I'll get out of here as soon as possible."

"That's probably for the best. Good night."

Hans lay on his back with his knees bent and realized Elise was right—the couch was too short. He stared at the ceiling and thought back to his fantasies about returning to Dresden. In those dreams, he'd step off the train, see Elise from a distance, and they'd rush toward each other. He'd embrace her, pick her up, and spin her around. She'd look exactly as she had in 1942, and everything would return to the way it had been back then, minus the Nazis, the genocide, and the war, of course. He now realized he was a fool who had seen too many Hollywood movies as a boy. His thoughts of this day had sustained him for fourteen years, and now he was just relieved that it was done.

CHAPTER 3

Elise entered the bedroom she shared with her mother and closed the door without turning on the light. She sat down on her bed and whispered, "Can I talk to you for a minute?" No response, just the ticking of the plastic alarm clock on the nightstand between their two beds. "I'd like you to try to be nice to Hans. I promise he won't be here very long."

Her mother whispered back, "He shouldn't be here at all. You have no obligation to let him stay with us just because you dated when you were teenagers. That was half a lifetime ago."

"I know, but he doesn't have anywhere else to go."

"That's not our problem. Plus, we don't even know who this person is. We just know some kid from fourteen years ago with the same name. He's barely recognizable."

"You're right about that. I wasn't sure it was even him when he got off the train. For some reason, I had pictured him coming back in his Wehrmacht uniform. I certainly wasn't expecting the Russian peasant clothes."

"I was expecting his squeaky teenage voice, and it startled me when he said, 'Hello, Frau Engel' in that gravelly one. And then there's his beard and his limp. I'm serious when I say I don't know who that man is." She was quiet for a moment, and then asked, "When you saw him, what was your first thought?"

Elise hesitated and then whispered, "I have to admit I was excited for a second."

"I was afraid of that, but I'm sure that feeling was just nostalgia for a world that no longer exists."

Elise nodded in the darkness. "What was the first thing you thought?"

"That we're going to have a strange man sleeping on our couch."

"I understand. I just thought having him here for a while would be something—different. It's not like we have a bunch of exciting stuff going on in our lives."

"Are you sure it's not because you want someone around who thinks you're interesting and pretty?"

"I doubt he thinks that. Even I don't think that. I know our relationship ended a long time ago."

"Yes, but does he?" Elise didn't respond. "How much are you going to tell him about what happened?"

Elise sat quietly for a moment and then said, "Nothing. I'm not going to tell him anything."

She slid under the blanket and lay her head on the pillow. Her mother was probably right, and there had to be boundaries. There were feelings she didn't want to feel, remembrances she didn't want to remember, and, most importantly, revelations she didn't want to reveal. The bombers had knocked down Dresden's physical walls, but the walls she had constructed inside her mind needed to remain standing.

She reflected on the day's events, especially seeing Hans's street. As she began to doze, her thoughts drifted back to the morning after the bombing . . .

She woke up on the floor with her back against a wall and a weight on her left arm. She turned her head back and forth and up and down but couldn't see anything, not even a twinkle of light. Was she blind? Had she been buried alive? She tried to rub her eyes with her right hand and immediately discovered she was still wearing goggles. Once she'd removed them she could see a faint light leaking through the pavement-level windows, providing just enough illumination for her to get her bearings.

She was in the basement, surrounded by the boxes of memorabilia, mementos, and memories her mother had amassed over the years. The accumulator of these items was sleeping on Elise's left arm, her wheezing the only evidence that she was alive. The basement was smoky, but it was easier to breathe than it had been earlier. The light outside didn't appear to be the glow from a fire, but it didn't look like sunlight either. Was it dawn? Dusk? How long had she been sleeping?

She closed her eyes and pieced together what she had seen, skipping over the vision of her father's final moments. After she had organized her memories, or at least the ones she wanted to keep, she opened her burning eyes and realized she should put her goggles back on. They were covered with soot, and wiping them on her dress didn't help because it was coated too. She tried to spit on them but couldn't produce any saliva.

She needed water, so she gently laid her mother on the floor and crawled to the bucket her father had brought down when the sirens began wailing. She scooped some water with cupped hands, swirled it around in her soot-coated mouth, and spit it on the floor. She swallowed the next scoop, and it felt like gargling with sawdust as it went down. After she'd rinsed the goggles, she put them back on, checked on her mother, and went upstairs.

It was too dark to perform a thorough damage assessment, but it appeared that other than some broken windows, singed curtains, a layer of soot, and the electricity and water no longer working, the stone house had survived remarkably well. She took a pillow and blanket to the basement, tucked them under and around her sleeping mother, and then went back upstairs. While it had been more than two years since she had heard from Hans, and she didn't even know if he was still alive, she had made him a promise and intended to keep it.

She walked out the front door and paused at the top of the porch steps. The afternoon before, she had seen cars buzzing by, neighbors chatting, and children in colorful costumes skittering to Fasching celebrations. The night before, she had heard sirens, planes, explosions, and screams.

Now, all was quiet and still. The morning sun, futilely attempting to penetrate the smoke and ash, silhouetted her neighbor's houses, at least the ones that still stood. She felt as if she were standing on her porch during a snowstorm, with snow filling the air and blanketing the ground. The snowflakes, though, were ashes, and the sounds weren't neighbors shoveling sidewalks or children throwing snowballs, but fires crackling and houses collapsing. Every sound was muffled by the buildings of Dresden, reduced to their ashy essence and floating in the air, making it difficult to gauge distance. Was that crackling fire a block away or next door? Was something collapsing down the street or in the next neighborhood? The scene was eerily peaceful, and for a moment, she thought she might be dead.

Her trance was broken when she doubled over with a violent cough. After hacking for a half minute and spitting on the porch, she wrapped a scarf around her head to cover her mouth and nose. She walked cautiously down the ash-covered steps, and after exiting through the still-warm wrought iron gate, she turned right, knowing that if she turned left she'd see her father.

She felt like she was walking in ankle-deep flour, and her shoes were soon full of ash. As she climbed over rubble and circled around craters, she began to see bodies, or parts of bodies . . . a decapitated boy in a Hitler Youth uniform next to his bicycle; a young couple cremated in their burned car, their bodies fused and the tires melted to the pavement; a woman cowering behind a fence while cradling a baby, both now barely recognizable as humans.

Halfway to Hans's house, a young soldier emerged from the fog, followed by a group of refugees who reminded Elise of the zombies she'd once seen in a movie. The figures included pajama-clad children with blankets over their shoulders and blinded men and women who had to be guided through the wasteland. The soldier informed Elise that survivors were gathering at a nearby park, where food, water, and medicine would soon be available. She nodded, stepped aside, and watched as the zombies continued their slog.

She arrived at what had been Hans's house, but the only thing left standing was the fireplace Hans's father had been so proud of. The remains of the building were still smoldering, so she walked down the block and cut through in order to get to the shelter. She knocked on the hatch but didn't hear a response. She grabbed the still-hot handle, and as she flung the hatch open, light from a kerosene lamp cut through the darkness. Hans's mother, standing at the bottom of the steps, barked, "What do you want?"

Elise lowered the scarf from her face and said, "Frau Becker, it's me, Elise."

Frau Becker hesitated and then said, more softly, "What do you want?"

"Can I come down?"

"No. We're fine. Go help people who need it."

"Can I come down for just a minute?" She didn't respond, so Elise walked down the steps. Greta, whimpering softly, was burrowed under a blanket beneath a cot, and Hans's father sat on a chair in the corner of the shelter. He was slouched forward with his hands behind his back, and it appeared that he had thrown up on himself.

"Is he all right?" Elise asked.

With her hands at her sides and fingers splayed, Frau

Becker said, "He doesn't like to be down here and he had a difficult night. He's fine now, and we'll get out of here as soon as things are better up there."

Elise walked toward him and saw that his hands were tied to the chair. She looked at Frau Becker and said, "He doesn't look fine." She took off her goggles, knelt beside him, and said, "Herr Becker? It's me, Elise."

He turned his head slightly toward her but didn't respond.

CHAPTER 4

Hans awoke with a start the next morning and sat bolt upright on the couch. He looked out the window and tried to determine where he was. A minute before, he had been lying in the snow in an open-air prison camp. The man lying beside him had been staring at him, and Hans had asked, "What do you want?" When he didn't respond, Hans realized the man wasn't staring—he was dead. His cheeks were sunken from malnutrition, his lips were swollen from typhus, his nose was blackened from frostbite, and clusters of lice had overrun his beard and eyebrows.

But now Hans was on a couch in an apartment. Had he been dreaming about the prison camp, or was he now dreaming about the apartment? He yelped when a voice behind him asked, "Are you all right?"

He jerked his head around and saw a woman standing in the kitchen. He studied her for several seconds, and as the pieces of his new reality settled into place, he realized it was Elise. He smiled weakly and said, "Yes, fine."

She furrowed her brow and asked, "Are you sure? Who were you talking to?"

"Sorry, nobody. Just a bad dream." She turned and went back to preparing breakfast. As his head cleared, he realized he had finally spent a night with Elise in the same residence after months of thinking about it in the early 1940s and over a decade of imagining it in the intervening years. It had not gone as he had fantasized.

Watching her, he observed that she still had the same upright posture he remembered, but something wasn't quite right. She reminded him of a well-constructed building that had narrowly missed being hit by a bomb, one that was still intact and appeared stable, but whose structure had been fundamentally damaged by the shock wave. The angles of such a building would never be perfectly perpendicular again and its framework would be permanently weakened. He stopped staring when she turned to put a bowl and cup on the table. She said, "I need to go to work, but I've made some coffee and oatmeal for you. The coffee isn't very good—sorry."

"I'm sure it's fine."

"Make sure you're not late to your Stasi appointment and that you answer every question and do whatever they ask. Mother won't be getting out of bed for a while, so you'll have time to get cleaned up before you go. Do you have what you need?"

"I should be all right for today."

"Make a list, and we can go out this weekend and try to buy whatever essentials you're missing."

"You're being much too generous."

She shrugged. "By the way, the hot water is intermittent, but it always comes on eventually."

After she left, Hans felt strange and alone as he ate in the silent apartment. He realized that he hadn't been by himself at any time in the prior fourteen years, and he now found the experience unsettling. As he looked at the sunlight peeking through the curtains, he also realized that he hadn't slept in a room with curtains since his boyhood home. But no birds were singing their dawn chorus outside this window because there weren't any trees. And no wind chimes either.

He shook his head to clear the cobwebs and then walked

to the tiny bathroom. He'd rarely had access to mirrors in captivity, and even if he had, he wouldn't have wanted to see what he looked like. So here he was—thirty-two years old. Eyes a bit too sunken, cheeks a bit too hollow, and scars a bit too numerous. All things considered, though, not too bad.

As he rotated his head and examined his face, he realized he didn't know where most of the scars had come from. In Stalingrad and in his first months of captivity, every scratch had become an infection and every infection had become a scar. He regretted not having stories about the scars that proved his gallantry and martial prowess, such as this one being from a duel and that one from saving a damsel in distress. Of course, maybe old soldiers never knew where their scars came from and they only made up stories. He'd have to work on that.

The first thing he did was shave—the beginning of what he hoped would be a fresh start. When he was done, he inspected the finished product and wondered if he looked like his dad. Maybe. He did some math and calculated that he had been seven years old when his father was this age. By this point in his father's life, he had returned from a war, moved away from home, and had a wife, a kid, a job, and a house. A real adult life . . .

A cough from the bedroom jolted him out of his thoughts. He shivered, finished getting ready, and left the apartment.

CHAPTER 5

Hans took a tram across the river to the Neustadt district and then walked to the Stasi headquarters on Bautzner Strasse. He was familiar with the nondescript five-story structure, as he was with most of the prewar buildings in Dresden, and knew it was originally a paper mill that had been converted to apartments in the 1930s. He wondered when it had been transitioned to its current purpose, and why a government agency would need such a large building.

The waiting room was empty except for a few unoccupied chairs. Hans approached a sliding reception window opposite the entrance and saw a woman wearing a headset and typing intently. A cord connected the headset to a machine, and he wondered if she was typing a transcript of the words that were coming out of it. He tapped on the window, but she didn't respond, so he tapped again, more loudly this time. She stopped typing, pressed a button on the machine, and huffed as she looked up at him. She took his name and told him to sit down.

Hans lingered at the window, fascinated by the modern office. In addition to the mysterious listening machine, her desk included a typewriter, a telephone, and a small device with numbered buttons—perhaps an adding machine of some sort? The office was illuminated by long tubes of light that were unlike any lightbulbs he had ever seen. The receptionist cleared her throat and glared at him, so he sat down as she resumed typing.

After a half hour, the door to the back offices opened, and out stepped a man Hans immediately recognized: Gerhard. His hairline had receded, a Stalin walrus mustache had replaced the Hitler toothbrush mustache, and his shape had devolved from an inverted pyramid to a pear. The lower buttons of his gray uniform tunic strained against his belly, and the top button of his shirt held on for dear life against his neck. His chin and the tops of his shoulders were still at the same height, but in 1941 his shoulder muscles had been built up to the level of his chin, and now his chin drooped to the level of his shoulders. It occurred to Hans that Gerhard must not be experiencing the same food shortages that made Dresden's population almost uniformly thin.

Gerhard smiled and said, "So nice to see you again, Herr Becker. Please come with me." Hans briefly froze but then got up and followed him down a long gray hallway with metal doors at regular intervals on each side. Gerhard's shoes squeaked with every step on the linoleum floor, and his girth prevented his arms from hanging straight down, making him resemble an arrow, with his head a round arrowhead.

They entered an office, and then Gerhard closed the door and motioned for Hans to sit. Gerhard sat down behind his desk in a chair that was significantly higher than Hans's. The small office, smelling of musty file folders, tobacco, and body odor, was jammed with metal file cabinets, and additional folders were stacked on top of the cabinets. Gerhard's desktop held just one pen, one ashtray, one pack of cigarettes, one lighter, and one folder.

Gerhard withdrew a cigarette from the pack and lit it, all while looking at Hans. As he exhaled, he blew the smoke toward Hans, not directly in his face, but close enough to be clearly intentional. Hans pulled his head back, blinking rapidly, and recognized the smell as the cheap but potent Machorka tobacco his Russian guards had smoked. Even though it was only midmorning, the ashtray was nearly full, and it was easy to deduce why the whiskers above Gerhard's upper lip were yellow. The cigarette butts were lined up in neat rows, and for a moment, Hans was reminded of another item he had seen lined up in that manner: corpses in body bags.

Hans stopped staring at the ashtray when Gerhard said, "Let's see what we have here." He opened the thick folder, and as he flipped through the pages with his stubby fingers, Hans wondered how there could be so much information about him. He frowned when he saw that the file included photos of his parents.

After several minutes, Gerhard closed the folder and said, "So you survived the war."

"Yes. I surrendered with the Sixth Army at Stalingrad."

"I see. Do you feel that the Germans who died there were heroes?"

This felt like a trick question, and Hans didn't know how to answer. He remained silent until Gerhard chuckled and said, "That's all right, I'm getting ahead of myself. There will be plenty of time to discuss these issues. Today we're just going to get details about your situation so we can follow up with you in the future."

Hans was relieved that he didn't have to answer the question and realized he had much to learn about the political landscape. He hoped Elise would be able to help him.

"I understand you spent last night at Elise Engel's apartment. Is that correct?"

Hans didn't understand how Gerhard could know this but responded, "Yes."

"Is it just Fraulein Engel and her mother who live there?"

"Yes."

Gerhard looked up from his papers. "They've certainly had a rough go of it, haven't they?"

"From what I've seen, it looks like everyone in Dresden has had a rough go of it."

"True, very true. Let's move on. Why were you held in the Soviet Union so long?"

"I have no idea. As you know, most of the prisoners were released by the late 1940s, but they held on to thousands of us. It was as if they wanted to keep a certain number and made up reasons to do so. They seemed to have a special hatred for Germans captured at Stalingrad."

"The Soviets told us that only war criminals were detained after 1949. What war crimes did you commit?" As he finished the question, he took another puff of his cigarette and blew the smoke toward Hans.

Hans recoiled and said, "I didn't commit any war crimes."

"Are you saying that our Soviet brothers are lying?"

"No, I'm just saying that I didn't commit any war crimes, and I don't know why they kept me for so long."

"Well, either you're wrong, or the Soviets are wrong. Who do you think I should believe?"

Hans shrugged.

"We've found that many prisoners who have returned to Germany in the past few years have anti-Soviet feelings. That surprised us because we expected that the men who had the most exposure to the superiority of the Soviet system would have the most favorable impression of it."

Hans wanted to say, "Maybe it's because they held us captive for a decade after the war was over," but resisted the urge. Instead, he just shrugged again.

Gerhard continued, "The Soviets consider you to be a war criminal, and therefore our government considers you to be a war criminal. Because of this, you'll be getting extra attention from my organization. Please let us know if you plan to leave

Dresden, and I recommend that you not associate with other war criminals."

"I'm not a war criminal."

"So you've said. By the way, I'm curious about something. Most of the late-returning POWs chose to go to the West, probably because as Fascists and war criminals, they'd fit in better there. Why did you come back here?"

It was a difficult question because Hans was beginning to think it had been a mistake. "It's my home," he said quietly.

"Whether it's your home or not, we have no place for Fascists and war criminals here. The good news is that because you chose to come here rather than going to the West, we believe that you have the potential to be rehabilitated. With the proper training and education, we can help you see the error of your ways and teach you how to become a good Socialist. Plus, if we let all the young people leave, who would do the work, right?" he asked with a smile.

Hans shrugged again.

"I'll be happy to help you on this journey. I should tell you that I saw your name and asked for your case specifically. You should feel honored."

"Thank you," Hans said, unsure what he was thanking him for.

Gerhard closed the file and said, "This has been a productive session, but we clearly have much work to do. Let's meet again next Monday." He crushed out his cigarette, lined up the butt with the other corpses, and stood. They walked back down the hallway toward the exit to the waiting room. As Hans was leaving, Gerhard said, "Make sure you tell Elise hello for me."

CHAPTER 6

As soon as he left the office, Hans realized he hadn't asked about housing or a job. He didn't want to go back, so those concerns would have to wait until the next week. His mind buzzed with questions. Why was he considered a war criminal? How could a zealous anti-Communist like Gerhard have become a Communist government official? And was Hans considered a coward for surrendering to the Communists or a hero for not fighting for Fascism? It was all so confusing.

He wandered aimlessly around Dresden for the next two hours, trying to adjust to his new surroundings—not just the buildings but the people. Amid all this destruction, they were going on with their lives as if everything was fine. Women ate lunch in cafés, men in business suits read newspapers on benches, and children played in yards. They acted like things were normal despite being surrounded by evidence of utter devastation. What had once stood in that vacant lot? What had that charred pile of rubble been? Had people died there? It was maddening—was anyone asking these questions? Nobody seemed to care.

He sat on a bench and watched people walk by. Most of them, even the children, walked with their heads down, and he realized that while the war hadn't personally touched individuals in many parts of the world, that was certainly not true of these Dresdeners. He started making up stories about the passersby based on the age they would've been during the war. He saw a young man, twenty-five or so, wearing overalls. He would've been fourteen at the war's end, so he was probably in the Hitler Youth and perhaps even in the military since boys were fighting by then. His dad was probably in his thirties for most of the war, so there was a good chance he had fought too. Had he survived the war? Had the boy's mom survived the bombing?

A thin woman of about thirty-five passed by holding the hand of a preteen girl. Had the daughter been conceived in the last years of the war? Was she born before the bombing? What had it been like for the mother to raise a child in the years immediately after the war?

A businessman in his fifties carrying a briefcase. Was he a factory supervisor during the war, and if so, what did his factory make? Tools for war? Tools for genocide? Probably one or the other. Or perhaps he had been an officer in the army. Had he abetted mass murderers? What were his secrets, and how did he live with them?

Next up was a sturdy woman in her midfifties carrying a bag of groceries. She would've been about forty-five at the war's end, so she might've had a son in the military. Did he survive the war? Maybe he was captured and she never found out what—Hans abruptly stopped when he realized he could be describing his own mother. Perhaps it was best not to play this game.

He lowered his head, rubbed his eyes and face, and was startled by the absence of a beard. He decided to walk back to the apartment, but as he stood up, he suddenly realized he didn't know where he was. He looked left and right but saw nothing familiar. He had explored Dresden hundreds of times as a kid and had never once felt lost, but now he stood motionless and became increasingly panicky. People passed him on the sidewalk, but he didn't approach them because they didn't seem approachable. He realized that he no longer knew the city or its citizens.

He picked a direction and started walking.

CHAPTER 7

After an hour, Hans found his way back to the apartment and tried half-heartedly and unsuccessfully to converse with Maria, who eventually shuffled off to her bedroom. With nothing else to do, he picked up a fashion and culture magazine lying on the coffee table. This type of periodical was not something that would've interested him before the war, but he was now intrigued because of his complete ignorance about these topics.

He flipped through and found an article about the disappearance of men's hats, which was something he'd noticed while people-watching earlier that day. The article noted that before the war, German men were rarely seen in public hatless, but now hats, especially among younger men, were an anomaly except in cold weather. Hans wondered when this change had taken place.

He began to think about the lost years when he'd had no access to news. He was completely isolated between his capture in 1943 and when he first started receiving mail in 1948. Even after that, news was sporadic and unreliable. Over the years, he had heard stories from prisoners captured late in the war and from Russian guards, but he never knew what to believe. And then, of course, there were the rumors. How many rumors had he heard about finally being sent home . . . 1945 . . . 1947 . . . 1949 . . . 1953 . . . 1955 . . .

The sound of keys in the door startled him, and he realized he had been staring at the hat article for quite some time. Minutes? Hours? He wasn't sure, but the sun had set and the apartment was nearly dark.

Elise turned on a light, set down her keys, purse, and a grocery bag, and sat in a chair facing Hans. "Where's my mom?"

"She went back to her room. I think I chased her away."

Elise rolled her eyes and then said, "You shaved. You look almost like yourself again."

"Yeah, well, I'm not sure if that's a good thing or a bad thing."

"How was your meeting?"

"It was short. They just asked for some basic information."

"Okay, good. Did you tell them where you're staying?"

"It was strange, but they already knew." Hans heard the *shush-shush-shush* of Maria's slippers. As she entered the room, Elise got up from the chair and moved to the couch next to Hans, allowing Maria to sit in her customary seat. Hans continued, "By the way, you'll never guess who's in charge of my case."

"Gerhard?" asked Elise.

"How did you know?"

"I knew he was in the Stasi, and I sometimes see him around."

"Ugh," said Maria, shaking her head.

"Seems like he's just as much of an asshole as he used to be," Hans said, immediately regretting that he had used a curse word.

"Shh," Elise said while signaling for him to be quiet.

Hans assumed her reaction was because he had cursed, and mouthed, "Sorry."

She leaned over to him and whispered, "We'll talk later." He nodded.

Maria asked, "What are we having for dinner?"

"I picked up bratwurst on the way home."

"So our two-person meat ration is going to be split three ways now?"

"Of course not. Hans will get a ration card too." She faced Hans and asked, "Did you get a card today?"

"No, I . . . I didn't know I was supposed to."

"That's all right, but you'll need to get one as soon as possible."

Maria shook her head.

After dinner, Elise cleaned up the dishes and then she and Hans put on their coats and left the apartment. When they got outside, Elise looked in all directions before they started walking. She said, "I'm going to talk quietly, so let me know if you can't hear me."

Hans furrowed his brow and nodded.

"Sorry for shushing you earlier, but I need to explain some things. The Stasi is the state security agency. They're similar to the Gestapo."

"The Gestapo? I assumed they went out of business at the end of the war."

"Well, they did, thank God. They were wiped out, and a lot of the members, including Gerhard's father, killed themselves. The Russians dealt with the rest, either by killing them or sending them to work camps, in some cases the same camps that the Nazis used. I don't think the Stasi are as evil as the Gestapo, but they know a lot more about what's going on than the Gestapo ever did. The Stasi have been around for a while, but a few years ago, they got more power after there was an uprising here. Did you hear about it?"

"The only news we heard was filtered through the Russians, and I don't think they'd want us to know about something like that."

A man walked toward them and Elise stopped talking.

After they passed him, Elise looked over her shoulder and then continued, "The uprising was briefly successful, and in Dresden, they were even able to take over the radio station and broadcast antigovernment messages for a while. I thought of you and all your radio experience."

Hans was happy that she had thought about him in the past decade, at least occasionally.

"Many of the participants in the uprising were former POWs, so now the government is paranoid about men returning from captivity."

"What was the uprising about?"

She lowered her voice even further, barely above a whisper. "Since we became two Germanys, the West has done much better than us. Most people don't like the government here but can't do anything about it."

"What happened to the uprising?"

"Soviet tanks crushed it, and afterward, the Stasi became much more powerful."

"I was thinking that their office building was awfully big for a government agency. And it looks like they're expanding it."

"That's the thing—it's not just an office building. The Soviets confiscated it after the war and used it as offices for their secret police, but they also converted parts of it into a prison. Three years ago they handed it over to the Stasi, and they've been expanding it ever since. The prison space has gotten larger and we hear scary stories about interrogations and torture, but you never know what to believe."

"It's sad to think that the German secret police need more space than the Soviet secret police did."

"I know. The Stasi keeps expanding and everyone is paranoid that they're being spied on. You're allowed to grumble about stuff more than you could with the Nazis, but the Stasi gets to decide when you've crossed the line. And to make matters worse, it seems like the entire Stasi is staffed with category fours."

Hans furrowed his brow and asked, "Category fours?"

"One of your theories was that there are four types of people, and the fourth category was those who don't know and don't know that they don't know. I expanded the theory to state that if an organization begins with a bunch of category fours, then they'll hire other category fours, and pretty soon the entire organization will be made up of them. Each individual doesn't know that he doesn't know, but he also doesn't recognize that his coworkers don't know."

"I guess I'm honored that somebody remembers one of my theories, but I'm not sure I like you making amendments without my permission." Hans looked at Elise and was happy to finally see her smile. "So how do the Stasi get their information?"

"They listen in on phone calls, open people's mail, and have a huge network of informants. People are afraid to say anything because any person could be an informant."

"Just so you know, I'm not an informant."

Elise smiled again. "No, I didn't think so, although if you were an informant, that's what I'd expect you to say. They also install listening devices in people's houses and apartments."

"Is that why you told me to be quiet earlier? Is it possible they're listening in?"

"It's unlikely, but now that they know where you're staying, I wouldn't be surprised if they tried. I think they'd need everyone to leave the apartment to set it up, and since my mom is always home, it would be difficult."

"Unless she's an informant too, right?" Hans said with a smile. "Maybe we're both informants, and you're our target."

"Sadly, it wouldn't be the first time family members spied on each other."

Hans thought about it for a minute and then said, "I'm

sorry to bring this attention onto you. Maybe I should leave now."

"That's all right—a few days more isn't going to matter. I'm just telling you all this so you know to watch what you say."

They walked on for a bit, and then Hans asked, "Why did your mom have that reaction about Gerhard? How does she even know him?"

"After you left, he asked me out aggressively and persistently, and my mom doesn't like him. There were so few young men here and so many girls that he had lots of options. I don't know why he was fixated on me."

Hans said, "Did he stay in Dresden for the entire war?" He immediately regretted missing the opportunity to compliment her.

"Yes, I think his dad got him a special assignment, helping to prepare for the defense of Dresden or something. As it turned out, there was never much of a battle here, so he spent the war doing nothing other than occasionally helping to round up Jews."

"What a swine. So why would they have a committed Nazi whose father was in the Gestapo be a Stasi agent? That doesn't make sense."

"When the Soviets took over and needed to set up a new government and security agency, they looked for men who were good at following orders, and many young Nazis fit that description. People in the Nazi government were dealt with harshly, but Gerhard wasn't in the government. So he just took some anti-Fascist classes and joined the Socialist Party, which is the only party, and they gave him a job. He actually seemed to embrace the new government even more enthusiastically than the Germans who were Communists before the war."

"So he never believed that anti-Communist stuff he spouted for all those years?"

"I think he only believes in power and is flexible about the rest of it. There's another reason he's a good fit for the Stasi, based on a joke that's going around. Why do the Stasi always work in groups of three?" Hans shrugged. "They get one who can read, one who can write, and one to keep an eye on the two intellectuals."

CHAPTER 8

Elise awoke early on Saturday but stayed in bed. Ordinarily, she would drink a cup of coffee and read a book on the couch, but Hans had disrupted her routine. His presence was even more disruptive for her mother, and Elise knew Hans would need to leave soon.

Eventually, she got dressed and went to the kitchen to make potato pancakes for herself and Hans. When they were nearly finished eating, Hans said, "I was hoping we could do something today if you're not busy."

Elise felt her body stiffen. "What did you have in mind?"

"I've walked around Dresden quite a bit in the past week, but so far I've avoided the Altstadt. I was hoping you'd join me on a tour, kind of like we did in 1940."

Elise frowned, looked down at her plate, and said, "Almost everything we saw that day was destroyed."

"I know, but I need to see it eventually, and I thought I should just get it over with all at once."

Elise looked up and their eyes met. She recognized that despite everything he'd been through, he still had a trace of the naive optimism he'd possessed before the war. The fact that he wanted to tour the Altstadt, especially in the context of their relationship in 1940, made her realize that he still believed there was hope for Dresden, or for the two of them, or both. She didn't want to be cruel, but perhaps the tour would make him realize that his old world no longer existed. The sooner he understood that, the better. She stood up to clear their plates and said, "All right. But you should expect to be disappointed."

Just like all those years before, they sat facing forward on the tram, with Elise in the window seat. As the bell clanged and the tram accelerated, Hans said, "When I was in captivity, I spent a lot of time thinking about our special moments together. Do you remember when we made that list of our favorite days?"

Elise remembered but shook her head no.

"On our six-month anniversary, we made a list, and over the years, I'd replay those days over and over in my head. I could kill hours doing that."

Elise felt the conversation might be headed toward a sweet, romantic place, so she tried to derail it. "I'm sure the boredom was awful."

"Yes, the boredom and not knowing when I'd be coming home were the worst parts. Actually, the death, disease, and starvation were pretty bad too. Come to think of it, it was all bad. I'm not sure there was a worst part. Anyway, I replayed those days and got to where I knew every step we took and pretty much every word we said."

"That sounds like a good way to kill time."

"Yes, it definitely was. I had a good friend for the past five years named Willi, and he liked it when I replayed these days in my head because otherwise, I'd be describing them out loud to him. I'm sure he was terribly bored with them."

"I feel sorry for Willi."

"He told me lots of stories too, so it was a fair exchange. Anyway, this is at the top of my list of favorite days. There aren't many days that can be described as perfect, but this is one of them."

She noticed that he used the present tense, and she was careful to use the past tense when she said, "Yes, that was fun."

She also noted that he didn't mention, and perhaps didn't remember, the assault on the Jew that they'd witnessed. It certainly wasn't a perfect day for that guy.

"After I found out you were still alive, I promised myself that if I ever made it home, we'd relive those days, and that's why I wanted to make sure I had them all memorized." He looked at her with a sad smile, and Elise turned away as she felt her eyes becoming misty.

Hans continued, "The second day on my list is the Striezelmarkt. They still do that, right?"

"Yes, but it's different because it's not a religious event anymore."

Hans furrowed his brow. "How do you have a Christmas festival without Christmas?" He shook his head. "Anyway, my last favorite is the Fasching celebration when you wore your princess costume."

Elise blanched and turned to the window. "Dresden doesn't celebrate Fasching anymore."

"Oh." He paused and then asked, "Are those days your favorites too?"

"I suppose so," she said, still facing the window.

CHAPTER 9

Hans didn't look out the window as they passed through the Altstadt and crossed the river, preferring to see it all at once. They exited the tram, walked to a spot near the place where they had been back in 1940, and sat on the ground. He looked down for several seconds, took a deep breath, and then finally raised his head.

He had expected to be startled or shocked or infuriated, but he wasn't any of those things. In the end, the ruined city wasn't startling or shocking or infuriating, perhaps because he had seen variations of it dozens of times, both during and after the war. Rubble was just rubble, he realized now, whether it had begun as the most beautiful city in Europe or an obscure town in Russia. It was like a corpse that had partially decomposed. Perhaps it had once been a beautiful young woman, or maybe an ugly old hag, but at this point, you couldn't tell, and truth be told, it didn't really matter. Like all corpses, Dresden was silent—the church bells were gone. The sky was gray, and a brown miasma of air pollution hovered over the remains.

Before the war, Hans had known every building, steeple, statue, fountain, and clock tower, and as he scanned what was left of the city now, he began to see things he recognized. The spire of the Hofkirche and the tower of the castle still stood to his right, but they now loomed over blackened, roofless shells. Many of the statues atop the Hofkirche had survived, and he could also identify a few other buildings and steeples, mainly in the distance. But the reminders of what the city had been only disheartened him because they proved these ruins were indeed Dresden and not just some random European city destroyed in the war.

He said, "The last time we were here, I rambled on about things not being permanent, so I guess I was right about that." He paused and then asked, "Isn't this the 750th anniversary of the city?"

"Yes. I think there's going to be a parade or something."

"It'll probably be challenging for the bands to march over the rubble." Elise didn't respond. "Do they have plans to rebuild the city?"

"Some people want to rebuild it like it was, but that would be expensive. The government feels that the old buildings were symbols of the inequality of our prewar society, so they wouldn't rebuild them even if they had the money. Some Socialists want to make Dresden into a model Socialist city because they'd literally be able to build it from the ground up. Nobody can agree on what to do, so they're doing almost nothing."

After a few minutes, he asked, "Should we walk across?"

"It's not going to look any better on the other side."

"I know, but I have to see it."

"Okay." She paused and then added, "You're the tour guide," repeating her comment from 1940. Hans got a lump in his throat as he realized she remembered parts of the day too. He stood and extended his hands to help her, just like he had in 1940, but she got up on her own. He quickly returned his hands to his side.

They crossed the bridge to the Hofkirche and the Dresden Castle, both of which looked worse up close. While the statues atop the church had survived, most of them were missing their heads, arms, or both. The ornate staircases inside the castle now led nowhere except the open sky. Some of the copper-plated walkways on the upper floors still existed, but the copper was frozen in a dripping pattern, like icicles. Elise told him that it had melted and dripped on people trying to flee. Hans knew the melting point of copper was high, and he wondered how hot the fire had been.

The clock on the castle's tower was stopped at 2:20. Elise told him that was when the inner workings had melted, shortly after the second wave of bombers. Hans was embarrassed by how little he knew about the bombing—he hadn't even realized there had been a second wave. And the clock had melted? He wondered again, how hot had it been?

The walls of the Semper Opera House still stood, but the interior was gutted. Hans was thankful that he and Elise had seen a performance there in 1941 because there wouldn't be shows there anytime soon. As they crossed the plaza, he noticed that "Adolf Hitler Square" had reverted back to its original name of "Theater Square," so at least there had been one improvement.

When they arrived at the Zwinger Palace and Gardens, Hans finally saw some reconstruction efforts. He said, "When we were here before, I saw all the happy couples walking arm in arm, and I hoped that would be us someday."

Elise just shrugged.

As they were about to leave, she asked, "Are you sure you want to keep going?"

"Yes, there are only two more stops. The next one is the synagogue ruins."

"I don't want to see that."

"Are the ruins still there?"

"They are, but . . . How much do you know about what happened to the Jews?"

"They showed us films about the camps and everything."

She looked down and said, "I don't want to see the synagogue."

"Okay, we'll skip that."

CHAPTER 10

Elise noticed that as the day progressed, they walked faster and spent less time at each site, which was the opposite of what had happened in 1940. She also noticed that Hans often walked with his head down, as if they were watching a horror movie and he was averting his eyes during the scary parts. They eventually reached the center of what had been the Altstadt, but was now a meadow littered with rubble mounds and grazing sheep. Laughter and the joyous peal of church bells had been replaced with baaing and the tinkle of cowbells, the aroma of baked goods with the stench of sheep dung, and the aura of happiness and vibrancy in the heart of a bustling city with a feeling of desolation and solitude in an abandoned wasteland.

As they entered what was once Neumarkt Square, they saw the ruins of the Frauenkirche, whose rubble had been heaped into the footprint of the original church. Hans asked, "Are they just going to leave it like that?"

"Some of the important pieces were numbered, taken away, and stored, with the idea that they'd eventually be used in a reconstruction. But for now, they've decided to leave it this way so people won't forget about the war, especially the destruction caused by the British and Americans."

Hans looked around. "Is there really a risk that people will forget about the war?" They walked to the Martin Luther statue. The rubble around it had been cleared so the original cobblestones were visible. "He looks awfully lonely here in the middle of nowhere, but I'm glad that something is still standing."

"It was knocked down too, but they put it back on its pedestal later."

"Do you remember meeting here at the Oktoberfest?"

Elise nodded. "Ruth was funny that night."

"Ruth! I haven't thought about her in ages. What happened to her?"

Without looking at Hans, Elise said flatly, "She killed herself after the war."

Hans flinched and looked back at the statue before they continued to the Frauenkirche. Elise said, "I heard that on the day after the bombing, the church was the only thing left standing on the square. Its sandstone was glowing and fires burned in it and all around it, but it lasted for more than a full day before finally collapsing. I remember thinking that you were right—it must've been extremely well constructed to survive that long."

He looked at the rubble and said, "I guess the stones have a lot more stories to tell than they did the last time we were here." He bent down, touched one of the blackened stones, then stood up and said, "Look at all these ruined buildings and think of the thousands of craftsmen and hundreds of years required to create them. And then a handful of Englishmen destroy it all in one night." He picked up a fragment of carved sandstone and said, "Someone spent a long time carving this and was probably proud of his work. And now it's all gone."

Elise wondered if he was thinking about his dad.

They walked around the perimeter of the church, and Hans occasionally stopped to touch a stone or pick up a chunk of masonry. He didn't speak, his shoulders sagged, and his limp became more pronounced. They circled back to where they started, and Hans said, "This was harder than I thought it would be, but I'm glad we did it. Thank you." Elise nodded. "Should we take the tram back?"

He looked heartbroken, and she wanted to hug him, but instead, she said, "We didn't take the tram back in 1940, so why would we take it now? I thought we were going to relive the day." She was instantly disappointed in herself for letting one of her walls down.

Hans looked away for a moment and appeared to wipe away a tear, but then turned back and said, "You're right, let's walk."

On the way back, Elise thought about how different the experience of the day had been for the two of them. She had witnessed every phase of Dresden's recent history, from magnificent city to jumble of burned bricks and bodies to the massive cleanup and sluggish reconstruction.

Hans knew what it had been before the war and now was seeing it as it was in 1956, but he hadn't seen it in 1945. He didn't know which buildings had held roasted corpses in their cellars, which ones had encased suffocated children, which ones had collapsed and buried people alive. He didn't know how much work had gone into putting out the fires and digging out the bodies from these silent, placid piles of rubble. The area they'd just left had been one of the main corpse collection sites, with thousands of them stacked ten high before being cremated.

These were things Elise couldn't unsee and couldn't forget, and she pictured them every time she saw the Altstadt. It seemed to her that by just viewing the end state, Hans was getting off easy.

CHAPTER 11

In his mind, Hans was in the prison camp immediately after his surrender, a place and time that haunted his dreams even more than Stalingrad. Dozens of men starved to death here every day. Walking into a hut he saw men huddled on the floor, apparently eating something, so he approached the circle, wondering where they had found food. He looked over the shoulder of the nearest man and saw he was picking raw meat off a bone, which under the circumstances was better than no meat at all. As he squeezed in to join the feast, he realized that the bone was a human femur.

Hans awoke on the couch, gasping for breath and drenched in sweat. He sat up, wiped the sweat from his face, and took several deep breaths. These dreams usually faded after a few minutes, and shortly afterward he would be unable to remember them. Slowly, his pulse and breathing returned to normal, and the vision was successfully reburied, at least until the next time he slept. Sometimes, these torments came to him during the day, but he was usually able to prevent them from creeping too far into his consciousness.

It was the Monday after his trip to the Altstadt with Elise. She had already left for work, so he got up to get ready for his appointment with Gerhard, attempting, as usual, to leave the apartment before Maria got out of bed. He knew Elise's mother was awake because he'd heard a horrific throat-clearing and coughing fit. The noise made him think of a series of barks from Cerberus while guarding the gates of hell, and he had no idea how it could be produced by such a frail woman. As it was every morning, that sound was his cue to leave. He wished, as he always did, that he had left before he heard it.

As he sat in Gerhard's office, Hans saw a portrait on the wall that he hadn't noticed during his first appointment. He had since learned more about his new country and now recognized it as Walter Ulbricht, the Socialist leader of the German Democratic Republic. Hans wondered if Gerhard's father had displayed a similar picture in his office, but of Hitler.

The desk still held one pen, one ashtray, one pack of cigarettes, and one lighter. But now it contained three folders instead of just one. Gerhard lit a cigarette, leaned back in his chair, and asked, "How was your weekend?"

"Fine." Elise had told him to keep his answers simple.

"Did you enjoy walking around Dresden with Elise? It looks different from what you remember, no?"

Hans tried not to show any emotion. Was he being followed all the time? "It was nice, thank you."

"Wonderful. So, have you started looking for a job?"

"I plan to start this week."

"Do you have any marketable skills? Other than war crimes, obviously. Those skills aren't marketable, at least not in the GDR," Gerhard said with a smirk.

Hans wanted to leap across the desk and strangle his interrogator, but he remembered Elise's advice about being careful. "I mostly did manual labor in Russia."

"I see. Wasn't your father some sort of manual laborer too?"

"Actually, he was a master mason."

"Like I said, a manual laborer. Can you give me examples of the work you did?"

"Early on, the Russians would attach ten or twelve prisoners to a plow, and we'd plow fields all day."

Gerhard took a drag from his cigarette and smiled. "So you were a jackass?"

Hans didn't react to the provocation. "All their animals were either being used in the war or had been eaten."

"Do you think pulling a plow is a useful skill in the GDR?"

"No, I was just giving you an example because you asked. For the past five years, I've mostly done rubble clearing and construction."

"Were you rebuilding what you and your Fascist friends destroyed during the war?"

"We were helping to repair the damage, yes."

"Well, that's certainly a more marketable skill than being a jackass."

Hans took a deep breath. "I also learned to speak Russian."

"Russian, that's very useful. There's always a need for translators, but I'm afraid that your history as a war criminal would disqualify you." Gerhard stubbed out his cigarette. "What else did you do while you were there? Did you take anti-Fascist classes?"

"Yes, everyone did."

"What did you learn?"

"We learned about the superiority of Stalinist ideology."

"Do you feel that you're an anti-Fascist?"

"Yes, definitely."

"Do you understand the horror that Fascism brought to our country and the world?"

"Yes." Hans couldn't help thinking about how similar this line of questioning was to Nazi indoctrination before the war.

"Do you think Fascism is dead?"

Hans knew this was a trick question and was prepared. "Fascism still exists in Western Germany and many other parts of the world."

"Indeed. Can you tell me where the Fascists who started the war lived?"

"They lived in the West."

"Correct. As you know, here in Dresden and in the rest of the East, we were victims of Nazism, not its supporters."

Hans frowned. Did Gerhard believe what he was saying? Was he lying to Hans, or was he lying to himself?

"Well, we don't want you to sit around all day and think of ways to cause trouble for the state. Idle hands are the Fascist's workshop," Gerhard said, looking as if he expected credit for his clever play on words. The best Hans could do was a half-hearted smile.

Gerhard continued, "I'm going to give you the address of the employment bureau. Go register there. As you've seen, there's a lot of construction work to be done, thanks to the capitalists and the Fascists. I should tell you, though, that there is a great deal of competition for these jobs. Many people now living in Dresden weren't here when you left, and quite a few of the Germans who moved here when the borders shifted are looking for construction jobs. However, unlike the West, we believe in full employment here." Gerhard moved the top folder, the thickest of the three, to the side. He opened up the next one and said, "What can you tell me about Elise?"

"Well, you know her from the old days, right?"

"Yes, of course. But what can you tell me about her now? Does she have any contacts with people in the West?"

"Not that I'm aware of."

"Do you think she plans on moving to the West?"

"Not as far as I know."

"If you hear something to the contrary, please tell me, okay?" Hans nodded. Gerhard put aside Elise's folder and opened the third folder. "And what can you tell me about Frau Engel?"

"Nothing, really. She's not healthy and mostly just stays in the apartment."

"I see. Given her inability to work, we wouldn't mind if she moved to the West," Gerhard said with a smile. He made a note in the file, closed it, and then stood up and led Hans back down the hallway. As they approached the exit, Gerhard said, "If I come across a job for a jackass, I'll let you know." He laughed, and as Hans left the office, he heard Gerhard repeating his jackass joke to the receptionist.

CHAPTER 12

That evening, Elise set bowls of potato soup in front of Hans and her mother and then sat down. Before he began to eat, Hans said, "The employment bureau thinks they'll be able to find construction work for me, but it'll be a few weeks before they can process the paperwork and assign me to a project."

"Does that mean you'll be moving out soon?" Elise's mother asked.

"Yes, I hope so."

Elise wasn't sure why she felt her heart sink.

"That's good," her mother continued. "This was never supposed to be a permanent arrangement, and now you've been here for more than a week."

"I know, and I'm sorry. It should be just a few more weeks."

After another sip of wine, she asked, "I'm curious. Why did they keep you in Russia for so long?"

Hans furrowed his brow, hesitated, and then said, "We were free labor. Whenever men became too unhealthy to work, they'd release them because they were no longer useful."

"So you were one of the strong ones?"

"I know it's hard to picture teenage me as one of the strong ones, but it wasn't so much being physically strong, it was more being able to fight off diseases. I got typhus once and had several bouts of dysentery, but I always recovered. When we were in Stalingrad, they bandaged my foot because I had frostbite, but when they took off the bandage three toes came with it. That's where my limp came from, but it didn't prevent me from working."

Elise cringed at this new information as her mother pressed Hans further. "When they released a big group of POWs in 1949, the government told us that the war was officially over because the only people still in captivity were war criminals. I was confused because I never thought of you as the war criminal type."

"Mother!"

"That's all right," Hans said. "Gerhard asked me the same question, and I'll give you the same answer. I honestly don't know what happened. There wasn't any formal judicial process with lawyers or judges or appeals. Who stayed and who got released always seemed arbitrary to us. There were definitely some bad men who were prisoners with me, but there were also a lot of us who didn't know what we had done wrong."

"From what we've heard, there were enough war crimes to go around for the whole lot of you."

Hans looked down and said, "You're not wrong. Some terrible things happened there."

"How did they treat you? The government told us that the Russians treated POWs well, probably better than they deserved."

Elise glared at her mother but then looked to Hans for an answer.

Hans lowered his eyes and said, "The first few years were the worst. We had no medicine and very little food, and everyone was already sick and starving when the Stalingrad battle ended. I don't know how many men died in the first few months after our surrender—thousands or maybe tens of thousands. I remember marching for what seemed like forever. Well, not really marching, more like stumbling and trying to stay upright. If you fell, you'd get a rifle butt in the back, and if you didn't get up, they'd shoot you. And it was so cold . . ." Hans's voice trailed off as he continued staring at his bowl.

Elise frowned at her mother, who shrugged and returned to eating. After a few moments, Elise stood up and said, "Hans, let's go for a walk."

Her words jarred him out of his trance. "What?"

"Let's go for a walk."

"Okay. I'll meet you downstairs." He got up, looked at Elise's mother, and said with a flash of anger in his eyes, "I didn't commit any war crimes." He then walked out of the apartment, closing the door with something that fell just short of a slam.

Elise sat down again and looked at her mother. "Why would you say those things?"

"I think we should understand what's going on with him, don't you? He's a complete stranger, who the Russians say is a war criminal, and we're pretending that everything is perfectly normal."

"He'll be gone in a few weeks."

"A lot of bad things can happen in a few weeks. How do we know he's not dangerous? I've heard stories of POWs coming back after what they've been through and being crazy. He might be crazy too or even violent. Surely you've heard him moaning and talking at night."

"I'm sure he's not crazy or violent. He's just lost. It's got to be incredibly disorienting to come back after all this time."

"I told you before, it's not our problem. By the way, you two seem to be talking a lot. You haven't told him about what happened while he was gone, have you?"

"No, and I don't intend to."

"Good. He doesn't need to know. It would probably make him even crazier."

Elise got up and put on her coat. As she was leaving, her mother said, "Also, he leaves whiskers in the sink. Men are disgusting."

Elise stifled a smile as she walked out the door.

As Elise exited the apartment building, she saw Hans pacing the sidewalk. She said, "Sorry. I'm not sure what got into her."

"She's right—I've overstayed my welcome."

"She's unhappy about everything. Don't take it personally." They started walking, but then he stopped and faced her. "I need to tell you something that I meant to say on my first day back, but things were too strange. It's about my last night here in 1942." Elise cringed. "That was the worst thing I did in my life up to that point, and the fact that I didn't have a chance to apologize has tormented me for the past fourteen years."

"You apologized in almost every letter you sent me."

"I know, but I want to apologize in person. I'm sorry."

"Okay. I don't want to talk about it anymore, so please don't bring it up again." She started walking.

Hans continued, "I also wanted to tell you that that was the last time I drank. I don't think alcohol and I are good for each other. Of course, I haven't had much access to it since then, but I promised myself I wouldn't touch it again." Elise nodded. "By the way, it was funny that your mom's questions were the same as Gerhard's. Maybe she really does work for the Stasi."

"That reminds me—how was your meeting this morning?"

Hans said a bit too loudly, "I swear one of these days I'm going to kill that bastard."

Elise looked around and then said, "Please don't talk like that."

"Sorry, but I can't stand him."

"Just remember what I said, and don't take the bait. He'd

like nothing more than to lock you up, so don't give him a reason."

"It's so maddening. My mom told me one time that if you're in a situation where the other person has all the power, your only goal should be to get out of that situation as quickly as possible. I try to remember that when I'm with Gerhard, but it's hard."

Two young women walked toward them, and out of habit, Hans and Elise stopped talking. After they passed, Hans said, "I notice that there aren't many couples here."

"It's hard to have couples if you don't have men." Elise knew Hans was desperate to learn about her romantic past, and she couldn't think of a way to derail the questions she knew were coming.

After a few more steps, he said, "So, did you get married or anything while I was gone? I won't be mad if you did."

"No."

"I know you said you'd wait for me, but obviously, I never imagined I'd be gone so long." Elise didn't respond. "I assume you had some boyfriends along the way."

Elise sighed and said, "There weren't any boyfriends either." She noticed a subtle but perceptible bounce in Hans's step, and it reminded her of the happiness he'd exhibited when they first started dating. Now, though, there was a hitch in the bounce due to the missing toes. She was sure he was thrilled to hear that she hadn't dated, and he'd probably want to learn more. She, on the other hand, just wanted to stop talking about it.

"How is that possible?"

"It's just math. You're good at math, right?" The question came out more snippily than she intended. "The men our age all went to war, so nobody was here except people like Gerhard. A lot of the men died, and most of the others became POWs.

Then after the war, most of the returning POWs went to the West."

The bounce in Hans's step diminished as the sting in Elise's voice sharpened. "There are more men in their fifties here than men in their thirties. Something like a third of the men born in the years we were born died in the war. It's just math. It's not that hard."

Hans said quietly, "I'm sorry. I didn't think about it."

"I'm sure you're happy I didn't have a boyfriend, but it wasn't because I was waiting for you. I didn't even know if you were alive for the first few years."

They walked on, the bounce in Hans's step now replaced by a stiff gait and short strides. Then he said, "Just so you know, I didn't have a boyfriend either."

Elise smiled but didn't let Hans see her.

CHAPTER 13

As she lay in bed that night, Elise heard moaning coming from the living room. She went to investigate, and when she turned on the light, she saw Hans lying on the floor behind the couch. He looked at her and shouted, "Get down!" while pointing frantically at the window. "There's a sniper up there!" His wild eyes reminded her of something, but for a moment she couldn't recall what it was. Then it came to her—it was the same look of terror that had flashed over her father at the end.

She turned off the light and stepped back into the hallway. After five minutes, she could hear Hans snoring, but she left him on the floor rather than risk waking him up. She returned to the bedroom, sat on her bed, and listened to her sleeping mother as her breath wheezed and whistled. She then got dressed, tiptoed past Hans, put on her coat, and left the apartment.

The moonlit streets were deserted, and she walked quickly to her destination, a rubble-strewn lot eight blocks from the apartment. She clambered over the debris and sat down on a pile of bricks that wasn't visible from the sidewalk. Painted on the remnants of a wall across from her was a message that had probably been there since 1945: *"Trudi—Wir sind zu Omas Haus gegangen. Treffe uns dort."* "Trudi—we have gone to Grandma's house. Meet us there." Elise wondered who Trudi was and who her grandma was and whether there had been a successful reunion. So many mysteries in Dresden. And ghosts.

She had been making these visits to Dresden's endless piles of rubble for years, always at night and always after her mother had gone to sleep. She had no specific agenda, and would often just sit and let her mind be empty. Other times she'd try to figure out what the rubble had been before the bombing—an apartment building? A house? A shop? There were always clues. Sometimes she'd also try to determine what had happened to the building. Had a high explosive bomb hit it, or had it burned and then collapsed? And why did one wall remain standing when all the others had fallen?

On clear, cold nights like this, she'd look into the sky and imagine bombers overhead. They were probably just kids in those planes, possibly even the same age as her. She wondered about the view from up there, especially for the men in the second wave. Surely they had seen that the city was already burning, yet they had dropped more bombs. Had they thought about what they were doing, or was it just a job? That night would torment her for the rest of her life, and as she gazed at the empty sky, she wondered if those men ever gave it a second thought.

She knew she'd find nothing of value in this lot or any other pile of rubble. Anything flammable would've already burned, anything valuable would've already been stolen, and anything edible would've already been scavenged. She had been one of those scavengers in the brutal postwar winters and had spent more time in lots like this than she liked to recall, searching for scraps of food or bits of coal. After the war, the German greeting had transitioned from "Heil Hitler" to *"Bleib übrig."* "Survive." The only goal of life then was to survive each day and then worry about the next day when it came. If it came.

In a strange way, she missed those days. Survival was a specific objective that had given her life a purpose and even a sense of excitement. Somewhere along the way, that had been lost. Perhaps that was why she was drawn to the rubble. Or maybe the rubble was simply a reflection of how she felt about herself.

In the early months, before the cleanup and reconstruction began, she had been able to see mounds of rubble for hundreds of meters in any direction. That view had reminded her of the sand castles she and Ludwig used to construct on the beach. She'd build the basic structure with sand, and Ludwig would add battlements and turrets with shells and rocks and driftwood. Like Dresden after the war, the finished product had never looked like a castle, or anything else, really. That hadn't mattered, though, because they knew it would eventually be washed away no matter how well it was constructed.

She grieved in the rubble for an hour and then walked home.

CHAPTER 14

As they finished dinner the following Friday, Elise said to Hans, "I'm sorry we don't have more sources of entertainment. We hope to get a television someday, but we can't afford it now."

Hans frowned and then looked at Maria to see if she knew what Elise was talking about, but she continued eating without looking up. "You're hoping to get a what?" he asked.

"A television," Elise repeated. A smile crossed her face, and then she started laughing. "You don't know what a television is, do you?"

Hans shook his head.

Elise laughed some more, and even Maria looked up and smiled. Elise said, "Sorry, I don't mean to laugh. Sometimes I forget how much has changed for you."

"So what is a television?"

Elise said, "It's like a radio, but it has pictures. Most people can't afford one, but there are stores in town that have them in their windows. People sometimes watch from the sidewalk, even though they can't hear anything."

"Can we go see one sometime?"

"Sure," said Elise. "Two years ago, when West Germany won the World Cup, crowds always formed in front of stores to watch the games. But once West Germany started doing well, the government shut down the broadcast."

Maria was more engaged than usual. "What else don't you know?" she asked with a devious smile.

"Well, I guess I don't know what I don't know."

"All right, Mother," Elise said, "let's think about what's changed since 1942."

"Do you know what a washing machine is?" Maria asked him.

"Well, I can guess, but I've never seen one."

Maria and Elise both laughed.

"Wait, I have one." Elise stood up, grabbed a piece of bread, put it into a slot on a silver box on the counter, and pulled down the box's handle. Hans had seen the silver box earlier but hadn't wanted to embarrass himself by asking what it was. Elise smiled and looked back and forth between Hans and Maria. Hans was anticipating what would happen with the silver box, and Maria and Elise were clearly anticipating what would happen with Hans.

After a minute, a piece of toast popped out of the silver box, and Hans jumped. Elise and Maria laughed hysterically. Hans was embarrassed, but he didn't want to spoil the fun. He had forgotten how captivating Elise's laugh was.

"Do you know what a jet airplane is?" Maria asked next. Hans shook his head.

"How about penicillin?" Elise tried. Another head shake.

"A helicopter?"

"A computer?"

"No." Hans was tiring of this game, but the other two seemed to be enjoying it, so he played along. Maria continued to laugh until she began coughing, and once she started she couldn't stop. Elise got her a glass of water, but she was coughing too hard to drink it.

Eventually, she managed to take a sip and then said, "I think that's enough for tonight." She took another drink of water and then downed the rest of her wine. "Thank you, Hans. You made my day." She paused and then added, "And if you need to stay here for a while until you get on your feet, that's okay." She got up and shuffled back to her room.

Hans and Elise moved to the couch, and he asked, "Is she going to be all right?"

"Yes, I think so. She hasn't laughed that much in a long time."

"Well, I'm glad I could help."

"I'm sorry. That was mean."

"No, it's fine. I guess I need to understand what's changed, and if I can provide some entertainment along the way, that's okay. It's all so strange, though. It's like I'm in a different world."

Elise hesitated and then asked, "Do you feel like Rip Van Winkle?" Hans frowned. "Before you left, you said you hoped to be like Rip Van Winkle, that you'd wake up and Hitler would be gone and you'd be living in a new country. Well, you got your wish."

Hans was silent for a moment and then said, "Oh yes, I remember. The Rip Van Winkle analogy. What a clever boy I was. The difference is that old Rip just had a few drinks and then fell asleep for twenty years. I would've much preferred that."

They sat quietly for a few minutes and then Hans said, "You know, a big part of the Rip Van Winkle story is that when Rip went to sleep, America was still a British colony, and the energy of the citizens was low. When he woke up, it was the United States, and everybody was energized and enthusiastic." He lowered his voice. "It seems like it's the other way around here. Everybody was energized when I was growing up, and now everybody seems listless."

"I guess that's true, but think about where that enthusiasm was directed. Low enthusiasm is preferable to high enthusiasm directed toward doing evil things."

Hans nodded. "Maybe someday we can find a place with high enthusiasm directed toward good things. Or at least not evil ones."

CHAPTER 15

A month later, on a chilly but pleasant Sunday afternoon, Hans and Elise sat on a bench in the courtyard of her apartment building. Elise's mother had ceased pushing Hans to move out, and Elise had accepted that unless he was pushed, he probably wasn't going to leave on his own. He was scheduled to start his new job the next day, and he said, "The thought of doing construction has got me thinking about my dad, and how little I know about his last few years," he said. "Don't you think we should talk about what happened while I was gone, both what happened here and what happened to me?"

Elise recoiled and hesitated before answering. "I don't know. You've only been ho"—she almost said "home" but changed it midword—"back for a little while. I'm sure you endured some horrible things, and I didn't know if you'd want to talk about them."

"I'm not sure either, but it seems strange that we talk every day, but not about anything important. If I don't know what happened while I was gone, I can't know who you are. It's like I was watching a movie where you were the star, and then I left the theater for an hour, and when I came back, I had lost the plot."

Elise stiffened. Her walls needed to remain standing. "Why don't you tell me what you want to whenever you're ready. If you never want to tell me, that's fine too."

"All right, but the same applies to you." He looked at her, but she looked away. "It's okay if you don't want to share, but can you make an exception and tell me about my parents?"

She turned and faced him. "I can tell you what I know, but it's not going to make you feel any better."

"I understand, but I've spent years wondering. I left in 1942, they died in 1945, and I know almost nothing about the time in between."

She looked down for a moment before she began. "After you left, things kept getting worse. The rationing got stricter, and our normal lives disappeared. I visited your parents about once a week and sometimes brought them something I had baked, and I could tell the stress was getting to them.

"During that first year, your mother treasured your letters and would read them over and over. She had a picture of you in your uniform on the mantel, and when we talked about you, I'd sometimes catch her staring at it. Your dad tracked the war's progress in newspapers and on his radio. Whenever it was safe, he'd listen to a nightly German-language newscast on the BBC at six o'clock. He also had a big map that he'd unroll on the kitchen table every night to mark the position of the Sixth Army."

Hans smiled. "I can picture him leaning over the map, drinking a beer, and cursing at all the unpronounceable Russian town names."

"It sounded like things were going well in the summer and autumn, and the government implied that if we captured Stalingrad, the war would basically be over. We were all excited, not just about the prospect of the war ending but about you being involved in the victory. But in December the tone of the broadcasts changed, and we knew something was wrong. Your mom got your last letter in mid-January."

"I think I wrote that right before Christmas. When did they find out I was a POW?"

Elise hesitated and then said, "They never found out. Germany and the Soviets weren't able to reach an agreement about sharing the names of POWs, so in both countries, the relatives didn't know who was alive and who was dead. The only thing the government told your parents was that the last time you were known to be alive was in Stalingrad on January 15, 1943."

"They didn't know I was alive?"

"You were listed as missing in action. Initially, the Nazis implied that the army in Stalingrad fought to the last man and that everybody died a hero for Germany. Your mom couldn't stop crying. But then rumors started circulating that many men had surrendered, and we began to wonder."

Hans stared at two women in the courtyard hanging dresses on a clothesline.

"I read that there were over a million German soldiers listed as missing in action throughout the war. By 1944, many people realized we were going to lose and turned their focus to getting their men back. Your mom joined a group that had been organized to push the government for information about their sons and husbands, but as you can imagine, the government wasn't responsive."

"Of course not."

"It was interesting to see your mother transition from being quiet to being so vocal about this issue. Unfortunately, her activism, plus your dad's lukewarm embrace of Nazism, caught the attention of the Gestapo. They were harassed pretty regularly."

"My mother, the rebel."

"She also became more religious in those last two years. I didn't go to church every Sunday, but I saw her there whenever I did. I think people turned to religion more as their faith in the government faded."

"I guess everyone has to believe in something, right?"

"I don't know, do they?" Hans looked at her quizzically, but she turned away. "She started going back to her village more often and sometimes helped out there since there were so few farmworkers. But she always came back because she was worried about your dad."

"How did he hold up?"

"At first, he tried to stay busy at work, but eventually it became impossible to get building materials. At that point, he was forced to work in an armaments factory, which he didn't like because it was indoors and he had to work fourteen-hour days."

"Yeah, that doesn't sound like something he'd enjoy."

"In late 1944, his radio broke, and since spare parts were no longer available, he couldn't listen anymore. I'm not sure he minded, though, because he knew where things were headed. He used to say, 'Enjoy the war because you're going to hate the peace.' Around that time, he was forced to work on constructing the Dresden defenses, and he was drafted into the Volkssturm."

"What's the Volkssturm?"

"Oh, right. It was a military unit made up of people who weren't qualified to be in the military, mostly older men. I went to your house once and saw him after a meeting. The Volkssturm didn't have enough uniforms, so your dad and some other veterans wore their uniforms from the previous war. He looked pretty stylish, even though the jacket didn't fit because he had lost too much weight."

"And what about Greta?"

"I think she missed you, but your mom did a good job of spoiling her. Greta followed her everywhere." Elise looked away as her voice cracked on the word "everywhere."

"I keep thinking about who might have identified their bodies," Hans said. "I realized there weren't many people who knew both of them since she rarely socialized and didn't know his work buddies, but then I thought about Herr Schmidt. I considered looking him up, but I don't know his first name. My dad just called him 'Schmidt' or sometimes 'that dummkopf Schmidt.'"

"I still don't understand why you're trying to find this out. Nobody died well during the bombings."

"I know, but I'm sad because there's so much information about their lives that's gone, and there's no way to get it back. Teenagers don't ask their parents about themselves because they assume there will be opportunities later on, but sometimes there aren't. How they died, at least, seems like something I should be able to figure out."

Elise didn't respond.

He paused and then said, "It's also strange that I don't have any pictures of them. How do you know a person even existed if you don't have pictures? We had an old family tintype from the late 1800s that included my great-grandfather. He had a bushy imperial mustache, was wearing a uniform from the war with France in 1870, and wasn't smiling or looking at the camera. Because we had the picture, he always seemed real to me, but the generations before him didn't because even if I knew their names, I didn't know what they looked like. Sometimes I'm afraid I'll forget what my parents looked like and they'll simply disappear. I thought about going to my parents' family farms to see if they have pictures or anything, but I don't know who still lives there."

"The farms were collectivized a few years ago, and most of the farmers left or were pushed off. They're probably gone."

Hans stared into the distance and nodded. "I always thought it was sad that the generations before my great-grandfather didn't seem to exist, but now it's like the generations right before me don't either."

CHAPTER 16

Nervous energy kept Hans awake that night, and as he lay on the couch thinking about his new job, he could almost envision living a life like his father's. Perhaps someday, he'd even have a wife and kids and be a normal grown-up in Dresden.

He got up before Elise and dressed quickly. Prior to walking out the door, he checked his pockets to ensure he had everything: wallet, identity card, and the apartment key Elise had made for him. He recalled his dad doing similar pocket checks before he went anywhere, but this was the first time Hans had done one. Things in your pockets indicated normal, everyday responsibility, and he was happy to finally have some of that.

The other passengers on the crowded tram seemed to experience the ride to their workplaces as ordinary and mundane, but for Hans it was thrilling. While doing construction hadn't been his dream when he was a kid, he was delighted to have this job now. He thought back to the close-knit teams his dad was once a part of, the men kidding each other during the day and socializing at night. Perhaps soon he'd even be able to expand his circle of friends beyond Elise and Maria.

He also anticipated the satisfaction and pride that came from creating something out of nothing. He knew he'd never be as talented as his father, but he'd acquired some skills over the years and was confident he'd be able to make a solid contribution. Just as importantly, he was excited to be a part of the reconstruction of his beloved city.

Hans wasn't familiar with the area on the outskirts of town that included the construction site, so he was concerned he'd be unable to find it. As it turned out, he saw it as soon as he stepped off the tram. He'd expected the project to be similar to what his father had worked on, houses or small apartment buildings, but what he saw was a monstrosity. The project consisted of six identical huge gray buildings in varying stages of completion. The grounds contained no trees, just acres of weeds, gravel, stacks of prefabricated concrete slabs, and the hulking eyesores.

At the entrance to the site, he stopped to look at a poster hanging on a fence. It showed five men standing on a hill overlooking a factory complex with the caption "Learning from the Soviet people means learning to win!" The factory complex included smokestacks, power lines, and quite a bit of air pollution, which seemed like an odd detail to feature in propaganda. One man held a red banner that promoted the Communist party, and all the men were fit, smiling, and enthusiastic. Hans turned to look at the actual men milling about his worksite. They appeared to be wan, aloof, and apathetic. Not really poster material.

Hans found a foreman, who told him where to go and what to do. His role was to stand on the concrete floor of one layer of the building while a crane lowered a slab for the wall of the next layer. He and several other men would align and secure the slab and then wait for the crane to deliver the next one. Hans realized that the end result of his efforts, a brand-new building, would be the same as his father's, but it didn't require the same level of skill, or any skill at all for that matter. Scores of men were doing identical work at the other buildings, each of them a tiny cog in a giant construction machine.

He spent the morning repeating the mind-numbing task,

and then they broke for lunch. While eating the sandwich Elise had packed for him, he tried to talk to the other workers. Most of them were refugees from Silesia, Prussia, and Czechoslovakia. There were native Dresdeners like him too, but none of them seemed to share Hans's civic pride. While many were veterans, they weren't inclined to talk about their experiences. In fact, once they found out he was a recently released POW, they didn't seem to want to talk to him at all.

Near the end of the lunch break, Hans saw several men pass around a flask, and they continued to drink when work resumed. They didn't offer any to Hans, and he wouldn't have taken it if they had. Hans was dismayed. His father had often drunk after work but would've considered it unprofessional to do so while on the job.

Over the course of the day, Hans learned more about the development. The buildings, called Plattenbau, were cheap and easy to construct. Every building was the same, and every apartment within every building was too. He admired the speed, efficiency, and economy that the structures represented. The only thing missing was beauty. He left the site that evening disheartened, his vision of working a fulfilling job as part of a fulfilling life further out of reach than it had been when the day started.

CHAPTER 17

That evening Elise could tell that Hans was unhappy, and after dinner, they went for a walk. He explained how disappointed he was in the quality of the architecture and the quality of the craftsmanship. And the quality of the workers, for that matter.

"I've read about the new construction," she said. "The idea is that the buildings should focus on equality rather than beauty."

"I don't know if they accomplished the equality part, but they definitely fulfilled their goal regarding beauty."

"I think they call the style 'brutalist' or 'Stalinist.' I can't remember which."

"Both words seem to fit." He paused and then said, "Everyone seemed to avoid me once they found out I had just gotten back."

"That doesn't surprise me. The government has been telling people that the late-returning POWs are war criminals, so those guys probably assume you're either a war criminal or a Stasi informant."

Hans shook his head. "I don't think I'm going to like this job."

"I'm sorry to hear that. At least the rubble at the site is cleared, right? It seems like that would be the worst part of trying to rebuild a city."

"I did plenty of that in Russia, and it's not fun."

"I did a lot of it here too."

Hans stopped and looked at her. "You cleared rubble?"

Elise hadn't intended to tell him anything about those years, but she had inadvertently lowered a wall, and he had immediately stepped over it. "That was my job for the first year after the war. Lots of women did it—they called us 'the women of the rubble.'"

Hans began walking again. "That doesn't seem like women's work."

"Someone did the math and calculated that in Dresden, there were forty cubic meters of rubble for every surviving resident. During the war, prisoners cleared some of it, but once it was over, they left. There was obviously a shortage of men, so women did much of the cleanup."

"I can't picture you clearing rubble."

"It certainly wasn't a job I ever thought I'd have. We looked ridiculous because there was no place to buy work clothes, so we wore our dresses. I'm sure my father was turning over in his grave." Elise immediately regretted the metaphor since her father didn't have a grave, but she kept talking. "We'd remove the bricks, and then kids would sort them by size, chip off the mortar, and stack them so they could be used in new construction. They built mini railroads throughout the city that carted away the debris that couldn't be reused. A few of those railroads are still being used."

"I never would've guessed we'd be doing the same work after the war," Hans said. "Hitler told us he'd create a bunch of new jobs, so I guess he was ultimately proven right." Elise smiled. "Do you notice that you look at rubble differently now?" he asked. "A pile of rubble used to just be a pile of rubble, but now when I look at it, I think about the most efficient way to clear it. Is there a particular side that's more accessible? Should you start at the top and throw the debris down, or should you eat away at the sides? Are the individual bricks or stones small enough for one person to carry, or will you need teams of people?"

"Yes! That's funny. I thought it was just me. It's not a pile of rubble—it's a project."

"Exactly," he said. "I think anytime you have expertise in something, it changes how you look at it. I remember a Mark Twain story I read when I was a kid. He wrote that when he was growing up, he noticed many beautiful, subtle details about the river. After he started working on boats, though, these same features became technical considerations for him to take into account for his job. He had to look at the river in practical terms, and he no longer appreciated its beauty."

"I don't think I ever read that, but it makes sense."

"He compared his job on the river with a doctor looking at a beautiful woman. He wondered if after the doctor learned all the scientific details of the body, he would lose the ability to look at it from the perspective of beauty."

Elise smiled again. "But was the pile of rubble that beautiful to begin with?"

"Well, I didn't say it was a perfect analogy. I will say, though, that I haven't lost the ability to look at a woman and see her beauty."

They glanced at each other briefly but then Elise turned away. She wasn't sure if that was supposed to be a compliment or what to think about it if it was, so she retreated to the safety of the rubble conversation. "Actually, the rubble was sort of beautiful sometimes. I remember crossing a street once on a sunny spring afternoon after a rain shower. The rubble had been cleared from the street, but mountains of it still lined both sides. When I got halfway across, I stopped and looked down the length of the street. For as far as I could see, the cobblestones glistened, making it look like a river flowing through a canyon. But nature hadn't created the walls of the canyon—humans had created them by destroying what we had built. I remember standing there and thinking, *What have we done?*" She paused, embarrassed, then glanced at Hans and said, "So anyway, I cleared rubble for about a year."

"I never pictured you as a rubble clearer or a textile-mill worker. Why didn't it work out for you to be a teacher?"

Elise stiffened and hesitated before answering. "I finished school the year after you left but couldn't attend university because of the labor shortage. Everybody had to work wherever they were needed, so for the last years of the war, I worked on the assembly line at the Zeiss factory making detonators and igniters for various weapons."

"Did you like it?"

"On my first day, I thought it was interesting to see how things were made, but by the end of the first week, I understood how they were made and was just bored. Plus, as time passed, more and more forced laborers were brought into the factory, and they were treated horribly. It was disturbing to see every day, especially because everything else was falling apart at the same time. The job ended with the bombing, and there wasn't much of an economy for the next few months. After the war, I cleared rubble until things stabilized. Many teachers had moved to the West, so the new government set up an accelerated program to train teachers quickly. I did the training and taught for a while, but I didn't like it."

"What didn't you like?"

She lowered her voice. "Do you remember we used to talk about how our teachers, even the ones who weren't Nazis, had to pretend they were? Well, it was the same thing here. We had to pretend to love Communism and say that all the Fascists were in Western Germany and everybody in the East had been anti-Fascist. It was the same old indoctrination but with a different underlying philosophy. Most people went along, but I couldn't, so I quit."

"I think you would've been a great teacher. Who knows, maybe you'll still do it someday."

They continued walking, but Elise didn't say anything else. Her original intention had been not to tell him anything about the missing years, and she feared that her walls, so carefully constructed, were starting to crumble. But perhaps it was okay if some of the little ones came down as long as the big ones stayed up.

CHAPTER 18

Hans had been in Dresden for three months when Elise got home from work one day and brought in the mail. "There's something here for you," she said. As she handed him the envelope, she whispered, "It looks like it's been opened." Hans got a chill. He appreciated Elise's increased openness when they spoke outside, but he also liked talking to her indoors because she sometimes whispered in his ear.

Hans looked curiously at the return address and then had a moment of recognition. "It's from my friend Willi. I hope you don't mind that I gave him your address. He wasn't sure where he'd be living, so we agreed that he'd send me a letter first with his address. It looks like he's in Nuremberg, where his parents live."

Hans took the letter out, read it, and put it back in the envelope. "He's visiting relatives in Chemnitz next month and wants to get together for lunch here in Dresden."

Elise said, "That sounds nice. But it's Karl-Marx-Stadt now."

"What's Karl-Marx-Stadt?"

"Chemnitz. They changed the name a few years ago."

Hans shook his head. "I think I'll do it, and you should come along. I'm sure he'd like to meet you after hearing my stories for all those years."

* * *

That evening Hans and Elise went for a walk, something they did routinely now that the warmer temperatures had arrived. Elise asked, "Was there anything else in the letter?"

"Not really. He probably knows my mail could be opened, so he didn't say too much." Elise nodded. "When they told us we'd be released, Willi encouraged me to move to the West instead of coming back here. We had heard that returning POWs were treated better there, but I never considered it because everything I know is here."

Hans hoped Elise would reassure him that he had made the correct decision, but all she said was, "It'll be nice for you guys to see each other again."

"Yes, and I think you'll like him. He's very smart."

"I'm sure I will. So what did you guys talk about for all those years?"

"We'd tell stories about things back home and discuss plans for when we got out. He also had to listen to my goofy thoughts and theories, just like you used to do."

"Did you come up with new ones?"

"Of course. I had nothing else to do, so I'd think about stuff all the time. Sometimes it was math related because then I'd have to use my brain and could fill a few hours. For example, if you fire a gun horizontally over an empty field at the same time that you drop a bullet from the same height, the bullets will hit the ground at the same time."

Elise thought about it a minute. "That doesn't sound right. Is that true?"

"I think so. Gravity exerts the same force on both bullets. Of course, I couldn't test that particular theory because the guards were reluctant to give us guns."

"Understandable. What else?"

"I spent a lot of time thinking about fate and the randomness of things. For instance, if a bomber is flying at three hundred kilometers per hour, it travels eighty meters every second.

So if the bombardier pushes his button at one moment, the bomb will hit a certain spot, but if he pushes it one second later, it'll hit a spot eighty meters away. Based on that choice, one house is spared, but a house down the block is destroyed. For that one second, the bombardier is a god, deciding who lives and who dies. After I learned my parents died in a bombing, I thought about that a lot."

Elise nodded but didn't say anything.

"The same idea holds true with rifles. If a Russian points his gun from a hundred meters away, he'll hit a certain target. But if he changes where he's pointing by just one degree, the bullet will hit two meters away from the original spot. That's the difference between hitting me and hitting the guy next to me."

"But it's not all fate, right? People can control their destinies, at least to a certain extent."

"I used to think that, but now I'm not sure. Everything seems so random. Most of the men in the Wehrmacht were better soldiers than me, yet I'm still here and they're all dead. My dad built the best bomb shelter in Dresden, but there are thousands of people walking around town and he's gone."

"After the war, I think a lot of people in Dresden started looking at life that way and just stopped trying."

"Like your mom?" He immediately regretted saying it.

Elise stopped short but didn't look at Hans. After a few seconds, she began walking again. "Yes, like my mom." After a pause, she said, "It's not her fault."

"I know. I'm sorry I said that."

"You're right—she has given up. You remember what she was like before you left?"

"I've never met anyone so full of life. Now she seems so . . . empty."

"She actually stayed optimistic for almost the entire war. Everything in her life had always worked out, so she assumed this would too. She believed it right up to the day when it was impossible to believe it anymore. It's like a cartoon character who runs off a cliff, looks around, and realizes there's no ground underneath him. Then he just plummets.

"Let me tell you some of what happened," she said. "Ludwig was near Leningrad for most of the war, but then they started getting pushed back, and his letters became more troubling and less frequent. He wrote his last letter in late January 1945, and we received it on February 13. Does that date mean anything to you?"

Hans shook his head.

"That was the date of the bombing. Ludwig wrote that he had been wounded in East Prussia, was being evacuated via ship, and would be sent home. Of course, my mom wasn't happy that he was wounded, but she was thrilled that he was returning. It was the happiest she'd been in months. Plus, it was Fasching, and she always loved that holiday.

"For a brief moment that day, I think she could see the end. Ludwig was on his way home, Dresden was undamaged, and the war was nearly over. We knew the Russians or Americans would get here soon, and we were obviously worried about that, but with my dad being a doctor, I think she believed we'd get special treatment. Then the bombing happened, and my dad died, and her dreams were destroyed. A few weeks later, we learned that Ludwig had also died. He didn't mention in his last letter the name of the ship he got on, probably because it seemed like an insignificant detail, but it was the *Wilhelm Gustloff*."

Hans looked at her uncomprehendingly.

"The *Wilhelm Gustloff* was a transport ship that was evacuating civilians and wounded soldiers. It was supposed to hold a couple of thousand people, but something like ten thousand were on board. It was sunk by a Russian submarine, and about nine thousand people died, including Ludwig."

"I can't believe I never heard of that ship."

"It was six times more people than died on the *Titanic*, but nobody ever talks about it. There was so much carnage in the last year of the war that the story just got lost."

"I'm so sorry to hear all of that, and I understand how difficult it must've been for you and your mom. Thanks for telling me."

"That's not even close to the end of the story. The first few years after the bombing and after the war were disastrous for her health. She suffered from smoke inhalation on the night of the fire, which led to her cough. The smoke also damaged her eyes and caused them to be sensitive to light, which is why she always sits with her back to the window now. As we moved from shelter to shelter, she got typhus, and after she got over that, she got dysentery. Several times, I thought she was going to die. Everyone was nearly starving to death, and there were no doctors and no medicine. We were all dying in the ruins, and nobody cared because we were the bad guys."

"Did you have any money?"

"I was able to salvage some coins and jewelry that hadn't been looted from the house, and over time I traded those for food on the black market. If we hadn't had those, I might've had to do what many of my girlfriends did and sell the only thing I could."

Hans looked at her and she looked back. He seemed almost to be holding his breath, but she could see he was doing his best not to let his emotions show. "But you didn't do that?"

"No," Elise said quietly. "But I don't judge the girls that did. It was that or starve."

Hans nodded solemnly. They walked on a bit further, and then he asked, "Didn't your father being a doctor help you?"

"No. In fact, it was the opposite. The Russians and the new government wanted to eliminate the upper-middle class. They also hated doctors since many of them were Nazis, and quite a few had been involved in war crimes. They had to be respectful to the few remaining ones because so many of them had gone to the West, but being the family of a dead doctor only made things worse for us."

"I'm so sorry."

"You don't need to be sorry. Everyone has a sad story, and it's easy to blame fate, but after the war, some people moved on and took control of their lives while others didn't. My mom hasn't, and given her age and her health, she probably never will." She walked on for a few more steps and then said, "I suppose I haven't either. But for me, I like to think that there's still time."

CHAPTER 19

Hans got in the habit of periodically wandering around Dresden, in part so he could get to know the transformed city and in part to give Elise and Maria some space. One day, he saw an older man limping toward him with his head down. Something was familiar about him, but Hans wasn't immediately able to determine what it was. Then, just as their paths were about to cross, he had a flash of recognition and called out, "Herr Schmidt!" The man raised his head and looked at him with a frown. "It's Hans Becker, August's son."

The frown persisted for a moment, but then the man's eyes brightened, and he hugged Hans. "Hans Becker! We thought you were dead. When did you get back?"

"A few months ago."

"How could they keep you men for so long? It's criminal," he said, shaking his head. "Wow—you're the spitting image of your dad, but better looking, of course. Hey, I was on my way to lunch. Please join me."

They walked to a nearby café and sat in a booth. They considered each other silently for a moment, and Hans worried that the lunch would be as awkward as his first dinner with Elise and Maria. Schmidt's hair was gray now and his cheeks were hollow, but the laugh lines in his face and the sparkle in his eyes were still there. Eventually, he broke the silence. "Have you told your stories to anyone?"

"What do you mean?"

"When I came home after my war, I didn't want to talk about it. I didn't think anybody would understand, but then I met your dad at a pub one night. He was his usual loudmouth self, but we hit it off immediately. We got to talking and ended up being the last two guys at the pub. By the way, that wasn't the only time we were the last two guys at the pub." He laughed with the same roar that Hans remembered from his youth.

Hans laughed too, and Schmidt continued. "Anyway, we discovered that we'd had similar wartime experiences and shared many of the same bad memories. As German men, we were supposed to pretend that everything was fine, and that's usually what we did. But sometimes, if either of us was going through a rough stretch, we'd confide in each other. I know my war was different from yours, but if you want to talk about it, I'd be happy to listen."

Hans looked out the window for a few seconds and then turned back. "If I wanted to write a memoir about my experiences, there's no way I could do it because all the events blur together and I'm not sure what happened when. It's more like I just have images. For instance, there's this one image I have of rolling eastward in the summer of 1942. I could look in any direction and not see any hills, or trees, or anything. It was like being in the ocean. The tanks and trucks and men churned up huge clouds of dust, and I remember being coated in it that entire summer.

"I also have an image of when we first reached Stalingrad. The city had been destroyed by Luftwaffe bombing, and as we approached we saw a huge column of black smoke going straight up into the sky. There must have been some atmospheric thing happening because the smoke flattened out near the top of the column, making it look like an enormous cross hovering over the city. Somebody joked that it was a monument for the world's biggest cemetery, although the joke turned out not to be funny.

"From Stalingrad, I mostly remember the paranoia and exhaustion. The Russians never seemed to run out of men. We used to say that every time we killed a Russian, two more rose up to take his place, like Hercules trying to kill the Hydra. And we never knew where they were. Snipers were on rooftops, raiders emerged from sewers, and we were constantly ambushed at night. I don't think I ever got more than an hour of uninterrupted sleep during the entire time I was there."

He looked out the window again. When he turned back to Schmidt, he realized he didn't know if he had paused for ten seconds or ten minutes. "I also remember passing through towns in my radio van after battles and seeing the results." Hans choked up as he said, "It was horrible."

"The carnage after a battle is unimaginable unless you've seen it."

"Yes, but in my case, it wasn't just the battle. It was the other stuff that had nothing to do with winning a battle. The stuff we were doing to the Russians. And the Jews."

Schmidt furrowed his brow. "I think a lot of those stories are just propaganda. In my war, the English claimed that Germans killed babies in Belgium or some such nonsense. I guess the winners get to make up whatever stories they want."

Hans frowned at him. "The stories weren't made up."

Schmidt sat quietly for a moment and then, changing the subject, said, "Where are you living now?"

"Do you remember Elise Engel?"

"The girl you dated before you left? She was the oboe player, right?" Schmidt grinned.

Hans smiled back. "Yes, the oboe player."

"You two are still together after all this time?"

"We're not together. She's letting me stay there, that's all."

Schmidt stared at him for a few seconds and then said, "You can't hide your feelings any better than your father could. Do you want to be more than roommates?"

"I think so, but everything is so different now. And we're so different. I'm not sure what she wants."

"Well, if you can figure out what a woman wants, you'll be the first. Women are hard enough to understand in normal circumstances, but Dresden in the last twelve years is not what I'd call normal circumstances." Schmidt stared at him. "How much do you know about the bombing?"

"Elise doesn't talk about it, but I can see the end result. I lived through plenty of bombardments during the war, so I've got a good idea of what it was like."

Schmidt looked down at his coffee cup for a moment, then raised his head. "No, you don't. I was in the Great War. I lived through artillery bombardments that lasted for weeks, gas attacks, and hand-to-hand combat, but I've never seen anything like what happened that night. I've read descriptions about what people think hell is like, and that night was worse." He paused. "I think you should know. It'll help you understand Dresden, and maybe it'll help you understand Elise too."

Hans hesitated and then nodded.

Schmidt took a deep breath. "Compared to other German cities, Dresden had it pretty good for most of the war. In the first part of the war, the bombers couldn't reach us, and by the time they could, they didn't seem to want to. We had convinced ourselves that we were special. People stopped taking precautions, and the military didn't defend us. The only person who still thought we were at risk was crazy old August. He worked on that shelter right up to the end."

Hans got choked up as he thought of how often he had ridiculed his dad about the shelter.

"Anyway, it was Shrove Tuesday. It had been a beautiful winter day, cold but sunny. Dresden tried to make everything seem normal, and after school, the kids ran around in their Fasching costumes. For a while, it was easy to forget how close the Russians and Americans were and what would happen when they got here. We believed their armies were our only threat.

"The air-raid sirens started about twenty minutes before ten o'clock that night. The sirens were going off almost every night by then, so most people assumed it was another false alarm. But when the bulletin came over the radio that we were the target, everybody rushed to their shelters. Knowing your father, I'm sure your parents had gone to their shelter right away."

Hans nodded.

"The first planes marked the city by dropping red and green flares that drifted slowly to the ground. They looked sort of like Christmas trees and were actually quite beautiful. I had always assumed that during an air raid, there'd be constant action—antiaircraft guns booming, Messerschmitts buzzing around trying to shoot down the bombers. But that's not what happened. The only things we could see were the Christmas trees drifting down, and the only sounds were the sirens and the bombers. It was mesmerizing and almost didn't seem real.

"The first wave of bombers dropped high explosives and incendiaries. The high explosives are designed to blow buildings apart, which allows the incendiaries to go inside the buildings rather than landing on roofs. That was the beginning of the firestorm. Do you know what a firestorm is?"

Hans shook his head.

"A fire needs oxygen to live, and a giant fire needs a lot of oxygen. Since the hot air rises, the fire pulls in cooler air from the sides. The result is hurricane-force winds strong enough to uproot trees, and the things closest to the fire, including people, get sucked up into the air as the heat rises. And because the fire takes all the available oxygen, it creates vacuums where breathing is impossible.

"Once the first wave was finished, the firefighters and volunteers exited their shelters. It was already going to be bad, but the second wave was what turned it into a catastrophe. Those planes came three hours later, and because most of the air-raid sirens were broken by then, many people, including the firefighters, were trapped out in the open.

"For me, the worst part was being in our apartment building's basement, which we used as a shelter. We were accustomed to going down there because of all the false alarms, and everybody had assigned seats and knew where to go. That night, though, there were thousands of refugees in Dresden who didn't know their way around and had nowhere to hide. A bunch of them crammed into our shelter, and by the time we closed the doors when the first bombs landed, we were standing shoulder to shoulder. The explosions knocked dust and plaster from the walls and ceiling, and then the lights went out. We stood there in total darkness, waiting and listening. Then it started getting warm and smoky, and it became harder to breathe, which is when panic set in. Every instinct tells you to leave, but you know there's nothing out there but fire.

"Some people panicked and tried to go up the stairs to get out, but there were people outside who were trying to get in. The collision of these two groups led to people being crushed or trampled to death on the stairs. That's also about the time it started getting lighter down there and we realized the building above us was on fire. More people tried to get out then, but by that time the stairwell was jammed with bodies."

Schmidt paused and stared at the table a moment before looking up again. "The next day, we searched our neighborhood for survivors. Whenever we opened a cellar door, we'd get hit with a blast of hot air, like opening an oven. Usually, dead bodies that are starting to decompose emit a strange, almost sweet, smell, but the smell from the shelters where people got roasted was different—it smelled like roast pork. I can't eat pork anymore."

Schmidt looked out the window and was silent for a minute. "The worst one was when we walked into a basement and people were lined up on benches, all dead, all roasted. The image I can't get out of my head is a pregnant woman whose belly had been split open during the roasting process. I could see her baby."

Another minute passed as Schmidt continued to look out the window. Then he took a deep breath and turned back to Hans. "There are many reasons why I said it was worse than combat. In combat, you're doing a job, as distasteful as it is. Men have fought wars for as long as there have been men, and there's a certain logic to it. Here, though, it was just a bunch of women, children, and old people minding their own business, with no ability to defend themselves. I'm sure you've seen horrible things, but this was worse than anything I've ever seen. Not even close. Walking around the next day, it all seemed unreal. The strangest part was the animals."

"Animals?"

"The zoo and the circus were both bombed, and some of the animals that didn't die were able to escape. At different times the next day, I saw a giraffe and a gorilla walking through the smoldering streets as if it were the most normal thing in the world."

The men sat quietly for a few minutes, and then Hans asked, "Do you know what happened to my parents?"

"I had my own things to deal with in the first couple of days, but I eventually went to your house, or what was left of it. The shelter was still there, but it was empty."

"So you weren't the one who identified their bodies?"

Schmidt frowned. "No. Why do you care who identified them?"

"I'd just like to know what happened to them."

"There's nothing but heartache down that path. There's no reason to find out."

"That's what Elise said too. I guess you're right."

The two men left the restaurant and stopped on the sidewalk. Schmidt reached for his wallet, took out a card, and handed it to Hans. "Here's my phone number. If you'd like, perhaps we can get together and talk over a beer sometime. Just a couple of old veterans limping around and swapping war stories. Don't worry—the stories will eventually get more dramatic, and you'll become more heroic."

"That would be great." As they shook hands, Hans asked the question that his father had always asked Schmidt. "So, do you have any jokes?"

Schmidt smiled, and his eyes glistened with tears. He said, "You're in luck because I do: What would happen if the desert became a Socialist country?"

"I don't know."

"Nothing for a while, but eventually the sand would become scarce." And with that, Schmidt erupted in his trademark laugh. Laughing at his own joke, just like in the old days. Hans laughed too.

They shook hands again and walked off in opposite directions.

CHAPTER 20

After her mother went to bed that night, Elise sat on the couch with Hans. He said, "I ran into Herr Schmidt today, and we had lunch together."

"Oh, that's great. I'm glad to hear he's alive."

"Yes, he seems to be doing pretty well. He told me some of the horrible details about the bombing. He said it was worse than combat."

Elise looked away. "I obviously don't know what combat is like, but yes, it was bad."

"I think I know more about what you went through and maybe have a better understanding of how things are now. Do you want to talk about your experiences?"

"No."

"Maybe it would help you get past them if you talked about them?"

"No."

Hans paused briefly before continuing. "He also said he wasn't the one who identified my parents' bodies. He agreed with you that I should drop it. It's just hard to let go without knowing."

Elise stood up. "I'm tired," she said. "I'll see you in the morning."

In her room minutes later, she got ready for bed, turned out the light, and crawled under the blanket. She didn't want to think about it, but her mind returned to the morning after the bombing . . .

August stared at Elise with vacant eyes, his chin and shirt caked with vomit. She stood up and faced Olga. "He's not well and you should get out of here. They're setting up an aid station nearby. I can help you get there."

"We're okay. He has enough supplies in here so we can last for a week."

"I know, but he needs medical attention."

"He's fine. He just has to get his strength back. He's much better than he was last night."

"He doesn't look fine. Please, let me help you." She knelt next to August and said, "Do you want to get out of here?" He gave a feeble nod.

Olga said, "I think this is a bad idea." Elise, however, had already untied August. Once she had put goggles on him, she helped him to his feet, led him to the exit, and supported him as he climbed the steps.

When she reached the top, she turned and saw Olga shaking her head as she put on her own goggles and attached Greta's collar and leash. When Olga reached the second step, from which she could see that the house was gone, she started crying. She lifted her goggles to wipe away her tears, and Greta, who was two steps higher, turned and licked her face.

Once she was out of the shelter, Olga faced the smoldering ruins of her home. After a moment, she walked toward an ash pile and bent down to examine a puddle of melted metal. It occurred to Elise that the puddle was the remains of the wind chimes. "It's too hot to try to salvage anything now," she said. "I'll come with you tomorrow and see if we can dig anything out. Let's go to the aid station." Olga turned and glared at her.

They began walking, with Elise supporting a mumbling August, and Olga leading Greta. As their trek continued, Elise found that she no longer needed to support him, and his mumbling had turned into distinct words, specifically curse words. "Those bastards. I knew this was going to happen. Those bastards."

Elise said, "Why would they bomb us? What's the point?"

August looked at her. "Those aren't the bastards I'm talking about. The bastards I'm talking about are in Berlin."

Elise was anxious to return to her mother, but the journey took longer than she had hoped. Navigating through the wasteland was easier for her than for August and Olga, and Greta kept stopping to sniff corpses and body parts. By the time they arrived at the neighborhood park that contained the aid station, it was noon, and the smoke had begun to dissipate. A metal archway over the entrance to the park held a sign that read *"Dafür danken wir unserem Führer"*—"For this we thank our Führer." August huffed and said, "Those words have never been truer."

Elise led the Beckers to a bench, where she brushed off the ash and had them sit down. She got cups of water for August and Olga, a wet towel for August to clean his face, and even a small bowl of water for Greta. A medic examined them and administered eye drops as an aid tent was erected beside them and additional refugees began to assemble.

Elise said, "I need to go back to my house, but I'll come check on you later today, okay?" August nodded and thanked her, but Olga looked away and continued to chew her fingernails. Elise patted Greta on her head, eliciting a tail wag, and began her walk home.

As she passed back under the sign thanking the Führer, she turned to take one more look at the Beckers. They stood out because August's blue work clothes and Olga's green checkered dress were the only things in the park that weren't covered in gray soot. Olga had stopped chewing her nails and was now petting Greta, who had jumped onto the bench and was lying with her head on Olga's lap. Elise thought the scene would make an interesting surrealist portrait—a middle-aged couple and their dog sitting quietly on a park bench, but wearing goggles. Despite everything else that had happened, she allowed herself a quick smile, knowing that the Beckers were safe and that she had fulfilled her commitment to Hans. But now it was time to go home.

Two blocks from her house, she saw a boy in an ash-coated Hitler Youth uniform walking briskly toward her through the hellscape. He was carrying a portable air-raid siren and cranking the handle to produce a noise similar to the regular sirens but quieter and with a higher pitch. Elise stopped and thought about how inappropriate it was for him to play with that device like it was a toy, given what the city had just been through. As he approached her, she noticed tears creating tiny rivulets on his ashy face.

She saw a handful of zombies who had stopped walking and were looking up into the sky, even though it was too smoky to see anything besides a fuzzy outline of the sun. Then she heard a sound about as loud as if a man were humming a monotonous note in the next room. But then it was like two men humming, and then a dozen, and then a hundred, and they were no longer in the next room, they were directly above her. The zombies came to life and scrambled to find shelter.

Elise staggered through the debris toward her house.

CHAPTER 21

Willi visited Dresden on a splendid late-spring Saturday. Hans and Elise arrived early at the designated meeting place, a café near the apartment, and since individual tables were rare in the communal GDR, they sat at the end of a long refectory table.

When Willi entered the café, Hans stood up and Elise followed suit. The men walked toward each other and hugged, peppering their embrace with several masculine slaps on the back. Willi was a bit shorter than Hans but was broader, and his muscles were rounder than Hans's ropy ones. He wore a tweed jacket and dress trousers, while Hans wore the only garments he owned, baggy work clothes.

"You look good!" said Willi.

"You too! I'm not used to seeing you clean-shaven and wearing clothes without holes in them."

"And with a real haircut. And no lice!"

The two men laughed, and then Hans turned to Elise and introduced her.

Willi shook her hand and said, "I think Hans exaggerated in some of the stories he told, but he certainly wasn't exaggerating when he said how pretty you are."

Elise hadn't received a compliment like that since the early 1940s and didn't immediately know how to respond. "Thank you. I . . . I've . . . heard a lot about you."

"And I've heard a lot about you. It's great that you two were able to get back together after all this time."

Elise frowned. Did he think she and Hans were a couple? It was possible that all he knew about their relationship was that they lived in the same apartment, so he probably assumed they were together. She didn't know how to disabuse him of that impression.

They sat down and ordered food, and Willi ordered a beer. The two men talked about former comrades, and while Willi knew more than Hans since most of the former prisoners had gone to the West, neither of them knew very much. They also reminisced about their time in captivity, and Elise was amazed at their ability to find humor in it. Both men laughed about events that sounded ghastly to her, but she wondered if some of their exuberance was a facade put on for her benefit. Willi laughed even more after finishing his second beer.

After nearly an hour, Willi turned to Elise. "I'm sorry, this must be boring for you."

"Not at all. I haven't heard these stories before."

"Well, you should know that you helped keep this guy alive. He talked about you all the time."

Elise blushed. "Well, I'm glad I could help."

"Over the years, we'd sometimes hear that we were going to be released, and the first thing Hans always talked about was seeing you again." Willi turned to a red-faced Hans. "What year was it that you were on the train to go home, but then they physically pulled you off?"

Hans replied quietly, "1953."

"Yes, 1953. That was a tough one." After an awkward silence, Willi said, "Why don't we go outside and get some fresh air? It's a nice day."

Hans said, "That's a great idea." He asked for the check, but when it arrived, Willi insisted on paying, and Hans didn't argue.

*   *   *

They left the café and made the twenty-minute walk to Prager Strasse. Because of the narrowness of the sidewalks, Elise mostly stayed behind the two men, which she didn't mind. She didn't have much to contribute to the conversation anyway. Once they reached the street, they sat on a bench, with Hans between Elise and Willi.

"I'm curious—we hear a lot about the Stasi," Willi said. "How powerful is it? For example, were you nervous talking in the restaurant?"

Sitting in the middle, Hans was in the awkward position of needing to swivel his head back and forth between the other two. He looked at Elise, but she didn't respond, so he swiveled back to Willi and said, "They definitely know a lot about what's happening. For example, they probably know I'm meeting with you, especially since you're a former POW and are visiting from the West."

Willi looked around. "So Big Brother is always watching?"

Hans looked at Elise, but she shrugged. He swiveled back to Willi and said, "Elise's big brother died in the war."

"Oh, I'm sorry to hear that. But I was referring to Big Brother from George Orwell."

Hans furrowed his brow. "Is that someone we know?"

"No, the author George Orwell. He wrote a book about a government that's constantly monitoring its citizens."

"Oh. I don't know that book, but that sounds like this government. You get used to it, though, right?" Hans said, swiveling to Elise.

"Yes. We've been dealing with it for a long time."

Willi looked at Hans. "So, are you glad you came back to the East?"

Hans turned to Elise, who hadn't anticipated that particular swivel. She wanted to look away or look down, but instead, she stared into his eyes. He raised his eyebrows as if pleading for her to say something, and for a fleeting moment, she wanted to reassure him, or embrace him, or maybe even run away with him forever. Instead, she remained impassive.

After a few seconds, Hans turned so he was facing directly ahead and said, "I'm still not sure."

"But what about all the things you were excited about returning to?" Willi looked at Elise as he asked the question, grinning amicably. Because Hans was still looking forward, he missed Willi's implication.

"It's difficult seeing Dresden like this. I know it's just a city, but I truly loved it. I dislike everything about it now."

"Well, that's not a nice thing to say with your girlfriend sitting right next to you," Willi said with a smile.

"I'm not his girlfriend," Elise said. "He's just living with us until he can find his own place." It came out more bluntly than she intended.

"Oh, sorry," Willi said. "I didn't know."

Still looking ahead, Hans said, "That's all right. I should've made that clear earlier."

After a moment of awkward silence, Willi said, "I know what you mean about Dresden. When I was driving in, I saw some hideous new construction. Is the idea that everyone is going to live in identical apartments?"

"That's the idea," Hans told him. "But I'm sure the bureaucrats will live in nicer places."

"Ah yes," Willi said. "All animals are equal, but some are more equal than others."

Hans smiled. "Did you come up with that?"

"Oh, no. That's from George Orwell again."

Hans looked at Elise, and she shrugged once more.

"You used to stump me with literary references," Willi said, "and now I'm stumping you."

"There are a lot of books we're not allowed to read here."

There was another pause, which Elise broke by asking, "What's it like in the West?"

"Well, it's certainly different from what you've described here. They had parades for us when we returned."

Hans stared at him. "Parades?"

"Yes. The government had pushed the Russians to release us for a long time, and when they finally did, there was a big celebration. The government financially compensated us based on how much time we spent in captivity, and everyone who returned was entitled to the same job they had when they left. If we didn't want to return to our old jobs, we got preferential treatment for new jobs or education." With each statement Willi made, Elise noticed that Hans seemed to sag a bit more into the bench.

"When we were gone," Willi continued, "organizations were set up that pushed for repatriation. The churches were involved, and every year there'd be a day of remembrance for the men who were still missing." He looked at Elise. "Did they do that here?"

"No. They just pretended the POWs didn't exist, which was easier than confronting the Soviets about it. I think people tried to forget the war, and the POWs were a daily reminder of it."

"I'm sorry to hear that," Willi said. "And by the way, I'm not saying everything is perfect there. It's all fast paced and competitive. The returning POWs are at a disadvantage because everyone who has been home all these years has gone to school or started a job. I'm at the bottom rung, and everybody my age is way ahead of me. Also, it sometimes feels like I'm in America rather than Germany. Their culture has taken over, and I don't care for it. When we left for the war, the American music we heard was Glenn Miller, and now it's Elvis Presley, which is a big downgrade. Do you get to hear him here?"

Hans looked at Elise, but she didn't know what Willi was talking about either. She shook her head.

"I have a twelve-year-old niece who listens to rock-and-roll music," Willi said, "and I don't understand the attraction. I guess it's partly because I barely know her, since I hadn't met her until four months ago."

"Do you have a television?" Elise asked.

"My parents do. There are a lot of amazing things in the West, and not just gadgets. Our new construction is much more impressive than what I've seen here, and every time I turn around, there's a new building going up. It would be a great place for a budding architect," Willi added with a smile. Hans looked to Elise, but neither of them said anything. "But don't take my word for it. The two of you should come visit me."

"I don't know if I'd be able to get a travel visa," Hans said.

"You can at least ask, right? Then you could compare the two places and make sure this is where you want to be."

"Yes, I'll do that," Hans said quietly.

Willi looked at Elise. "You should talk this guy into moving to the West. And I know you're not his girlfriend, but you should come with him."

Elise nodded feebly but didn't say anything. She then took advantage of the pause in the conversation to say, "You two should finish catching up without me listening in. I'm going to walk home."

She stood up, and the two men did the same. Willi hugged her and said, "It was great to meet you after all this time. I feel like I already know you."

Elise said, "It was nice to meet you too."

Willi's display of affection apparently compelled Hans to make one too, because he hugged her for the first time since he'd gotten off the train. When they separated, Hans said, "I'll be back in a while," and then he turned toward Willi.

On her walk home, Elise thought about how dejected Hans had looked, and for the first time in years, she almost cried. But she didn't.

CHAPTER 22

The men sat back down, and as Willi watched Elise walk away, he said, "She seems great." Hans nodded, relieved that he no longer needed to swivel. "I'm sorry for what I said about her being your girlfriend. I assumed that since you're living together . . ."

"That's all right. It was a reasonable assumption. I didn't mention anything in my letter because I hoped that by the time you got here, she'd be my girlfriend. I realize now it was stupid to think we'd still have a romantic relationship after all these years."

"These things take time."

"I know. I just . . . I guess I'm just confused. I've told her stuff about my time away, but she's told me almost nothing about what happened to her. I don't want to push, but it's difficult to get to know her if she's keeping secrets."

They sat quietly for a minute. Then Hans asked, "Are things really that good in the West?"

Willi didn't immediately answer. "Everything I said is true, and I do think you should move there," he said after a moment. "But it's been hard. Everyone does and says the right things, but I don't fit in. I run into people I haven't seen since before I left, and they always act like they're happy to see me, but I can tell they think I'm an outsider. And then they go back to making their money and buying their cars and building their lives as if the war hadn't happened."

"It's the same here, but without the money and the cars."

"And I feel so—incompetent. Everyone our age spent the last decade learning things, but I still have the skills and knowledge of an eighteen-year-old. I look at people who never left Germany, who have had ten years to rebuild their lives, and I hate them. For them, the war has been over for a decade, but for me it just ended this year. Actually, in some ways, it still hasn't ended." He turned to Hans. "Do you wake up screaming?"

Hans frowned. "No, but sometimes I wake up covered in sweat, and once I woke up on the floor behind the couch. I don't think Elise and her mom have noticed. Also, I often lose time. Hours will go by, and I don't know where they went."

"I didn't want to say this in front of Elise," Willi said, "but I think I might be a little crazy. I always have nightmares, and sometimes I yell at my parents for no reason. I don't know what's wrong with me."

"It'll probably go away in time." Hans thought back to the anxiety attacks his father experienced twenty years after his war and realized he didn't believe what he had just said. "It's like there's a gap between remembering and forgetting. There's a bunch of stuff I remember, and then there are all these things that I think I've forgotten, but then something will happen, and I'll realize that I haven't. I'll hear a car backfire or a little kid scream, and a horrible memory will resurface. I haven't forgotten it at all—the memories are just lurking and waiting to ambush me."

Willi nodded. "I always imagined that I'd come home, get married, and have kids, but now the thought of those things terrifies me. I've met some girls, but it's been so long since I dated that I don't know what to do with them, especially since they're much more aggressive than they used to be. I dreamed about being with a girl for ten years, but now I look for reasons not to go out with them."

They sat on the bench for a few more minutes. Finally, Willi said, "I'm sorry to be so depressing, but I don't have anyone to talk to about this stuff. There are some veterans' groups, but they've been meeting for years, and I don't fit in there either."

"Veterans' groups aren't allowed here," Hans said. "The authorities are apparently worried that if too many veterans get together, they'll start conspiring against the government or something."

"It's outrageous that you spent thirteen years behind barbed wire, and then you come home and are still basically a prisoner."

Hans thought for a minute and then asked, "How do people move from the East to the West?"

"I was hoping you'd want to know, so I did some research before coming here. The easiest way is to be old. The East is happy to let retired people move to the West because they're no longer productive."

"I don't want to wait that long."

"Of course not. For young people, there are several ways. One is to get a visa to visit the West and never return. The second is to go to Berlin. There's no barrier between East and West Berlin, and thousands of people travel back and forth every day for work or other reasons. You can simply walk across the border and then request asylum."

"Those both sound straightforward."

"If those two approaches don't work for some reason, there's a third way. East Germany began fortifying their border with West Germany a few years ago, and they imply that it's impenetrable. The truth is, there are still places to cross, but it's dangerous because if they catch you, they'll shoot you."

Hans pondered the options. "I always assumed I'd live in Dresden when I was released, but now I'm not sure."

"Well, at a minimum, you should visit and see what you think."

"Okay, I'll try to get a visa."

"And let's stay in touch. It's good to have someone to talk to." Willi stood up. "But I need to go now. My pass to be in the East is good for only one day, and I still need to see my cousins."

They embraced, shook hands, and walked to Willi's car. After Hans watched him drive away, he trudged back to the apartment with his hands in his pockets and his head down. The weather had gotten chillier over the course of the day.

CHAPTER 23

As Hans opened the door to the apartment, Elise rose from the couch and turned to face him. "Hello," she said.

"Hello," he replied, without making eye contact.

He walked in, and they both sat down on the couch. "He seems nice," she said.

"Yes, he's great." Hans looked out the window instead of at Elise.

"What did you talk about after I left?"

"He said things in the West aren't quite as wonderful as he implied. He's having a hard time fitting in."

"That's certainly understandable."

Hans glanced at her and gave a quick smile but then returned to looking out the window. He said quietly, "I'm thinking about moving to the West."

Elise stiffened. "Just because of what Willi said?"

"No, because of everything. Willi only confirmed what I was already thinking."

"Oh, okay." She paused and then asked, "Do you regret coming here?"

Hans looked down at his hands. "I had to come here. Everything I knew and loved was in Dresden, and I had to see if it was still here. But it's not. Everything's gone."

"I know this hasn't been what you hoped for, and I'm sorry if I'm one of the reasons."

"It's not your fault, it's mine. My stupid, childish fantasies led me to believe something that was impossible." He shook his head. "The thought of coming back here and reliving all my favorite days? Ridiculous. Who thinks like that? That was never going to happen."

"Sorry—I could've been nicer that day."

"That's not the issue. I've thought about this a lot in the past few weeks, and the real problem is that for the past fourteen years, I've been using you. Some POWs used religion to get through the difficult times, but I used you. It worked, but in hindsight, it was never realistic and wasn't fair to you. I realize now that it wasn't even you as a person, it was you as a fantasy. We're completely different people than when I left, but I stayed in love with this pretend idealized version of you the entire time. I developed elaborate plans in my head for our lives together after I got back. I even designed a house for us to live in." He shook his head again and said once more, "Ridiculous."

He paused and then added, "I'm sorry I put you through this, and I'm especially sorry I put your mom through it. She didn't need this disruption after everything that's happened to her."

Elise took a moment before speaking. "It's all so strange," she said finally, "and I'm not sure how I'm supposed to act or what you expect of me." She touched his arm. "But I'm glad you're here."

Hans held back tears as he looked directly at her for the first time in the conversation. He leaned over to hug her, and she hugged him back. When he released her, she turned her back and rested against him with her head on his chest. They remained in that position for a half hour, and for the first time since his return to Dresden, Hans was happy.

Elise eventually said, "It's not terrible here, you know. It's not that there's a lot of bad stuff—there's just not very much good stuff. It's kind of . . . gray." After a few more minutes, she sat up and whispered in his ear, "Maybe you're right—maybe you should move to the West."

Hans didn't understand what she was suggesting. They had just shared their first affectionate moment since his return, so did she mean that both of them would go? Or all three of them? Or was she just trying to get rid of him? He knew he should ask her to clarify, but instead, he simply said, "Okay."

She leaned over and whispered again. "But we need to get a better understanding of what things are like there."

Now she was saying "we." What did she mean? He found it challenging to separate what she was saying from the fact that she was whispering in his ear right after leaning up against him. It was difficult to concentrate.

She pulled away and said, "Let's go for a walk."

When they reached the sidewalk, Elise said quietly, "It makes me sad to see how the government treats POWs, and it makes sense that you would consider leaving. But it's not a decision you should make lightly, because if you go, you won't be allowed to come back. I think you need to learn more."

"But how can I do that?"

"Yes, that's the problem. It's difficult to make phone calls to the West, and Willi won't be able to visit regularly, so that just leaves letters or a visit."

"Do you think I'd be able to get a visa?"

"I don't know the process, but people sometimes go, so there must be a way. Maybe you can ask Gerhard at your meeting on Monday?"

"Okay, I'll do that. I don't know how he'll respond, but I'll ask. And as for letters, aren't my letters going to be opened?"

"Any letters that come to you or from you will probably be opened, and I'm sure they're looking at my mail and Mother's mail now too. But as I was waiting for you to come back, I had an idea. My aunt Agnes lives on the east side of town. She had a heart attack a few years ago and is sickly and basically home-bound. I can take your letters to her and have her mail them, and then have Willi use her address to mail letters to you. Then when I go see her, I can pick them up."

"Are you sure it's not dangerous for Aunt Agnes?"

"I visit her sometimes anyway, so it won't be suspicious. And I'm sure she'd be happy to see me more often."

Upon returning to the apartment, they wrote a letter to Willi. They thanked him for visiting and asked him more questions about the West—the government bonuses, the guaranteed jobs, the opportunities to go to university. Lastly, they explained their communication plan involving Aunt Agnes. Elise then phoned her aunt and told her she'd visit the next day. Before Hans lay down on the couch that night, Elise hugged him.

CHAPTER 24

After lunch the next day, Elise took the letter and departed for her aunt's house, leaving Hans and her mother in the living room. Once Elise was gone, Hans turned to Maria and said, "I wanted to tell you that I've learned more about the bombing, and I'm sorry I wasn't more sympathetic to you earlier. It must've been terrible."

Maria frowned and looked at him through her thick glasses but waited a few moments before answering. "Get me a glass of wine, would you?" she said at last. Hans thought it was early to start drinking, even for her, but he poured the wine and brought it to her.

She took a sip and said, "I'm actually the one who needs to apologize. I've been unpleasant toward you, but it's not because of anything you've done."

"I know I've disrupted your routine."

"It's not that. I'm embarrassed by what I've become, and I'd prefer not to be seen in this condition. Also, you're an everyday reminder of my old life. The house, the dinners, the porcelain, the piano, the friends. That life was perfect for me, and I was perfect for it."

"You were an amazing hostess."

"But it was all a lie, wasn't it? And every day, we learn more about the truth." She took another drink of wine. "I must've seen what was happening back then, but I somehow managed to ignore it. Sometimes when I'm sitting here, and you probably think I'm not doing anything, I'm actually reconstructing those days, one piece at a time, trying to figure out how I could've overlooked the evil that surrounded me that in hindsight is so obvious."

Hans thought he should be supportive somehow, but he personally shared many of the same misgivings. After a few minutes of silence, she took a deep breath and said, "Elise seems happier with you here, and she's even letting her hair grow out, which is usually a sign. Women cut their hair short when they're mad at men. But she's still my little girl, and I need to watch out for her. I feel that I need to understand what you did in the war."

"I was a radio operator and—"

"No, I don't care what you tell other people. I want to know what you really did. Did you kill anybody?"

Hans furrowed his brow. "No, I was mostly behind the lines until the end at Stalingrad."

"Did you see people get killed?"

"Of course. It was a war."

"Did you see civilians get killed?"

He gave her a long look. "Yes."

"A lot of them?"

"Yes, a lot of them."

"Who killed them?"

"We did—the army. Sometimes we'd go through villages after the frontline troops had been there and we'd see buildings on fire with people screaming inside. Other times we'd see entire families, including children, hanging from trees."

"I see." She leaned back in her chair.

"There were units that followed along behind us. Einsatzgruppen, they were called. Their job was to find the Jews and other undesirables in the conquered towns and villages."

"And what did they do when they found these Jews and other undesirables?"

"Sometimes they killed them right away, but other times they rounded them up and sent them to camps."

"Do you know what happened at the camps?"

"I didn't at the time, but when I was a prisoner, they made us watch films of what was going on there."

"So you didn't know what was happening?"

"No, I wasn't involved in the really bad stuff."

"Ah, but you were involved, weren't you? Did you do any-thing to try to stop it?"

Hans looked down at his hands in his lap. "No, I didn't."

She leaned forward. "I understand." She paused. "Neither did I." They sat quietly for a few minutes, and then she asked, "Did Elise tell you about her father?"

"In what sense?"

"How he died, and I suppose how he lived too. Those two things are related."

"All I know is that he died in the bombing."

"I think it'll help you to understand her if you know what happened that night." She took a deep breath. "Max had just gotten back from work and we were about to have a small cel-ebration because we'd learned that Ludwig was coming home, but then we heard the air-raid sirens. At first we assumed it was another false alarm, but then a radio alert told us it was real. We hurried down to the basement, and Max brought a bucket of water and some goggles he had taken from the hospital.

"You might remember the narrow horizontal windows that were at pavement level at the front of our house. When we heard the bombs exploding, we huddled in the corner, behind some boxes and as far away from the windows as possible. After about a half hour, the explosions stopped, but it started getting brighter and warmer. When we realized the city was on fire, Max's first impulse was to go to the hospital."

"It wasn't to take care of you and Elise?"

"He thought we were safe in the basement, and if there was ever a night when he could save countless lives, that was it. But it kept getting hotter, and the wind began to howl and whistle through the windows."

"And he left anyway?"

"We begged him to stay, but he felt compelled to go. He always had a doctor's bag packed in case he needed to be at the hospital for an extended time, and he had brought it with him to the basement. He clearly had intended to go to the hospital the whole time."

She had a brief coughing fit but then took a gulp of wine and continued. "He went up the stairs and out the front door. Elise and I were both crying, and even though it was hotter near the windows, we stood there to watch him leave. Debris and orange embers were blowing horizontally down the sidewalk, and it sounded like the world was screaming.

"Our car was parked across the street, and despite all the obvious danger, I thought he'd be able to get to it. We saw him as he reached the bottom of the porch steps, and my first thought was that he looked ridiculous. He had put on his hat, scarf, and long winter coat even though he obviously didn't need them anymore. His coat and scarf billowed out behind him, and he was holding his bag with one hand while trying to keep his fedora on with the other. He was walking on his tiptoes, and I realized the sidewalk must be hot and the heat was going right through his wingtips.

"He walked hunched over, twisting left and right to dodge embers. Seeing it all through the window's glass made it feel like we were watching a movie on a screen and that it wasn't real. When he stepped from the cobblestone sidewalk to the asphalt street, his pace slowed, his walking pattern changed, and then he stopped. It took me a few seconds to realize that the asphalt had melted and become tar, and his shoes were stuck. He tried to get them unstuck but couldn't. He threw down his bag to free his hands, and I remember his hat blowing away. Elise wanted to help, but I grabbed her and wouldn't let her go.

"The melted tar burned through his shoes and started burning his feet. For a brief second, he glanced at the house with a look of terror, but I don't know if he could see us in the window. His burning feet must've become unbearable, so he dropped to his hands and knees, but then his hands and knees started burning, and he collapsed the rest of the way. His coat burst into flames, and he melted into the asphalt." Hans had broken eye contact with Maria and instead was staring at the photograph on the side table. It showed Dr. Engel on the beach—healthy, smiling, and surrounded by his perfect family.

Tears rolled down Maria's cheeks. "By this point, it was too hot near the window, so Elise and I went back to the corner behind the boxes. At the time I didn't really think about what I had seen because I was sure I was going to die too. In hindsight, perhaps that would've been better.

"I fell asleep, probably due to lack of oxygen, and when I woke up, Elise was gone. For a moment, I thought I had lost my daughter and husband on the same day, not yet knowing that my son was already dead. But then I realized I had a pillow and blanket that weren't there the night before, so I knew she must've gone to get help." Hans wondered if that was when Elise had gone to check on his parents and felt a twinge of guilt because she had been with them instead of Maria.

"While I waited for Elise to return, I emptied a big storage box and carried it outside to collect Max's remains. When I reached the body, I saw that some of him was stuck to the asphalt, and the rest had shrunk and become mummified. It turned out the box I'd brought was too big, and what was left of him would've fit inside a baby's cradle. I stared at the slop for several minutes but couldn't bring myself to try to scrape him off the asphalt. One of the reasons we don't go to that neighborhood anymore is that I'm afraid I'll see a shadow of him on the street." She took another drink of wine, longer this time. "None of what I've told you so far is the worst part. Do you want to know the worst part?"

"No, I don't think so."

She ignored him and continued. "We keep learning more about what German doctors were doing in those years. The horrible experiments, the forced sterilizations, the euthanasia. I don't believe that Max participated in those things, but there is no doubt he knew about them. Is that why he was so morose in those last few years? I think of the person he was in the 1920s and early 1930s, when we'd go out drinking and dancing, and then I think of the person he had become by the late thirties and forties. What was he involved in?

"He never explained to me why he was working so much or what was going through his head, and now all these terrible reports are coming out. It breaks my heart to think he knew what was going on and didn't do anything to stop it. Was I married to a bad man? More than anything else, this is what I can't get past.

"But it's all part of the larger picture, isn't it? I remember being angry in the first few years after the war, raging against what the Allies had done to Germany. Elise told me about the anarchy in the streets, the black market, the theft, assault, and murder. It was a complete disintegration of the world's most civilized country, and I was furious. But as I've learned more, it's clear that the collapse of Germany's civilization had happened years earlier, even before the war." She paused. "We should've done more when we still could."

"What could you have done?"

"More than I did, which was nothing. I didn't directly cause bad things to happen, and perhaps Max didn't either, but we were part of the scaffolding that supported the structure.

Maybe Dresden and Germany got what they deserved. Maybe I did too."

She drank down the last bit of her wine. "I've never talked to Elise about her father, and I'd appreciate it if you wouldn't either. She worshipped him, and it would kill her to think he was participating in or at least ignoring what the Nazis were doing." Hans nodded.

She got up slowly and shuffled to her room. Hans remained on the couch, feeling nauseous.

Several hours later, Elise returned with a strudel that Aunt Agnes had baked for them. Over dinner, she shared stories about her aunt and said she planned to visit her more often. As she said this, she winked at Hans, tacitly informing him that Agnes had agreed to their plan.

Hans smiled, but after hearing the story of Elise's father's death, he found that he looked at her differently. He was relieved to finally understand why she was so reluctant to talk about her experiences, but he couldn't get the image of Max's last moments out of his head. She probably couldn't either, and he decided it was indeed best if he didn't find out how his own parents had died. His new focus would be on visiting the West and determining his future, even though he still didn't know if Elise planned on being a part of it.

CHAPTER 25

As Hans sat down in Gerhard's office the next day, he saw the usual desk setup: one pen, one ashtray, one pack of cigarettes, one lighter, and three folders. Gerhard asked, "How was your week, Herr Becker?"

"Very nice, thank you."

"And work is going well?"

"Yes, I worked four days last week."

"And how was your visit with Herr Wessel on Saturday?"

Hans had assumed that Gerhard would know about Willi's visit. "It was nice."

"The Soviets held him with you, is that correct?"

"Yes, we were in the same camps for the last five years."

"And what war crimes did he commit?"

"To the best of my knowledge, he didn't commit any war crimes."

"That seems to be your response whenever I ask you questions like that. Because he moved to the West, I don't have a file on him, but I'm guessing you're wrong about his character." Hans didn't respond. "What did the two of you talk about?"

"We just reminisced about the old days."

"I recommend you not make a habit of spending time with war criminals from the West."

"I understand, and this won't be a regular occurrence. I

was hoping, though, to visit him once, and I'd like to understand how to get a visa."

Gerhard frowned, set down his papers, and crushed out his cigarette. "Why would you want to do that?"

"He's my friend, and we have a lot of history together."

"You don't have any reason to visit the West because of your occupation, so we can't let you go for that. Do you have any relatives in the West?"

"No."

"I see. People who have occupational purposes or relatives in the West are sometimes allowed to visit, but otherwise, we discourage it. The West has dangerous elements, and exposure to them isn't healthy. Plus, having a war criminal from the East visiting a war criminal in the West—that sounds like a bad idea."

Hans clenched his fists but remained silent.

Gerhard stared at him. "Are you sure you believe everything you've told me about the superiority of Socialism? Sometimes I get the feeling you're just telling me what you think I want to hear, and now you're asking me to visit the West. Some people visit the West and don't come back. You aren't thinking about doing something like that, are you?"

"No, I just want to visit my friend."

"You know it's a crime to even plan an unauthorized move to the West, don't you?"

"No, I didn't know that."

"We know you were a Fascist and a war criminal, yet I felt we'd made good progress in helping you see the error of your ways. But now I'm concerned that you've been lying the whole time. This is very troubling."

Hans realized he should've thought this through before bringing it up to Gerhard. He had gotten caught up in the excitement of the past two days and had come to the meeting unprepared.

"I'm afraid visiting the West is quite impossible for you, and we'll clearly need to redouble our efforts concerning your anti-Fascist education." Gerhard shook his head and began making notes. After a few seconds, he looked up from his papers and said, "So disappointing. I guess the apple doesn't fall far from the tree."

Hans flinched. The smirk on Gerhard's face compelled him to blurt out, "Are you implying something about my father?"

"Herr Becker, it's clear that the Nazi regime was evil, but your father wasn't just a bad Nazi, he was a bad German. He probably got what he deserved."

"And I hope that someday you get what you deserve. Just like *your* father."

Gerhard blanched at this, and Hans immediately realized he had gone too far. The two men stared at each other for a few seconds, but then Gerhard broke eye contact and looked down at his papers. For that brief moment, it occurred to Hans that perhaps Gerhard missed his father as much as Hans missed his.

Gerhard looked up again, smiled broadly, and said, "Oh, Hans. Always making poor decisions, just like your father. And your mother too, for that matter. She was such a simple woman yet made so many terrible choices." He shook his head. "I fear that you are a security risk to the state, and we must therefore increase our surveillance of you. I'm not going to arrest you today, although I'd be justified in doing so. You and I go way back, so I'll leave you out of prison for old times' sake. One more misstep, though, and you're done. And by the way, if we ever find you in Berlin, or on the way to Berlin, or discover that you've even said the word 'Berlin,' that will be the end of you. Don't even think about crossing to the West from there. We always know where you are." The smile had left his face.

CHAPTER 26

Hans wobbled out of the Stasi office and into the blazing midday sun, stopping on the sidewalk to regain his balance and composure. He took a deep breath and closed his eyes, his face tingling and stars dancing on the inside of his eyelids. He hadn't prepared for the meeting and now felt like a boxer who'd been knocked out. He'd realized early in the match that his foe had all the power, and at that point he should've just shielded himself to make it through the fight. Instead, he'd thrown a wild punch that landed but then opened him up for a vicious counterblow. As he stood on the sidewalk, he was only stunned, but he knew the pain would come later.

As the stars in his eyes flickered out and the ringing in his ears abated, he walked toward the river and sat on a chunk of broken masonry. He had ruined everything. Now he didn't need to worry about whether Elise would go with him to the West because he wasn't going anyway.

The sun glistened off the Elbe as his thoughts floated back to Stalingrad.

His squad had gone without water for days but were unable to reach the Volga because of Russian snipers. Thousands of civilians still lived in the ruins of the city, and Hans's sergeant recruited one of them, a boy, to help. It was difficult to guess the boy's age because he was so filthy and gaunt, but Hans estimated he was nine or ten. Despite the language barrier, his sergeant was able to communicate that he'd give the child a crust of bread if he'd go to the river and fill their canteens. The boy was clearly starving, and his family probably was too, so he accepted the deal.

He was too scrawny to support a shoulder strap or belt, so the Germans attached seven canteens to a length of rope for him to carry. Hans watched as the boy, canteens in hand, leaped over rubble, crawled through craters, and scaled walls, like a mouse running, jumping, and scampering over every obstacle in its path. Hans lost sight of him as he neared the river, but ten minutes later, the boy reappeared, not quite as nimble now that the canteens were full. When Hans's sergeant gave him the bread, he put it in his pocket, either saving it for later or keeping it for his family.

A neighboring squad witnessed the boy's success and offered him the same deal. Again he made it to the river and returned successfully, cheered on by the Germans. He smiled and pocketed another piece of bread. On his third trip, he was shot by a Russian sniper, the empty canteens clattering in the rubble and a dark splotch spreading over the thigh of his tattered pants. He glanced back to the German lines and then looked the other way toward the Russian positions, apparently uncertain which way to go. A sniper's bullet to his head eliminated the need to make a decision.

By that point in the war, Hans had seen tragedies and atrocities, horrors and evil, but this event bothered him more than any other. The Russians would prefer to kill a starving Russian boy than allow the Germans a sip of water. He remembered thinking that maybe Hitler was right—maybe the Russians were animals.

But later, after he'd had time to sift through his memories and make sense of them, or at least as much sense as was possible in war, he'd reconsidered his opinion. A month before the incident with the boy, Hans had been with his radio van a kilometer behind the lines. An Einsatzgruppen unit was searching for Jews that day, and Hans had watched as they broke down the door to a half-ruined house. He heard screaming, and then a soldier emerged carrying a baby, with a Russian woman crying and clinging to the soldier's arm. A Russian man followed them, prodded by a German soldier with a gun to his back. When the woman tried to grab her baby, a soldier smashed her in the face with the butt of his rifle, knocking her down. The Russian man scrambled forward to protect her and was shot by the Germans. Then they shot the mother and the baby.

Hans had witnessed atrocities like that before and had become somewhat numb to them. In the years since, though, a thought had struck him. At the time, the Battle of Stalingrad was nearing its climax, and the outcome was still very much in doubt. The most important battle of the war, the battle that would decide Germany's fate, was raging, and Germany had prioritized using valuable troops, perfectly capable soldiers, to go door to door looking for Jews. So who were the real animals?

He spent the afternoon staring at the river, and by the time he emerged from his stupor, the sun had begun to set behind the blackened spire of the Hofkirche. On his walk to the apartment, he thought back to his first meeting with Gerhard. Afterward, he had watched as people passed by, seemingly oblivious to the devastation all around them. He'd wondered how they could go about their lives like that, but now he understood, especially after his talk with Elise's mother.

Thinking about the pile of rubble might make a person think about why the city was bombed, and thinking about why the city was bombed might make a person think about the war, and thinking about the war might make a person think about the horrors of the Nazis. Who could do that and keep getting up every day? Maria thought about the rubble and the bombing and the war and the Nazis all the time, and look where it had gotten her. Perhaps people weren't crazy to ignore the piles of rubble; perhaps ignoring the piles of rubble was the only way to stay sane.

CHAPTER 27

Months rolled by, routines were established, and somewhere along the way, Elise realized, Hans had transitioned from being a houseguest to a roommate. She sometimes felt that she and Hans were like an old married couple, affectionate toward each other but without the passion of their youth. Even though they had skipped all the steps between being passionate teenagers and an old couple, Elise had decided that's where their relationship had to stay. Nobody, not even Hans, was allowed past her last few walls.

One brisk September Sunday evening, Hans and Elise went for a walk to discuss Willi's letters she had picked up earlier that day. She had read them while still at her aunt's, and Hans read them when she got home.

"Willi is certainly persistent about having you move to the West, isn't he?"

"Well, I think he wants both of us to move. It's funny that he now writes to 'Hans and Elise' rather than just 'Hans.'"

"I suppose we started it by signing both our names in our letters to him."

A man walked toward them, and they stopped talking. Elise hadn't noticed any increased surveillance since Hans's disastrous meeting with Gerhard, but she knew they had to remain vigilant. Perhaps the Stasi had found new ways to monitor them, or maybe Gerhard's words had been an idle threat.

The man walked past them, and Elise continued speaking. "Willi makes a compelling case."

"Yes, but I don't see how it can happen. I've been trying to be nice and deferential to Gerhard, but he has all the power and hasn't changed his position at all."

"I know, but thousands of people have already fled to the West, and more are leaving every day. I hear stories about people going from East Berlin to West Berlin, and it seems so easy."

"Gerhard has made it clear that I can't go to Berlin."

"Yes, but if you really wanted to go to the West, it seems like you could find a way."

"What's hard is that I know they're watching me, but I don't know how. If they caught me trying to leave, I'd be in real trouble."

"Do you think about it, though?" Elise asked.

"Think about what?"

"Moving to the West and starting over."

Hans paused before speaking. "I try not to because I know it can't happen. Do you?"

"I don't know. Sometimes, I suppose."

"I thought you wanted to stay here."

"I did for a long time, but now I'm not sure. There are so many bad memories. Having you here has forced me to look at Dresden differently, and now it makes me sad."

"What about your mother?"

"I think she would move if we asked her. She leaves the apartment so rarely that she might not even notice a difference."

They walked on in silence, and after a while Hans asked, "When you think about it, what do you envision?"

Elise wasn't sure she wanted to answer the question but eventually said, "You could go to school to learn architecture, and I could go to school to learn to teach. Then we could both get jobs doing what we want to do, and we wouldn't have to look over our shoulders to see if anyone was following us." As she said this, she looked over her shoulder to see if anyone was following them.

"That's a nice picture."

"And you could get a dog. It makes me sad that you never got a chance to see Greta again after you left. You'd be a great dog owner." Elise purposely didn't mention marriage or kids because that wasn't part of what she imagined. At least not usually.

"In prison, we always had something to look forward to—getting out," Hans said. "Almost every waking moment was consumed with that thought. Everything was going to be all right as soon as we got out. But now that I'm out, I don't know what I'm supposed to look forward to."

"Someone once told me that nothing is permanent and things are always changing," Elise said with a little smile. "So maybe change is the thing you should look forward to."

CHAPTER 28

One chilly, rainy afternoon in mid-October while Elise was at work, Maria and Hans sat down to relax and listen to music in the apartment. They were in agreement that no great music had been composed in the twentieth century, so it was always easy for Hans to find records they both enjoyed. That day he had chosen "The Blue Danube" waltz by Strauss, and as he settled himself on the couch and began reading a book, he unconsciously swayed his head to the music.

Maria looked at him and smiled. "Do you know how to waltz, Hans?"

He lowered his book. "I'm afraid I don't know how to dance at all."

"Well, if you're going to be my daughter's boyfriend, you'll need to learn a few things."

Hans wasn't sure where this was going and certainly didn't consider himself Elise's boyfriend, but he said, "Okay."

She struggled up from her chair and said, "Move the furniture against the walls. This apartment is too small to be a proper ballroom."

Hans cleared as much space as possible. As he went to restart the record, Maria stopped him. "We don't need to hear the music yet. First, you need to learn the steps. Come over here." Hans walked back and stood in front of her. "Waltzes are in three-four time, and the dance itself is simple. Watch my feet. On the first beat, my right foot goes backward, so what should you do?"

Hans had no idea what she was talking about. "My right foot goes backward too?"

"No, no, no. If my right foot goes backward, then your left foot goes forward so they're still next to each other. Let's try." She moved her right foot backward, and a half beat later, Hans moved his left foot forward. "All right, that was a bit late, but you get the idea. On the second beat, my left foot slides to the left." She continued demonstrating the six basic waltz steps.

Hans slowly caught on. His movements weren't graceful, and Maria's toes were going to be sore from being stepped on by Hans's big feet, but he eventually got to the point where he was doing something that bore a rough resemblance to a waltz.

She said, "Okay, let's try it with music."

Hans went to the record player and placed the needle at the beginning. As the record started, he quickly realized that dancing to the music was much more difficult than performing the steps in silence. Once again, though, he figured it out. He restarted the record multiple times, and by the last time, he was actually enjoying himself.

Maria said, "All right, you seem to have it. Now it's simply a matter of practice, so you get smoother. You don't want to be thinking about it; it should just come naturally." Hans assumed she'd have to rest now, but instead, she said, "Start the record over and watch."

While Hans walked to the record player, Maria took off her glasses and set them on the table. She also released her hair from its customary bun and let it fall past her shoulders. As the music was about to begin, she pretended that her dance partner was leading her to the floor. She turned and curtsied while holding out the sides of her housecoat.

Hans sat on the couch, and as the music played, Maria

glided around the apartment, her feet appearing to float above the floor. She had her arm around an imaginary partner, and for a moment, Hans could picture her in prewar Dresden with Dr. Engel, drinking martinis, laughing, and dancing. She seemed to see herself there too, and for the first time since he'd arrived, he saw a genuine smile on her face.

Elise got home from work near the end of the song, and as she opened the door, it bumped into a chair. She squeezed in and looked confused by the music, the improvised dance floor, and the smile on her mother's face. "What's going on in here?" she asked.

Maria continued to dance, and soon a tear rolled down Elise's cheek. Before long, she was crying in earnest. The record finished, and Maria stopped dancing. She had difficulty catching her breath but said, "I was teaching Hans here how to waltz. I think there's hope for him yet."

Elise wiped the tears from her cheeks.

"Oh, Hans," Maria said. "If you could've seen me back then!" Her breathing was labored, and she held her hand to her chest as she picked up her glasses and shuffled to her room.

Elise followed her without speaking to Hans.

CHAPTER 29

At dinner, Elise smiled as her mother shared stories about her prewar adventures, but she couldn't help mourning everything that had been lost. As she lay in bed that night, she wondered what Hans thought of the improvised dance recital. It had been difficult for her to watch because of her mother's missing partner, but it was probably even harder for him, having no parents at all. She didn't want to think about why he didn't have any parents, but as she fell asleep she drifted back to 1945 again . . .

As the roar of the planes intensified, Elise stumbled home and barged through the front door. She found her mother standing at the porcelain display case, cleaning soot from the glass with a feather duster. She seemed oblivious to the drone of the bombers even though it sounded like they were directly overhead.

Elise yelled, "They're coming again!" Her mother, goggles hanging around her neck, furrowed her brow and remained motionless but didn't resist when Elise herded her down the stairs. The humming of the planes vibrated the air and their noise was soon joined by the whistling of falling bombs. Humming and whistling—two pleasant sounds when heard in a very different context.

They once again huddled in their sanctuary in the corner

of the basement, tucked behind stacks of boxes. The bombs didn't land very close this time, and the droning soon faded. Not knowing if there would be another raid, they stayed in the basement the rest of the day and slept there that night.

The morning sunlight through the basement windows the next day was brighter than the day before, and Elise didn't see evidence of additional fires in the city. Perhaps there was nothing left to burn. They ventured up from the basement, and she continued to the second floor to perform another damage assessment, more thorough this time now that there was more light. When she came back downstairs, she saw her mother sitting at the piano. The nearby window had been blasted inward, causing glass shards and wood splinters to gouge the piano and allowing soot to enter and coat everything in the room.

Elise watched as her mother raised the keyboard cover, revealing clean, undamaged keys. She began to play "Für Elise," which Elise had often requested when she was a little girl. The first eight notes of the tune were sweet and lovely and perfect, but the ninth note, an A, was a dull thud. No resonance, no timbre, just a thud. She started again, but on the ninth note, another thud. "Something's wrong with the piano," she said.

It was obvious to Elise what was wrong with the piano, and she became concerned that the smoke had damaged her mother's eyes. As her mother was about to start the tune a third time, she was overcome by a violent coughing fit, and Elise added respiratory problems to her concerns about her mother's health. When the coughing stopped, Elise said, "I need to check on the Beckers. Will you be okay here by yourself?" Her mother nodded and Elise left the house.

The prior afternoon's raid hadn't further damaged the neighborhood, and cleanup efforts were underway. Teams searched for humans, alive and dead, and the latter were hoisted into the backs of trucks. Refugees carried their possessions and children, or pushed them in carts, heading to the undamaged suburbs or rural villages. The Beckers were fortunate that their hometown wasn't too far away, and Elise recalled Hans's idyllic descriptions of their village. Not such a bad place to be right now. She knew transportation would be difficult for a while and hoped her mother wouldn't mind if the Beckers stayed with them for a few days.

Fifty meters from the park, she stepped on a large piece of metal that was partially buried in ash. She looked down and saw it was part of the archway that had marked the entrance to the park the day before. She frowned and wondered how it had gotten there but kept walking. When she arrived at the entrance, she stopped. Something was wrong. For a moment, she wondered if her disorientation was due to the fact that it was brighter than the day before and things always looked different in the daylight. No, it was more than that. She didn't recall there being so many splintered trees and so much wreckage and debris. But then she realized the biggest change—the aid tent was gone, and in its place was a crater.

To the left of the crater, a two-meter-high gray mass rested atop a series of pallets. As she walked toward it, Elise could see items jutting out, but it wasn't until she was right next to the mass that she could identify the items—a lower leg bent at a grotesque angle, a long blond ponytail dangling toward the ground, a child's arm that hadn't been adequately tucked into the heap. The corpses included men and women, boys and girls. Some were naked, some wore winter clothes, and others were in pajamas. Elise stared, and for a moment she contemplated the random decisions, coincidences, and misfortunes that resulted in all these Dresdeners being so intimately linked for their tragic, horrific, undignified end.

She stopped staring, looked past the mass, and saw three

parallel rows of face-up corpses that had been laid out on the ground. People were drifting up and down the rows, searching for loved ones. They looked like customers at a butcher shop, perusing the display case for the best cut of meat. They lingered at each body, perhaps to identify, perhaps out of morbid curiosity, or maybe just to contemplate the fragility of the human form.

A truck stopped near the rows, and two Hitler Youth boys climbed into the back. They heaved additional corpses to the ground, where other boys picked them up and added them to the rows. The process of collecting, organizing, identifying, and eliminating the dead seemed very efficient, and Elise realized that Germany had probably mastered it over the preceding five years. She also realized this was no longer an aid station—it was a morgue.

She approached a young officer who was holding a clipboard and asked, "What happened to the aid station that was here yesterday?"

"It got hit by some stray bombs. We decided to use this site to burn bodies since there were already quite a few here, and now we're trying to identify as many as possible before we cremate them. Do you know anyone here?" Before she could answer, Elise heard a bark from halfway down one of the rows, and when she looked to the sound, she saw Greta. Elise walked toward her but already knew what she would find. And already knew the answer to the officer's question.

Greta had her head down but looked up at Elise with pathetic eyes. She managed a single tail wag when Elise scratched behind her ears but then lowered her eyes and whimpered. Greta was next to Olga, and Olga was next to August. Compared to many of the corpses, the Beckers looked undamaged. They could've just been sleeping.

She stared at their bodies and was startled when the officer asked, "Do you know them?"

"Yes. It's August and Olga Becker." The officer wrote down the names. "Do you know what happened to them?"

"We pulled them from that pile of rubble," he said, pointing to a collapsed building. "The way we found the bodies, it looked like the man was trying to protect the woman, and the woman was trying to protect the dog. They didn't get crushed when the building collapsed but were buried alive, and I guess they eventually ran out of oxygen. The dog either didn't need as much or else she found an air pocket. She hasn't left the lady's side."

A soldier holding a flamethrower approached the gray mass. The other boys and men moved away as the soldier pointed the nozzle and pulled the trigger, releasing a fountain of fire. After five seconds, he stopped, moved to the other side of the mass, and sprayed it for another five seconds. The smell of gasoline and roasting flesh filled the air.

The officer next to Elise whistled, and two Hitler Youth boys dutifully trotted over to perform their grim task. One picked up August by the wrists, the other by the ankles, and they carried him to the pyre. They swung him back and forth, saying, *"Eins, zwei, drei,"* and then tossed him into the fire. Elise watched as he burned, hair and clothes first and then flesh.

The boys came back for Olga, but as they approached her, Greta stood up, bared her teeth, and growled. When the first boy reached down to grab Olga's ankles, Greta bit his hand. Elise saw the officer draw his pistol, but then closed her eyes tightly before she heard the shot and the yelp. After disposing of Olga, one of the boys came back for Greta. Her fur sizzled on the fire.

Elise felt strangely removed from the entire incident and began numbly walking back to her neighborhood. Rather than going home, though, she went to the shelter in the Beckers' backyard. She opened the hatch, climbed down, and sat on a cot, the same one she and Hans had shared the night before he left. On the pillow was the framed picture of Hans in his uniform that his mother had displayed on the fireplace mantel. Elise wondered if she'd brought it to the shelter during every air-raid warning. It had been more than two years since they'd last heard from him, but his mother was sure he was still alive.

Everything was in order. "Beckers Bunker" was still painted on the wall. Greta's water and food bowls were full—she had probably been too anxious to eat. The buckets of sand and jugs of water were in place, and the shelves were laden with canned food. The light bulb was on, indicating that electricity had been restored to the neighborhood. She caught a whiff of kerosene, but for the first time since the bombing, she was able to take a deep breath without coughing. The shelter appeared to be the only thing in the city that wasn't coated with ash, and it might very well have been the safest place in Dresden.

Elise buried her head in her hands and began to cry as she realized what she had done.

CHAPTER 30

The next morning, Hans awoke and heard Elise sobbing, so he walked down the hall and peeked into the bedroom. She was sitting on the side of her bed facing her mother, who was lying perfectly still on her back. Maria's face was drawn and white and Hans immediately knew that she was dead.

He walked in, bent down, and put his arm around Elise. She patted the bed next to her and he sat down. "The truth is," Elise said, "she died in 1945 and has just been going through the motions ever since. She's with my father now. This is better." She looked at him. "Can we sit here a while?"

They stayed in that position for an hour, Elise with her head down, sobbing quietly, and Hans with his arm around her. The ticking of the alarm clock on the nightstand seemed unnaturally loud to Hans, and for some reason, he thought back to the ticking of the grandfather clock at the Engels' house on the night he first met them.

This was the first time he had been in the bedroom, and as he looked around, he noticed a porcelain figurine on the windowsill. He recognized it as the ballerina that Maria had described as looking like Elise on that first night. It was now chipped, and the lace dress was mostly broken off, but the yellow hair and green eyes told him it was the same one.

Eventually, Elise raised her head and wiped away her tears. "She never talked about it," she said, "but I think she'd want to be cremated, given everything else that's happened." Hans nodded. She paused and turned to face him. "There's something you should know. This might not be the right time to tell you, but for some reason, I feel compelled to do so."

Hans assumed she was going to describe the night of the bombing and said, "Your mom told me about how your dad died. I can't imagine how horrible that must have been for both of you." He squeezed her, but she didn't respond.

"That's not what I was going to tell you. This will be difficult for you to hear, but I think it's important that you know." She took a deep breath, looked back at her mom, and began. "Our house was damaged in the bombing, but we could still live in it. We probably should've moved to a refugee facility, but we loved that house so much and couldn't bear to leave it. Shortly after the war ended, we left and never went back."

"Your mom said it was difficult to look at the street because of what happened to your dad."

"That's not the only reason we wanted to forget the house. It's not even the main reason."

Hans was confused. What could be worse than watching your husband or father melt into the asphalt? He tightened his arm around Elise, thinking about how odd it was to be having a conversation in front of her mother's corpse.

"For the last few months of the war, we prayed that the Americans would get here before the Russians, but they stopped eighty kilometers away. So we knew our fate would be in the hands of the Russians, and every day we could hear artillery explosions from the east getting closer.

"But then, at the very end, it got eerily quiet and almost calm. We were accustomed to the government controlling every aspect of our lives, and suddenly, there was nothing. No police, no radio, no newspaper. The German soldiers took off their uniforms and melted away, and there were no more bombs or planes or tanks. Trams were abandoned in the middle of the street as if frozen in time. People rarely left their houses or talked to neighbors, and when they did they spoke softly, even though we didn't have to worry about the Gestapo anymore. We'd still hear the occasional explosion or see a Russian plane flying overhead, but other than that it was quiet.

"The war was over for the soldiers, but we knew it wasn't over for us. The Russians arrived the same day the war ended, and there wasn't even a battle other than a few small gunfights. Mother and I took food and water and went to our hiding place in the back of the basement, behind some boxes and next to the dollhouse I played with when I was a kid. We could see the boots of the Russians through the windows and watched as the first wave marched through town without stopping." She took a deep breath. "But then a second wave arrived."

Hans felt a knot developing in his stomach.

"That group was undisciplined and rowdy. Throughout that day and night, they partied in the streets, drinking and singing and sometimes firing their guns. The next morning they broke down the front door of our house and came in. We could hear them opening and closing cabinets. I assumed they were looking for alcohol. At one point, we heard a crash, which we found out later was the porcelain display case being tipped over. They all seemed to think it was hilarious.

"They found my dad's wine and liquor collection and celebrated in our house for most of the day. The only time things settled down was when a soldier played part of a Tchaikovsky concerto on our piano. He was quite good, and for a while, it was quiet except for those muffled notes. Then one of the other soldiers shot up the piano, and the party started again.

"That afternoon, a soldier came down to the basement. He opened a bunch of boxes but seemed frustrated to find only old clothes and toys, so he went back upstairs, and we breathed a sigh of relief. I was hiding next to the dollhouse, and for the rest of that day, I studied it to keep my mind off what was happening. It was so detailed—the windows had curtains, the beds had blankets, and the dining room table sat under a chandelier and was set with tiny plates and silverware.

"Even though the basement was pretty dark, I could see the perfect miniature world the dollhouse depicted—everything beautiful, everything in its place, and a big, happy family. When I was little, I'd imagined that would be my life someday, but here I was in a filthy, dark basement, hiding behind a representation of a world I knew I'd never live in." She stopped speaking, and Hans hoped that was the end of the story and that she was just describing her disappointment in the way her life had turned out. But he knew there was more.

Her hands were in her lap, and he could see her beginning to fidget. "That night, two soldiers came down with flashlights and bottles of wine. At first, they just looked in the same boxes that had already been opened, but they didn't stop there. I couldn't see my mom in the darkness, but I heard her start to make little noises in her throat, and I realized she needed to cough. I reached out and squeezed her hands to encourage her to hold it in, but I knew it was just a matter of time. After several minutes, she gave us away. As soon as the Russians heard her, they started knocking boxes out of the way, and then their flashlights were in our faces. One of them kicked the dollhouse, shattering my fantasy world, before grabbing me."

Hans removed his arm from her shoulder, not because he didn't want to be supportive, but because he didn't want her to notice his trembling.

"It went on for several days, with me tied up in the basement. The soldiers were drunk and filthy, and they reeked. I've never been able to forget that smell." Elise was now holding her arms so that each hand was rubbing the scars on the opposite wrist. It was then that he realized the scars weren't from a fire—they were from a rope.

"This happened to many of the women and girls here, and

in a way, we were fortunate because they didn't do anything to Mother. I'm not sure why, because they generally had no qualms about taking older women, or young girls either. It happened to Ruth's eighty-year-old grandmother, and to Ruth. She couldn't deal with it, and that's why she killed herself."

"Did your mother know what happened to you?"

"Yes, they made her watch." She paused. "I suppose it was good that my dad didn't live to see it because he probably would've tried to stop them and they would've killed him. He'd be dead either way, but at least he didn't have that as his last memory." Hans was becoming lightheaded, and his heart felt like it was going to explode.

"Unfortunately, that's not the end of the story, because I got pregnant. Most girls in my situation ended their pregnancies, but I decided not to. I eventually gave birth to a boy and named him Max, but he was two months early and very unhealthy. We were all sick and starving, and it was a terrible winter. He died in less than a week." Hans felt like a veil had descended over his brain, and even though Elise was speaking slowly, the information was coming in too quickly for him to process.

"After all that, I never dated, partly because there weren't many men around, but mostly because I wasn't interested. Most girls seemed to get past what happened to them or at least pretended to, but I never could. Maybe my life was too perfect before everything happened, so my fall was steeper."

Hans looked at the porcelain ballerina and recalled what Maria had said about its creation. The lace was very delicate at the beginning of the process, but then intense fire hardened it. Maybe Maria saved it because it reminded her of Elise even more after everything she had been through. Of course, even though it was hardened, it wasn't unbreakable. Or unbroken.

Elise took a deep breath, shook her head and said, "I need

to deal with her body. Why don't you go for a walk." It wasn't a request, it was a command.

Hans grabbed his coat and walked down the stairs and out the door, stopping on the sidewalk. The chilly October air was bracing. He stood up straight, took a deep breath, and then vomited in the gutter.

CHAPTER 31

Elise made the requisite call and the authorities arrived quickly and performed their tasks with typical German efficiency. After they left with her mother, she sat on the couch and alternated between looking out the window and glancing at her mother's empty chair. She'd known this day would come and assumed she'd feel heartbroken and grief stricken. Instead, she mostly just felt hollow. She had never been separated from her mother for more than a few days, and now she'd never see her again. The apartment already seemed eerily quiet, and she knew it would take years, or maybe forever, to get used to not having her around.

But she also felt something beyond the hollowness. She eventually identified this feeling as relief. She hated herself for thinking in those terms, but she couldn't deny that a tremendous burden had been lifted from her shoulders. Eleven years earlier, the bombing and its aftermath had forced an abrupt and complete reversal in her relationship with her mother. From that point on, her mother no longer took care of her; she took care of her mother. Elise had always enjoyed her company, and the responsibility was never onerous. But she had also known that as long as her mother was alive, neither of them would be able to escape the events of 1945.

She gradually became aware of a third emotion and realized that it related to Hans. She had never talked to anyone—not even her mother—about the Russians, the pregnancy, or her son's death. Those events were safeguarded by so many walls that it was almost as if they'd happened to a different person.

She therefore had no idea what had compelled her to open up to Hans. While she was speaking, it had felt like she'd become disembodied and was watching herself talk rather than doing the actual talking. Some details, like the soldier playing Tchaikovsky, were things she had forgotten about, but once she started speaking, the memories had poured out. She had finally knocked down the walls she had constructed so carefully over the years. It occurred to her now that they hadn't just kept people out but had also prevented her from moving forward. One wall still stood, of course, but she didn't think telling Hans about the circumstances of his parents' deaths would do either of them any good.

A little after noon, her thoughts were interrupted by the sound of a key in the door. She turned and saw Hans at the threshold. He hesitated, apparently trying to assess the situation, then walked in and sat on the couch. He put his arm around her, and she leaned against him and rested her head on his chest. They stayed in that position for several hours.

As the shadows began to form in the late afternoon, Elise said without looking up, "I don't know why I told you all that, especially in that moment. I'm sorry if it upset you."

"I'm glad you told me."

They remained there for another half hour, and then Elise sat up, looked at Hans, and whispered, "I want to leave Dresden. Both of us. As soon as possible."

"We can't."

She frowned at him for a few seconds and then said, "Let's go outside."

When they reached the sidewalk, Elise faced him, and said, "I've been thinking about something for a few weeks, and there's not a nice way to say it, so I apologize in advance.

I realized that you've never really made a decision. Your parents and teachers told you what to do, then the army told you what to do, and then the Russians told you what to do. You're thirty-three years old, and you've never made a major decision in your life. And now Gerhard is telling you what to do, and you don't know how to disobey."

The words came out more harshly than she intended, and she studied Hans to discern his reaction. He broke eye contact and looked past her, perhaps searching unsuccessfully for a rebuttal. She continued, "I'm sorry if that sounds heartless, but I don't think you know what to do without instructions. You're mad at Dresden for being unable to decide what to do with the destroyed buildings and instead just leaving them as piles of rubble, but isn't that what you're doing? Not making an effort to make things better?"

Eventually, he said, "Perhaps you're right."

That night, they wrote a letter to Willi to ask if he knew of other places to cross the border besides Berlin.

CHAPTER 32

Maria's death, Elise's secrets, and the hasty and somewhat reckless decision to escape to the West were disconcerting for Hans. Over the following weeks, he monitored Elise's emotional state, worried that her desire to move was simply a fleeting impulse. He occasionally observed her staring wistfully at her mother's empty chair, but in general she seemed to recover more quickly than he had expected. And her determination to leave Dresden only intensified.

She also became more open toward Hans. It was as if she had a limited amount of energy to share with the world, and now that her mother was gone, she had more to give to him. They talked about their lost years and all the other topics they had avoided up to that point. As they ate dinner in a café one evening, she asked, "Do you feel that you've finally adjusted to being home?"

"Mostly, but sometimes it still seems like a different world. For example, when we were growing up, we saw or heard Hitler, Himmler, Goebbels, and Göring literally every day, and now they're all gone. Doesn't it almost seem like they were cartoon villains and weren't even real? When I see photographs from those years, I have to remind myself that it all really happened."

"It certainly would've been better for all of us if they hadn't been real."

"Agreed, but we all followed them, didn't we? When I was in the Hitler Youth, I remember thinking that the other boys were just pretending to be violent monsters, but once I was in the army, I found out I was wrong. Back then, I thought most people were basically good, but now I'm not even sure about that. There's a continuum, I think, that runs from naive to optimistic to realistic to cynical to bitter. The 1941 Hans was definitely naive. When I think about that guy, I hate him, but I also sort of miss him."

"Why do you hate that guy? I thought he was great."

"He was so stupid. If there was a category before 'naive,' he would've been in it."

"Where are you on the continuum now?"

"I've bounced around quite a bit in the past fourteen years. After about a week in the army, I jumped from naive to realistic, skipping right past optimistic. Most of the time in captivity, I was cynical, but dreams of coming home kept me from becoming bitter. I'll admit that in my first few weeks here, I slipped into bitterness, but now I'm moving back in the other direction. I think I'm probably realistic again, and trying to get to optimistic."

"I hope I can help you get there." Elise smiled and reached across the table to squeeze his hand. "It's strange to be in our thirties, isn't it? It's like our twenties didn't happen—we skipped that decade. My mom used to talk about how much fun she had in her twenties, when life was full of possibilities. For me, my twenties were just a waste of time."

"They say that man is the only animal that knows it's going to die, so we have a built-in mechanism that makes us hate wasting time."

"I never thought about that, but I guess it makes sense."

"Plus, doesn't it seem like life moves faster as we get older? When I was a kid, a year seemed to last forever. But even in the prison camps, the years passed more quickly as I got older."

"Maybe it's because when you're ten, a year is ten percent of your life, but now it's only three percent?"

"Could be. It's sort of like a record player. The needle starts on the outside, and it seems like it takes forever to make it around one time, but then as the record plays, the needle moves inward, and the circle gets smaller. Everything gets compressed. It seems like it takes less time, but in reality, it's going at thirty-three revolutions per minute the whole way."

Elise nodded. "But then you get to the end of the record, and it's just a repetitive scratchy noise, even though the record is still spinning."

"Yes, that's what we should try to avoid." Hans paused and then said, "As part of my attempt to be more optimistic, I've decided to focus on looking forward rather than backward since there's nothing back there but sadness. I've also decided that there's no point in trying to find out what happened to my parents. It doesn't matter—they're gone now."

Elise looked away, and her eyes filled with tears. After a few seconds, she took a deep breath, looked at him, and said, "I think that's the right decision. I agree with you about not looking back, and I'll admit I've been guilty of it too. It was strange what happened here after the war. Some people our age seemed thrilled just to be alive, and rather than being depressed, they celebrated. Dancing all night, laughing, drinking when they could find something, listening to jazz music. And I'm not talking about a few years after—I'm talking about a few weeks after. They were all living for the moment as if nothing had happened, but I couldn't do that. I couldn't stop looking backward.

"And then once things stabilized, I got into a rut. I sometimes think it's like sledding down a hill, like we used to do at Waldschlösschen. The first time you go down, the sled can go in any direction. The second time, you can still go in several directions, but there's a good chance you'll end up in the same tracks as the first time. By the hundredth time, you know the sled will go straight down the same tracks, and it becomes less thrilling and more boring. That's been my life for the past ten years."

That night, Elise told Hans he could sleep in her mother's bed. The beds remained separated, but they finally slept in the same room. Hans looked at this as another step toward not wasting time.

CHAPTER 33

Elise had rarely been out of Dresden since the war, so she enjoyed her train ride to Karl-Marx-Stadt, at least in those moments when she could forget that the trip's purpose was to plan a crime. Willi had written that it was too complicated, and too risky, to explain what he wanted to say in a letter and suggested they meet in person while he was visiting his cousins in the GDR. Since Hans still didn't know how much, or in what ways, he was being surveilled, they had agreed that Elise would go.

She stepped off the train and immediately saw Willi, who was easily recognizable as a Westerner because the blue jeans he wore were rare in the East. They hugged, walked to his car, and drove to a café for lunch. Willi talked about his new job and new apartment, but they refrained from discussing the escape plan since they were in a public place. Toward the end of lunch, Elise said, "Tell me what it was like in prison. Hans doesn't share much."

Willi looked at her for a few seconds. "It's difficult to describe, which might be why he doesn't talk about it. Usually, even unhappy people can find joy in small things, but prisoners don't have any small things or simple pleasures. We had no possessions and no privacy. And I sometimes felt we were like dogs. Dogs have no say about what, when, or how much they eat, and it was the same with us.

"In the first few years, we talked about food all the time, but later on, things improved and we weren't as concerned about starving to death. At that point the conversations shifted to women. Most of the guys bragged about their girlfriends back home. Hans was always quiet in those groups, but if I got him in a one-on-one conversation, he'd talk about you for hours. With most guys, you could tell they were leaving out the bad stuff, maybe because they didn't want to share it or maybe because they didn't want to think about it. When Hans talked, though, it seemed like he didn't think there was any bad stuff. Whenever he told his stories, I was jealous because I didn't have anyone like you at home."

Elise blushed and looked down at her coffee cup, flattered but embarrassed.

Willi lowered his voice and said, "I'm glad you two are planning this, but I hope I haven't oversold it. It's not going to be perfect there." Elise nodded. "There's a German author our age named Borchert who fought in Russia, and he wrote something that really struck me. I liked it so much I memorized it. It goes, 'We are the generation without ties and without depth. Our depth is the abyss. We are the generation without happiness, without home and without farewell. Our sun is narrow, our love cruel and our youth is without youth. And we are the generation without limit, without restraint and without protection—thrown out of the playpen of childhood into a world made for us by those who now despise us because of it.'"

Elise stared at him for several seconds and then asked him to repeat it. When he finished, she said, "Our youth is without youth." She was quiet for a few more seconds and then said, "I think Hans and I both gave up on things being perfect a long time ago, and we'd be more than happy to just have things be better."

After lunch, they got back in his car so they could talk in private. Willi said, "Are you sure you can't go to Berlin? It's the easiest way to cross."

"The Stasi said he'll be arrested on sight if he goes there."

"If you can't get a visa and can't go through Berlin, that just leaves the border. There are places to cross, but it's dangerous. You understand that, right?" Elise nodded. "Okay. I've been able to ask some questions back home about the best way to do this."

Willi went on to describe what he had learned. Five kilometers before they reached the border, they'd encounter a prohibited zone. People lived and worked in this zone, but it was illegal to enter without a special permit. If they made it through the prohibited zone and reached the border, they'd find a ten-meter-wide control strip that was patrolled by Soviet and East German soldiers. Here, the trees had been cut down, and the strip was plowed and raked so the guards could see the footprints of anyone who tried to cross. Whenever footprints were found, that border sector would be put on alert until the source was discovered.

The government had spent the last four years fortifying the border with barbed wire, watchtowers, and guard dogs, making large stretches of it nearly impenetrable. Other sectors, though, hadn't yet been secured, especially in remote areas with rough terrain. With input from refugees he knew in the West, Willi had identified one of these areas at the southern end of the border, near the town of Hof. This location had the added advantage of being the closest border area to Dresden and also to Nuremberg, where Willi lived.

"Do you have a car?" Willi asked.

"My aunt has one that I can probably borrow."

"Well, this won't be borrowing because she's not going to get it back."

"That'll be fine. It's an old car from before the war, and she doesn't drive anymore."

Willi nodded, withdrew a piece of paper from his jacket pocket, and unfolded it. It contained handwritten lines and images but no words. "I didn't put any names on this map in case I got searched or in case you get searched. You'll need to memorize the names of the places I tell you today and then associate them with the markings on the map."

Elise nodded.

"This area is heavily wooded and hilly. This main road here," Willi said as he pointed to a line on the map, "runs parallel to the border and lies just outside the prohibited zone, so you're allowed to drive on it. Several smaller roads branch off the main road and lead to the border, but they're in the prohibited zone and would require a permit to drive on. If you look right here, though, there's an old farm road that's not used anymore. It goes about three kilometers into the forest, where you'll encounter a barricade of logs and rocks. From that point to the border, they tore up the road to make it impassable, so you'll need to leave the car at the barricade and walk the remaining two kilometers."

"Have you seen this road?"

"Yes, I drove on it a few weeks ago. It's not in great shape, but it'll work for your purposes. The forest is thick, so you'll get swallowed up by it after about fifty meters, and nobody will know you're back there. Once you start walking, make sure you stay on the road even though it's torn up, and make sure you do this in the daytime. You don't want to get lost in the woods, especially in the winter. You'll know you're approaching the control strip when you see that the trees are cut down. When you get to the clearing, there will be a gate immediately in front of you. It's a relic from the time before they tore up the road. Most of this area has barbed wire, but they left the gate where the road used to be. All you need to do is duck under it."

"Won't there be a guard at the gate?"

"The nearest guard station I saw is about three kilometers away, so probably not."

Elise nodded nervously. "So if we're able to cross, we'll be in the West in the middle of winter without a car."

"That's where I come in. The road that's torn up on the east side of the border still exists on the west side, so after you cross, you just need to walk on the road, and I'll meet you in my car. I can't drive all the way to the border, but I can get to within about a hundred meters. I drove to that spot last week and didn't have any problems. That's also how I know there isn't a guard, or at least there wasn't last week." Willi returned to the map and told her the names of every road, village, and landmark. He made her repeat the names multiple times to ensure she had them memorized.

"Once you've decided when you'll do this, send me a letter, but instead of dating it with the current date, write the date you plan on leaving. I'll be waiting for you in my car on the west side. You should know that the border keeps getting more secure, and they build new watchtowers and fences every day. Everything on that map is accurate as of a few weeks ago, but it could look completely different in a couple of months. For all I know, it could look different already. Plus, I think the Eastern governments are all on edge with everything happening in Hungary."

Elise furrowed her brow and said, "Hungary?"

"You people really are cut off from the news. There was an uprising in Hungary that started about a month ago, but Soviet tanks came in and crushed it."

"We didn't hear about Hungary, but we've seen that story play out before."

"Yes, I know. Anyway, my point is that if you're going to do this, the sooner the better. But please be careful."

"Yes, we will."

He started the car, put it in gear, and headed back to the railway station.

CHAPTER 34

While Elise was gone, Hans paced tiny circles in the cramped apartment. He wondered whether she'd return excited about escaping to the West or discouraged by the realization that it was too dangerous. She had left that morning energized and enthusiastic, and Hans hoped Willi wouldn't say anything to dull her newfound vitality. But at the same time, a small part of him wanted her to come back and tell him it wasn't going to work.

Tired of pacing, he sat on the couch and looked out the window. His lingering doubt wasn't about the escape itself—he had already beaten the odds many times and was confident they could make it. His concern was about living in the West. He had been in Dresden, a city he knew thoroughly, for nearly a year and was just now becoming reacclimated to it. Would he be able to succeed in a place he'd never even seen, much less lived in? He was more frightened of that than of crossing the border.

When the door opened two hours later, Elise entered with a smile and sat on the couch next to him. As she whispered Willi's plan and showed him the map, her enthusiasm became contagious, and by the time she finished, all of Hans's doubts were extinguished. They wrote a letter to Willi, and even though it was December 10, they dated the letter December 17.

Elise would visit her aunt on December 16 and then drive

Agnes's car back, parking near the apartment. The next day, Hans would go to his Monday morning meeting with Gerhard, and Elise would wait in the car around the corner from the Stasi office. They'd leave immediately, allowing them to reach the border by midafternoon and giving them time to navigate the woods before dark. They thought that since Hans would have just met with Gerhard, that would be the least likely time for him to be followed. It would also give him several weeks before his next scheduled meeting, which with any luck would be when Gerhard discovered that Hans was gone. Hans smiled at the thought of Gerhard's face when he realized what had happened.

On their last Saturday evening in Dresden, Hans and Elise held hands as they walked to the Striezelmarkt, just like they had all those years before. Many of the apartments they passed had candles in their windows, but they were now mostly electric imitations, and the sense of anticipation and excitement he had felt sixteen years earlier was gone.

They entered the market and strolled arm in arm among the stalls. It wasn't nearly as crowded as Hans remembered, perhaps because many of the former festivalgoers had either moved to the West or were dead. They ordered a Christstollen and two hot chocolates and sat down on a bench. Elise said, "It's not the same, is it?"

"No, and I'm trying to figure out what's different."

"I guess having piles of rubble nearby spoils the spirit of the thing a bit."

"Yes, that's certainly part of it." He looked around for a moment. "The Striezelmarkt has definitely changed, but I suppose we've changed a lot too."

"We were just children the last time we were here."

"We were naive and stupid, but in hindsight, so was Dresden."

They sat for a few more minutes, and then Elise asked, "Are you going to miss it?"

"All this time, I believed we had to be in Dresden to be a couple. This is where everything happened before, so this is where it had to happen again. But now I'm convinced that it can happen anywhere except here."

Elise nodded. "It's still strange to think that we'll never see any of it again."

"Some people like to go back to their old neighborhoods and picture themselves when they were little in the house they grew up in, the places they used to play, or the school they attended. But for me, all those things are gone. I can't picture a young me in Dresden because it no longer exists." He paused, but Elise didn't respond. He leaned over and whispered, "I can't wait to get out of Dresden."

Elise stood, reached down, and pulled him up by his hands. They embraced. And kept embracing.

That night, they finally pushed the two beds together.

When Hans awoke on Sunday, he looked at Elise sleeping and smiled. He felt they were finally a complete couple. He wished they could spend the day together, but they had a crime to commit and a dictatorship to flee. After Elise awoke and they ate breakfast, she left to get Agnes's car.

Hans waited nervously in the apartment. He put his few possessions into the canvas bag he had been issued at the POW transition center and then kept checking the bag to make sure he hadn't forgotten anything.

Elise returned in the late afternoon, and before she could sit down, Hans walked to her and whispered, "Did everything work out?"

"Yes, everything's perfect," she whispered back. "I took a meandering route home to make sure I wasn't being followed. My driving skills are a bit rusty, and the car isn't in great shape since it's been sitting in a shed for a decade, but I was able to fill it with fuel and it seems to run okay."

"I'm sure it'll be fine. I put my stuff in that bag, so just add your things whenever you want."

"Okay, I have two items I definitely want to include." She walked back to the bedroom and returned with a smile. In her right hand was the broken porcelain ballerina, and in her left was the "Für Elise" music box from the 1940 Striezelmarkt.

Elise handed Hans the music box, but she stopped him as he started to wind it. "It doesn't work anymore. It still looks good, but somewhere along the line, it stopped playing music. Some internal parts must've been damaged or something."

Hans smiled as he looked at it for a moment, and then put it in the bag.

They went to bed that night excited that the following day they'd start their new lives.

CHAPTER 35

The next morning, Elise took the canvas bag and kissed Hans before leaving the apartment. Shortly afterward, Hans took one last look around and then left for the Stasi office. He promised himself he'd keep his composure no matter what Gerhard did to provoke him. With any luck, after today he'd never have to see that swine again.

He was still concerned that their plan had been detected and repeatedly glanced over his shoulder as he walked to the office. Everything seemed normal. At the office, the receptionist was her usual condescending self. Everything still seemed normal.

After a half hour, Gerhard called him back to his office, where they sat on opposite sides of the desk. The desk held one pen, one ashtray, one pack of cigarettes, one lighter, and three folders. Normal.

Gerhard lit a cigarette, leaned back, and asked, "So, how have things been going for you?"

"Fine."

Gerhard rested his cigarette in the ashtray and opened the top folder. "How much have you been working?"

"I average about four days a week. I wish it was more, but they don't always have projects for me."

Gerhard made some notes and said, "Very good. It sounds like things are going well, and this can be a short meeting."

Hans was relieved, but his heart was still racing.

Gerhard closed the folder and leaned back in his chair. "As long as you're here, though, I'd like to get your thoughts on some things. How do you like Dresden? Do you feel that you've adjusted well?"

"It's been a difficult transition, but I'm getting into regular routines now."

"Good. I know I've been harsh with you, but I hope you understand that returning POWs have caused all sorts of trouble here, so we need to keep an eye on them."

"I understand."

"Are you still interested in visiting the West?"

"No, no. That was a passing fancy. I was going through a tough time, but now I'm happy to be here."

"All right, no hard feelings. You can go." Gerhard took one more drag on his cigarette and then stubbed it out.

Hans grabbed his coat and stood up, but then Gerhard said, "Sorry, I forgot to go through the other files. Just a formality. Please sit for a minute."

Gerhard lit another cigarette, moved Hans's file to the side, and opened the second file. "How is Elise doing?"

"She was sad when her mother died, of course, but she seems okay now."

"Yes, we heard about her mother. What a shame. We've officially closed her file." He moved Elise's folder to the side and opened the third folder. Hans's heart skipped a beat—if they'd closed Maria's file, what was in the third folder?

Gerhard looked up and asked, "Do you know Agnes Wilhelm?"

The blood drained from Hans's face, and his hands started shaking. "Um, I think that's the name of Elise's aunt."

"Do you know why Elise has been visiting her so often?"

"She's old and in poor health. Elise doesn't have many relatives, and I think she just wants to keep her company."

"I see. And you, of course, know Willi Wessel. We've spoken about him before."

"Yes," he said weakly.

"Why would a POW friend of yours from the West be writing letters to Elise's aunt?"

Hans paused. How had they been found out? "I didn't know he'd been writing letters. Maybe they're related somehow?"

"Could be, could be." Gerhard flipped through the file for several minutes and then looked up and asked, "Do you know why Elise took Aunt Agnes's car yesterday?"

Hans tried to maintain eye contact but then looked away. "I . . . I think she borrowed it to go see some of her more distant relatives who live out in the country."

"Oh, wonderful, that sounds nice. Family is so important." Gerhard paused and then said, "The problem is that's not what dear old Aunt Agnes told us when we brought her in for questioning last night. It took a bit of prodding, but she informed us the two of you intend to move to the West. I assume you got the car so you could drive to Berlin and cross there. We've specifically talked about Berlin, Hans, and you know you're not allowed to go there, right?"

Hans didn't reply.

"I should tell you that this has all been rather embarrassing for me. I went out of my way to take your case, and I believed we had an understanding. You can imagine how this looks to my coworkers. You've been assuring me that you like it here, and then we find out you're planning to leave." Gerhard shook his head. "I have two pieces of news for you, and I'm afraid you're not going to like either of them. First, we're placing you and your coconspirator, Elise Engel, under arrest. Second, we in the Stasi like to think we know everything about everyone, but I'm afraid that's not entirely true. We didn't realize that poor old Aunt Agnes had a heart condition, and unfortunately, she died while being questioned. I'm sorry for your loss, and

I'll pass along my condolences to Elise when I see her, which should be very soon.

"We need to know your accomplices, and we need to know if there are other plots against the state that your war criminal friends are planning. Is there anything you'd like to share with me now to save us some time and trouble later?"

Hans feebly shook his head.

Gerhard stubbed out his cigarette. "Okay, if that's the way you want to do it, then let me outline your schedule for the balance of the day. I am now officially placing you under arrest. I'll transfer you from here to a receiving room, where we'll confirm all your personal details, take your photo, and confiscate your clothes and personal belongings. Standard administrative stuff. I know my organization has a bad reputation, but almost everything we do here is quite mundane. Lots of filling out forms and filing reports.

"We do, though, have several purpose-built and impressive interrogation rooms. We prefer not to use these methods, and I find it all distasteful. However, some of my colleagues seem to relish that aspect of the job, and they truly excel at it. I don't think you, and especially Elise, will particularly enjoy your interactions with them, but I'm afraid there's nothing to be done about it. Unless, of course, you want to divulge some information now."

Hans remained silent.

"In that case, I'd like to introduce you to my colleagues."

Gerhard stood up, and Hans did the same. Gerhard stepped out from behind his desk and started to lead Hans toward the door. As soon as he was within reach, Hans lunged and shoved him against the wall.

Hans placed both hands around Gerhard's neck, and the two men locked eyes, one man resolute and the other terrified. As Hans looked at Gerhard's round face, it began to morph into Gerhard's face from when they were teenagers, with the ridiculous Hitler mustache. That face changed further and became Hitler's face, then the face of Hans's Hitler Youth leader, then his sergeant in the Wehrmacht, and then his sadistic Russian guard. He felt so much hate beyond that—hate for the Russian soldiers doing whatever they wanted to Elise and for the bombardier playing god with Hans's parents—but Hans didn't know what any of those others looked like. Gerhard's face would have to be a stand-in for them.

Gerhard tried to loosen Hans's hands, but Hans's grip was too tight. He then tried to punch Hans, but his arms were too short. His eyes bulged, and his face purpled as his thrashing weakened and slowed, like a windup doll losing its power. Hans kept him pinned against the wall long after it was clear he was dead.

Hans released one hand and then the other, and Gerhard's body crumpled to the floor. He expected guards to burst in when they heard the thud, but the steel door must've muffled the sound. Presumably, that was its purpose. He kicked Gerhard in the ribs once for old times' sake. Things had certainly changed since they were teenagers; *I am no longer a sheep, and you are no longer alive*, Hans thought. For a brief moment, he was pleased that he had finally composed a retort to Gerhard's "If you're not a wolf, then you're a sheep" taunt, even if it had taken sixteen years.

He hovered over the open-eyed corpse for several minutes, and as the adrenaline drained out of his brain, the probable consequences of his actions settled in. He knew he'd almost certainly be apprehended as soon as he opened the door, but he decided to conceal Gerhard's body anyway. He dragged it to the other side of the desk, stuffed it underneath, and then squatted down and stared at it for a minute. Even though Hans knew his own immediate future likely included torture and death, he smiled as he looked into Gerhard's lifeless, terrified eyes.

He walked to the door, took a deep breath, and slowly opened it. He expected burly guards to be stationed there but didn't see anyone. He poked his head through the doorway and peered out, looking both ways, but the hallway was empty. The only noise was the sound of typewriters clicking away in unseen offices. He glanced back at the desk, dumbfounded that Gerhard had assumed he wouldn't need assistance. Hans savored the fact that Gerhard's arrogance had finally caught up to him. The Hans who Gerhard had pushed around in the early 1940s would've meekly surrendered, but people change. The dead man under the desk hadn't learned that lesson until it was too late.

He walked quickly down the hallway and peeked out the door to the lobby. The only person he saw was the receptionist through the sliding window, and she continued typing without looking up. Surely it couldn't be this easy.

He hastened out of the building and turned left, toward where he hoped Elise was parked.

CHAPTER 36

Even though the car wasn't running, Elise gripped the steering wheel tightly as she waited for Hans. She stared out the windshield in the direction from which she expected him but periodically glanced out the back and side windows to ensure nobody was monitoring her. The windows were grimy, and she wished she would've thought to clean them.

After twenty minutes, Hans turned the corner and walked toward the car. She'd thought he would look nervous and distressed, but he appeared calm and composed. And almost—cocky? He opened the passenger door with a loud creak, and as he sat down, dust puffed up from the cracked leather seats. Before he even closed the door, he said, "Drive fast but don't speed or be reckless. I'll explain after we get going."

She was desperate to know what had happened but followed his instructions. After starting the car, she depressed the clutch and shifted to first gear, but as she released the clutch, the car stalled. When she turned the key to restart it, the engine whirred but didn't catch, and out of the corner of her eye she saw Hans grimace. It eventually turned over, but when she tried to drive, the gears ground and it stalled again. A man turned the corner from where Hans had been and looked into the car as he walked by. She could see Hans spread his fingers like he always did when he was stressed.

She restarted the car and lurched out of the parking space,

her heart racing as she shifted to second gear and then third. They were finally moving, and she couldn't wait any longer. "Is everything all right?"

"Let's get out of the city, and then I'll explain."

Elise could tell things were definitely not all right. She drove through Dresden and the western suburbs and eventually reached the autobahn. Hans took a deep breath and said, "I'm going to tell you some disturbing things, but you need to keep driving. Can you do that?"

"Yes, please just tell me."

"Everything started fine, and I thought we were almost done, but then Gerhard asked me about Aunt Agnes."

Elise's eyes widened. "What?"

"He knew about Willi's letters, and he knew you took her car."

"Oh my God," said Elise.

"He also told me that during her interrogation, your aunt had a heart attack and died." She glanced at Hans and saw that his look of composure had changed to a look of concern. "Do you want me to drive? I can probably figure it out."

Elise's eyes moistened, but she didn't cry. "No, you don't have time to learn."

"There's more. Gerhard said he knew we were trying to escape and that he was going to arrest us. He implied we'd be tortured."

Elise had to remind herself to keep breathing. "How did you get out?"

Hans hesitated and then said, "I killed him."

Elise glanced at him, thinking he might be making a terrible joke. "You killed him?"

"Yes, I strangled him. His face turned blue, and his eyes bugged out. And then he died."

"You killed a Stasi agent and just walked out?"

"Nobody seemed to notice, but they will soon enough. Of

course, if he was as much of a jackass to his coworkers as he was to everyone else, maybe they won't care. But we probably shouldn't count on that."

"You killed a Stasi agent," she repeated.

"I hid the body under his desk, so anybody who looks in won't immediately see him. We'll have a head start, but I don't know if it'll be five minutes or five hours."

"I guess we should assume it'll be only five minutes. We can make it to the border in two hours, but the murder of a Stasi agent will raise some alarms." Elise's hands were throbbing, and she realized she was strangling the steering wheel. She took a deep breath and tried to relax. "Are you okay?"

"It's strange, but I feel fine. I know I should feel bad for killing another human being, but I don't. Not at all." He paused and then said, "I fought in the deadliest war in history, but I never killed anyone until today."

Elise drove silently for ten minutes, trying to absorb what Hans had told her. Then she asked, "If they've been intercepting letters, do they know where we're crossing?"

Hans didn't immediately answer. "We never put that in a letter. Gerhard seemed to think we'd try to get out through Berlin, so I guess that helps a little."

As they raced westward, it began to snow.

CHAPTER 37

The cracked and brittle windshield wipers were nearly useless, and the snow forced Elise to drive cautiously, so they neared the prohibited zone later than they had planned. Fortunately, Hans, who was keeping careful watch, hadn't yet seen any police, army units, or other indications that the security apparatus of the state was on alert.

Like Elise, Hans had memorized the names of the towns along the route, and he tracked their progress on Willi's map. Shortly after they'd exited the autobahn and joined the rural road, he identified the village that was their final landmark before the farm road. Elise slowed down as they strained to spot the turnoff in the snowy landscape.

Finally, Hans pointed and shouted, "There!"

Elise slammed on the brakes, and the car fishtailed to a stop, nearly sliding into the ditch along the side of the road. They scanned the area to ensure nobody was around, and then she backed up ten meters and turned onto the farm road.

As Elise drove slowly into the forest, Hans looked over his shoulder to make sure they weren't being followed and immediately recognized a problem. He turned to Elise and said, "We're leaving tracks in the snow." She nodded but continued to focus on her driving. "Willi was right that these woods are dense, but I'm sure someone will notice tire tracks on a road that isn't supposed to be used."

The combination of bald tires and the slick, poorly maintained road forced Elise to drive carefully, and it took twenty minutes to cover the three kilometers to the barricade. As they got out and started walking, Hans looked back at the tire tracks and footprints in the snow. It couldn't be more obvious where they were going or what they were doing. They tried to walk quickly, but the torn-up, snow-covered road was treacherous, and its curves and hills meant that the distance to the border was longer than the two kilometers they had anticipated.

In other circumstances, Hans thought, the scene would have been lovely. His view down the road was like a tunnel, with blue spruce trees on both sides and a snow-laden canopy overhead. The dense foliage darkened the tunnel, though, producing a sense of foreboding and making the trek more hazardous.

After an hour of hiking, Hans saw some light and an end to the tunnel two hundred meters ahead. He looked at Elise, and they both smiled and quickened their paces. As they neared the clearing, he saw the gate and nearly started running. When they were fifty meters away, though, a border guard walked into view and stopped in front of the gate.

They dove to the side of the road and huddled in the snow behind a tree. There was no indication that the guard had seen them, so after a minute, Hans peeked out from behind the tree. The guard was leaning against the gate, smoking a cigarette. Hans whispered, "It's darker in the woods than in the clearing, so I don't think he saw us."

"What should we do?"

"Maybe he's just on a patrol and will leave soon. Let's wait."

For the next fifteen minutes, Hans kept periodically peeking around the tree. The guard walked to the left and then to the right but always returned to lean against the gate. Hans looked at Elise shivering in the snow and regretted the unsuitability of her attire. So as not to raise suspicions when she left the apartment that morning, she had worn what she always wore—a dress and leather flats. The snow was ankle deep and had spilled into her shoes, and her coat wasn't nearly heavy enough for a winter hike in a Bavarian forest.

Elise whispered, "It doesn't seem like he's going to leave."

"I don't know what to do. We can't stay here all night—we'll freeze to death. And we can't go back because I'm sure they're searching for us by now. We could try to look for other crossing points, but Willi said most of this area is fenced."

"So, what does that leave us?"

"We need to get through here somehow, if for no other reason than this is where Willi is waiting for us. Let's get closer and see what we're up against. He won't see us if we stay in the woods." They crept cautiously through the snow and stopped in the forest twenty meters from the gate.

From that distance, Hans could see that the guard was a Soviet soldier wearing the brown uniform that Hans had become familiar with during his years in Russia. He had an AK-47 slung over his shoulder and periodically stamped his black boots, looking as cold and miserable as Hans felt. He was leaning against a red-and-white-striped boom gate that had blocked the road back when it was a road. As Willi had said, it would be easy to duck under it if they could get that far.

They decided to wait and see if he'd leave, but Hans knew time was their enemy. At three thirty, it was already getting dark, and he regretted that they had planned this adventure for one of the shortest days of the year; sunset would arrive shortly after four o'clock.

The blanket of snow in the thick forest muffled sound, leaving only the barking of dogs somewhere in the distance. Hans opened the canvas bag on the off chance that it contained something that might help them get out of this predicament, but all he saw were the music box, the porcelain ballerina, and some toiletries. Also, at some point Elise had added the photograph of her family that had been displayed at the apartment. Nothing in the bag would be of use to them here in the forest.

As he closed the bag and resumed staring at the guard, Hans suddenly realized that he had missed a precious opportunity hours earlier. He should've taken the photographs of his parents that were in Gerhard's folder before he left his office. Why hadn't he thought of that?

As the barking of the dogs got louder, his mind drifted to a vision of the house that he'd someday build for Elise and himself that included a fireplace with a mantel, perhaps similar to the one his father had constructed. On the mantel they could've displayed the photographs of her family and his parents, but that was no longer possible because he hadn't thought to grab the photos. But maybe the rest of the fantasy would come true? And perhaps there would be photographs of their children? It was all within reach now, just on the other side of the gate . . .

Hans was jolted out of his trance when Elise touched his arm. He looked at her and for a brief moment was reminded of her face on that cold evening at the Striezelmarkt all those years before, smiling while holding the music box to her ear. But she wasn't smiling now and instead looked terrified. She pointed in the direction of the farm road, and when he heard the barking, he realized what it meant. They were being tracked.

The acoustics in the snowy forest were deceptive, so he couldn't tell how far away the dogs were, but he knew they didn't have much time. He looked at the guard, who was smoking a cigarette and seemed oblivious to the barking, and whispered, "We need to do something. They'll be here soon, and we won't be able to hide."

"But what can we do?"

Hans looked at the guard and whispered, "I think I can take him."

Elise shook her head. "He has a gun, and you don't. I don't see how that's possible."

"I'll have the element of surprise, plus the added motivation of knowing what will happen if those dogs catch up to us."

"No, that's crazy. You'll get shot."

"You said a while ago that I don't make decisions. Well, I'm making this one."

Elise just looked at him.

"But if something happens, you have to promise you'll go on without me."

"I'm not going to go without you."

"You have to. If they capture you, you'll be tortured and killed. Do you promise?"

She hesitated and then finally nodded. But all she said was, "We're so close. We have to make it."

"We'll make it. Willi is sitting in a nice warm car only a hundred meters away from us." He smiled and said, "Maybe someday we'll look back on this, and I'll consider it to be one of my favorite days, and then we can relive it."

Elise smiled back but also started crying. "I don't think it'll be on my list."

Hans handed her the canvas bag, and they crept forward as the barking of dogs was joined by the voices of men. When they reached the edge of the woods, Hans saw that the guard had finally realized something was wrong. He dropped his cigarette in the snow, and as he took the rifle off his shoulder, Hans sprang from his crouch and sprinted the last ten meters toward him. In the gloaming, the guard couldn't accurately aim at the tall, thin figure about to attack him and instead fired wildly in Hans's direction. Elise ducked as bullets whistled past her and into the trees. Hans tackled the guard, pinned him, and pummeled him with his fists until he was un-conscious. Blood pooled in the snow.

Hans looked over his shoulder and shouted, "Let's go!" Elise ran from the woods toward the gate.

EPILOGUE

2005

Hans drove his new Mercedes sedan on the autobahn toward Dresden, occasionally glancing at his eighty-one-year-old mother in the passenger seat. Their journey had been inspired by a newspaper article he'd seen a month earlier about the reopening of a church in Dresden called the Frauenkirche.

The article stated that the reconstruction began in 1993 and took more than twelve years to complete, partly because modern engineers, even with their high-tech computing power, found it difficult to replicate what their eighteenth-century predecessors had created. Wherever possible, the builders had used the original stones, performing painstaking analysis so as to place them exactly where they had been before the destruction of 1945. The completed church was constructed predominantly of light tan sandstone, but it was peppered with the black of the original stones.

When Hans first showed the article to his mother, she hadn't reacted, but a week later, she'd told him she'd like to see the Frauenkirche. He'd been surprised because she never talked about Dresden and had never shown any interest in visiting it. She had few keepsakes from her youth, just a music box that didn't work and a broken porcelain ballerina. Now that his kids had moved out, Hans was in the process of purging the family's household possessions, and he figured the music box and ballerina were just two more items destined for the landfill after his mother passed. Her only other memento was an old, badly damaged photograph of her family on a beach. Hans had recently had it scanned and reprinted, but it hadn't turned out very well.

She'd never seemed interested in politics but sixteen years earlier had been transfixed by the fall of the Berlin Wall. One evening as they watched the events unfold on television, she began to cry. Hans couldn't remember her ever showing that much emotion, and he was touched when his father, who was significantly taller than her, knelt next to her chair and let her cry on his shoulder.

His father's health had deteriorated throughout the 1990s due in part to the lingering effects of the poor nutrition and appalling conditions he'd endured in the Soviet POW camps. He died of cancer in 2002, and shortly thereafter, Hans's mother had moved in with him and his wife. She was a considerate houseguest, and most days she stayed in her basement apartment and only came up for meals. She seemed a bit sad and lonely, but those traits had always been an aspect of her personality. Hans recalled that when he was a kid, he had sometimes seen her staring out a window for long spells. He'd often wondered what she was thinking about or recollecting.

Since she so rarely asked for anything, Hans realized that her request for a trip to Dresden was important to her. He had invited the rest of the family to come along, but his kids, his sister, and his nieces all had other things to do. So it would be just the two of them, and he was eager for the opportunity to find out more about her past. If he didn't learn things now, at some point they'd be lost forever. While Germany as a whole would prefer to forget those years, he felt it was important to keep the history alive at the individual level.

During the first part of their three-hour drive on a chilly but clear November morning, Hans asked about her time in Dresden, but although she answered his specific questions, she didn't elaborate or volunteer any information. At one point, he joked, "I read that former East German citizens are now allowed to review their old Stasi files. While we're here, should we take a look at yours and see if you have any deep, dark secrets you've been hiding from us?"

"No!" she said abruptly. She looked at him, and when she saw he was smiling, said, "I'm sure there's nothing interesting in there." She turned her head and looked out her window.

They drove on in silence for a while, but eventually, Hans asked if she'd like to listen to the CD he had purchased. Before the trip, his mother's only request was that he buy a Beethoven CD, specifically one that included "Für Elise." As the Mercedes glided forward on cruise control, he opened the case and slid the disc into the dashboard player.

Hans wasn't familiar with classical music and was therefore surprised that he knew most of the songs. They had become part of the fabric of the culture, and everyone knew them, even if they didn't know they were by Beethoven. To his added surprise, he found that he enjoyed them.

Eventually, Hans read the title "Für Elise" on the CD player's digital display. "Oh, I know this song!" he said, glancing at his mother as it began. But she didn't respond and instead just stared out the passenger window.

When it was finished, she asked him to play it again, so he pressed the replay button. When it finished a second time, she asked him to play it once more. He cast a sideways glance and saw her eyes glistening.

After the third listen, she didn't say anything, so he let

the CD move on to the next tune. He lowered the volume and asked, "Is it a coincidence that you're named Elise?"

"Your grandparents named me after the song. They enjoyed Beethoven."

And just like that, Hans learned something about his grandparents. All he'd known before then was that his grandfather was a doctor who'd died in the Dresden bombing and his grandmother had died in East Germany after the war.

She continued, "Your uncle was named Ludwig, after Beethoven." Hans sometimes forgot he had an uncle since he'd died well before Hans was born and his mother rarely mentioned him. "Your grandmother was a good piano player," she said with a catch in her voice, "and an amazing dancer."

Excited to finally have a conversation going, Hans urged her on. "Did you play an instrument?"

"Yes, I played the oboe in the orchestra." She hesitated a moment, and Hans looked forward to learning more. Then she said, "It was nice that your children played instruments. Let me see, Eduard played the trumpet, and Eva played the flute, right?" Hans realized his mother was doing what she always did when she didn't want to talk about herself—she was asking questions. His window to learn more appeared to have closed.

Hans had conducted online research in preparation for their visit, so he knew to park as close to the Altstadt as possible. He pulled a wheelchair, which his mother needed for long distances, out of the trunk, unfolded it next to the passenger door, and helped her into it. He had printed a map with a recommended one-day itinerary for Dresden tourists and leaned over to show it to her. "This suggests we start with the Frauenkirche."

"No, we need to start by going across the river to look at the entire city." He was taken aback because she was always very accommodating, but he would of course do whatever she wanted. He studied the map, looked up at the street signs, and then looked down at the map again before she said, "You don't need the map. I know where to go. Head down this street and then turn left in two blocks, and we'll cross the river on the Augustus Bridge."

They trekked to the north side of the river, and she asked that he roll her to a meadow directly across from the city center. He sat down on the cold ground next to her. From this vantage point, it was easy to see why the city was so famous. Planners had decided to rebuild the city's core to make it look like it had before the war, and they appeared to have been successful. The only things marring the vista were the scaffolding and cranes dotting the skyline, but Hans figured that was the price of progress.

He knew, though, that since 1945 Dresden's fame had not been due to its skyline. He tried to envision bombers overhead and the city in flames, but it was difficult to do given the peaceful world he'd grown up in. It was nearly inconceivable to him that England and America had tried to burn down Germany so recently that people his mother's age had been alive to witness it. He glanced at her and tried to picture her as a young woman during the bombing, but he didn't know what she'd looked like then. After five minutes, he said, "It's beautiful. You haven't seen it since 1956?"

"Yes, that's the last time I was here. That's also the year your father was released from the POW camp." He wanted to ask about his father's time as a POW, but he knew this was a sensitive subject since those experiences had tormented him for his entire life.

Ten minutes later, she said, "We can go back across the river now."

Hans replied, "Okay, you're the tour guide." She jerked her

head toward him and furrowed her brow for a second but then returned her gaze to the skyline. He didn't know what he had said that would've caused that reaction.

As they continued on their journey, it was clear to Hans that she had a definite itinerary in mind. They stopped at the Hofkirche, the castle, the Semper Opera House, and the Zwinger Palace and Gardens. Everywhere they went, he was impressed with the quality of the reconstruction. It was difficult to tell which buildings were original and which had been rebuilt, although the original ones were often blackened. Despite the cold, Hans noticed that his mother had left the top button of her coat unbuttoned. This was a strange quirk of hers, and she had once told him the rationale, but he had long since forgotten it.

They headed east and arrived at the New Synagogue, which had been built on the site of the one that was destroyed on Kristallnacht. While most of Dresden had been reconstructed to match its prewar appearance, the New Synagogue most definitely had not. It was an entirely modern building, built in the shape of a cube. Hans rolled his mother to a spot near the entrance and then sat on a bench next to her.

He didn't ask questions, even though he had always wondered what his relatives knew about the Holocaust. Just like he couldn't imagine English airmen intentionally burning down Dresden, he also couldn't imagine German citizens intentionally burning down the old synagogue that had stood right in front of where they were now sitting. And the burning of the synagogue was nothing compared to what came after. He believed that blaming the Holocaust on a country obscured the fact that it had been perpetrated by individuals, but who were those individuals? Had his mother been one of them, or his father, or his grandparents?

He glanced at his mother and saw her wiping away tears. She hadn't been much more than a child when it happened, and she was an old lady now. He decided this wasn't the right time to talk about it, although he realized and accepted that there would probably never be a right time. Whatever memories, regrets, or demons she had were destined to remain hers forever.

After twenty minutes, she nodded to him, and they moved on to the Frauenkirche, pausing as they entered the square in front of the church. Hans stayed behind the wheelchair and tried to view the square, bustling with Dresdeners and tourists, through her eyes. A backpacking American girl in her late teens or early twenties approached Hans and asked him to take a photo of her and her friend. Hans lined up the shot with the church in the background, and as he took the picture, the girls stuck out their tongues and made peace signs. He returned their camera and faced his mother, who suddenly looked terribly small and sad and old, sitting in her wheelchair as the crowd swirled around her.

He was momentarily choked up, but after he took a deep breath, they started forward across the cobblestones again, stopping in front of a statue. Hans read the plaque and discovered it was Martin Luther, but when he turned to tell his mother, it was obvious she already knew. And for the first time since entering the square, she had a bit of a smile on her face.

Just before the entrance to the church, she asked him to veer off to the side, toward some black stones to the right of the door. She got out of the wheelchair, walked the last few steps to the wall, and reached out. At first, Hans thought she had lost her balance and was trying to steady herself, but then he saw that she was just feeling the stones. Her wrinkled, veiny hand stroked one black stone and then the next, and he realized the stones must have some significance for her.

He looked at her quizzically and she said, "I like to feel the stones in these old buildings. Each of them was carved by a craftsman who . . ." Her voice trailed off as a field trip of nine- and ten-year-olds stopped next to them. Hans eaves-dropped as the children's teacher explained why the stones were different colors, and he was proud of himself because he already knew. The students seemed uninterested, with several boys elbowing each other and two girls whispering secrets. After a few minutes, the group moved into the church, and Hans turned back to his mother.

"Sorry. What were you saying about craftsmen?"

"Nothing. It's not important. We can go inside." They walked into the church, leaving the wheelchair outside. As they entered the nave, they both looked up at the light coming in through the dome. She touched the back of each pew for support as they walked slowly up the aisle, and when they were directly under the dome, she sat down. Hans sat next to her. The church was crowded with sightseers, and because it was now more of a tourist attraction than a house of worship, the two of them could talk.

Hans asked, "So, does Dresden look different from when you left?"

She smiled and said, "Oh yes. I barely recognize it."

She seemed more comfortable talking than she had been earlier, so he continued. "Did Dad spend much time in Dresden?"

She thought about it for a moment and then said, "As far as I know, he was only here once, in 1956."

"I thought 1956 was the year you left here."

"Yes, it was. Your dad had come to visit our friend Hans earlier that year, and then he helped us escape."

"And I know you've already told me this, but who was this Hans guy I'm named after?"

She looked away for a moment, tears again filling her eyes. "He . . ." She swallowed hard, paused, and then continued. "He was a friend of mine from growing up here, and then he and your father were in a POW camp together. He was a very good friend to both of us, so we agreed to name you after him."

Hans sensed that there might be a family scandal involved but didn't pursue it. Instead, he asked, "And he escaped with you?"

"Well, he tried. We were shot at as we crossed, and a bullet nicked an artery in his leg. He made it across but bled to death before your father and I could get him to the hospital."

"What happened after you crossed?"

"I didn't have a place to live, so your father let me stay with him. We found that we were a good match, and we got married a year after I arrived, and then you were born a year after that."

Hans nodded and looked at the magnificent altar, but when he glanced at his mother, he saw that she was looking straight up at the dome. She had a hint of a smile, and he wondered what she was thinking about.

After sitting in the pew for a half hour, she touched his arm to let him know they could leave. They walked back outside, and she sat down in her wheelchair. They rolled a good distance from the church, and then Hans stopped and stepped to the front of the chair. "So, what did you think? Did they do a good job?"

"Yes, it's beautiful."

"Is there anything else you want to see now that you're in your hometown? We still have some time."

"There's nothing else here. I'm ready to go home now."

ACKNOWLEDGMENTS

Many thanks to my friends and relatives who took the time to read and comment on early drafts of this book, including Sharon Anderson, Ted Barnhart, Julie Gerut, Jeff Hoffmann, Matt Irons, Jennifer Kassebaum, Dave Klages, Marc Levine, Fred Peronto, and Jim Post.

Also thanks to my wife, Anne Marie, and my children, Matthew and Ally, who encouraged me to finish this project. It wouldn't have happened without them.

ABOUT THE AUTHOR

Mark grew up in the St. Louis area before receiving his bachelor's degree from the University of Illinois and his master's degree from Northwestern University. He has had a lifelong passion for reading and history, particularly military history, and the idea for this book can be traced back decades to when he first read that the Soviet Union detained some of their German POWs for more than a decade after the end of World War II. He recalls thinking that the story of those POWs would make an interesting novel, but it took years of research and a visit to Dresden before this book came to fruition. He currently lives with his family in the Chicago suburbs.

www.ingramcontent.com/pod-product-compliance
Lightning Source LLC
Chambersburg PA
CBHW020239010826
48973CB00006B/1574